LATE HARVEST

LATE HARVEST

Barbara Masterton

SOUVENIR PRESS

ISBN 0 285 62840 2

Photoset in Great Britain by
Rowland Phototypesetting Ltd,
Bury St Edmunds, Suffolk
Printed in Great Britain by
Richard Clay Ltd,
Bungay, Suffolk

Chapter One

May was her favourite month. Winter is well and truly over and, no matter how disappointing the spring, one may hope for better things. There was another reason for her partiality. May was the only month which did not have sad associations for her. The rest had been marred by tragedy and she supposed that it was too much to expect that in the handful of years she anticipated was left of God's gift to her, May would remain unblemished. This year it had slipped away unscathed. Today was her twenty-fifth wedding anniversary and tomorrow was the first of June.

The telephone rang beside the bed. As she was reaching for the receiver, her husband entered the room with a cup of tea and the morning paper.

'Grandma? What time is your appointment?'

'Ten o'clock,' she told her grand-daughter.

'Right! See you!' The caller was gone.

'That was Samantha. She is taking me to the hairdresser.'

He placed the tea and newspaper beside the telephone and crossed the bedroom to open the curtains about a metre, just enough to brighten the room to its four corners. 'It's sunny,' he said.

They smiled at one another with satisfaction. It was going to be a good day for them both.

'Twenty-five years,' he remarked thoughtfully, sitting on the side of the bed and watching her sip her tea.

'Most couples our age would be celebrating far more years than that,' she observed. 'Forty or more.'

'Would we have liked one another when we were young, do you think?' he asked.

She put down her cup and picked up the paper, settling herself more comfortably against the pillows. 'Liked, definitely, but I don't know about loved,' she said. 'I changed a lot between twenty and forty. No doubt you did as well.'

That old adage, life begins at forty, had been proved in her case, although it would have been truer to say that she had started living all over again. For three years after her first husband had died, she had experienced the lonely existence of one who grieves inconsolably. Then she had met Bart. He was ten years older than she was and living a similar loneliness, having been a widower for four years. He had been contemplating moving from the large family house into something smaller, a flat perhaps, but could not bear parting from the constant reminders of happier times. However, he had been quite prepared to move when he married Una, even eager to do so. It had not seemed proper to bring her into his first wife's home. His children had found it easier to accept her in a place of her own.

'Have you finished packing?' he asked.

Una regarded him over the paper. 'Almost. What time must we leave?'

I thought we would have tea at the hotel, so we'll leave about three. It's only about half an hour's drive. Then you'll have plenty of time to get ready for this evening.'

They had invited the family to join them at the airport hotel for dinner. In the morning they were flying off to Singapore for a month's stay with Bart's younger daughter and her husband.

He got up from the bed, leaving her to read in peace.

'What time is it now?' she enquired, without looking up.

He paused by the door to consult his watch. 'Ten past eight.'

'Don't mow the lawn yet,' she warned. 'It's too early to start making such a noise.'

Bart left the room without answering. He wanted to leave

the garden as tidy as possible for his son-in-law, who had promised to look after it while he was away.

Samantha's small red car drew up before the house at twenty minutes to ten. Immediately, Una hurried out along the garden path, which was bordered by dense masses of lily-of-the-valley. Next to the gate, the laburnum was coming into full, pendulous bloom.

'I won't wait for you, Gran,' Samantha said, as Una got in beside her. 'I'll call back to pick you up in about thirty minutes. I have to go somewhere.'

Una wondered if she should ask where. She and Bart were supposed to be keeping an eye on this lively young lady while her parents were in Singapore, but it was proving difficult to draw the line between interested concern and downright interference.

'Excited about tonight?' Samantha asked, as they drove towards the centre of the county town. 'I am. I've got a new dress.'

Una looked forward to seeing it. 'Where did you get it?' she asked.

'My friend's great-grandmother. She's a lot older than you and has some fantastic stuff hoarded away in moth balls. We persuaded her to part with a few things. She couldn't wear them, even if she wanted to. She's huge. She must have been really thin once, though. The dress is great, about nineteen-thirty, I should think. May I borrow your long string of pearls to wear with it? I'll look after them, honestly.'

Una readily assented.

'Thanks, Gran.'

Samantha cared about clothes and loved making an impact in something out of the ordinary. She wore the kind of things that other people admired but would not have the courage to wear, and she wore them with aplomb. She had a mop of tight fair curls on the top of her head and the rest of her hair, two shades darker, resembled an old-fashioned short back and sides. She adored ear-rings, the larger the better, and today

9

was sporting giant hoops in bright orange, which swung with every movement of her head. She was dressed in a baggy white top, shiny black pants and flat, orange canvas shoes.

'I'll miss you while you're away,' she said. 'I shan't be able to drop in for a feed when I'm broke.'

'I'll leave plenty in the freezer,' Una promised. 'Just don't entertain all your zany friends there.'

'As if I would!' Samantha declared, grinning. She shared a shabby flat in an unfashionable part of the town with two girl-friends, who were with her at the College of Art and Technology. Her parents had bought the car for her and were maintaining it, because they did not want her walking around that area on her own, particularly at night.

'What are you going to have done to it?' she asked Una, when they drew up outside the hairdresser's.

'Just trimmed and blow-dried, the same as usual,' Una answered, amused.

'Stick in the mud!' Samantha exclaimed, cheerfully. 'See you in about half an hour, then.'

'I may not be ready,' Una warned her as she left the car.

'That's all right. I'll probably be late anyway.' And off she went.

Una had been attending the same hairdressing salon for many years. The staff of young women was constantly changing and every two or three years the décor suffered a metamorphosis, when the pot plants were replaced or dusted and rearranged. Even the name of the establishment had changed several times. Only Una remained constant. Fashion in hair styles came and went, leaving her untouched by them. Her grey hair, which had once been a rich brunette, was naturally wavy. It was trimmed once a month and encouraged to keep off her forehead and behind her ears.

This morning, while she was waiting to have her hair washed, she noticed that there was a different young lady behind the counter with the busy telephone and bottles of conditioner. She remembered she must ask her to cancel her next appointment. She was soon sitting quietly beneath the deft scissors of the woman who usually cut her hair. Her name was Cynthia, but Una, unlike most of her regular clients, never used it. She disliked conversing for the sake of it and had no desire to impart her life story in monthly instalments to a comparative stranger. Instead, she gazed dispassionately at her own reflection in the wall mirror, while she was being transformed beneath therapeutic hands from an ugly, wet-haired harridan, with face finely etched by the advancing years, into someone much more attractive, with shining waves brushed back from a face subtly softened, on which the age lines were no longer so evident. It was a minor miracle, which never failed to boost her morale and make these visits bearable. She always tipped generously, because she was so relieved when the ordeal was over. She had to stop herself from doing the same thing after a session in the dentist's chair.

She left quickly and then spent almost a quarter of an hour walking up and down the street, waiting for Samantha.

Bart had started mowing the extensive lawns at the back and front of the house at nine o'clock on the dot. He reckoned that even on a Saturday morning people should be up and about their daily business by then. Although in retirement, he could never remain in bed after seven-thirty. When he had finished the mowing, he went along with the edging shears and then began trimming the hedge with the electric clippers. He did not want to leave anything for his son-in-law to do immediately, otherwise he would be fed up by the time four weeks had elapsed. His younger daughter had urged them to stay with her for three months, but Bart would not, even though there was no good reason why they could not stay indefinitely. He was just one of those people who thought that the best part of a holiday, no matter how enjoyable, was the return home, and if he had not longed to see her again, he would have settled for a week in Scotland. That was what he preferred: two or three short breaks a year, instead of one long haul. At least they would be back in time to pick the soft fruit.

Samantha stayed for lunch and had a sandwich with them. She looked in the refrigerator and obligingly offered to eat up the remains of an apple pie and a plate of rice pudding, so that Una would be saved the task of throwing them in the dustbin. She opened a large tin of evaporated milk to pour over both desserts and then wrapped cling film over the holes to make it easier to transport what was left back to her 'pad', as she called the flat. When she had departed, with the chamois leather bag containing Una's pearls stuffed into the pocket of her thick white cotton sweater, Una went upstairs to check the suitcases and make sure they had everything they needed in the overnight bag.

Bart wandered round the house, fastening windows and pulling plugs from sockets, reluctant as always to perform the ritual of closing down the home, even temporarily.

They had very little unpacking to do at the hotel. Una hung her dress for the evening in the bathroom, so that the light creasing would disappear in the steam from their baths. Bart hung his newest suit in the closet, then they went down into the pink-carpeted lounge for tea. It was a quiet period and there were not many people about. Apart from themselves, there was only one other couple taking tea, accompanied by two young children who were arguing noisily and persistently over a plate of cakes.

'It will be wonderful to have the family here this evening,' Bart remarked. 'I shall miss Angela. One always thinks more about those who are absent on such occasions. Still, we shall be seeing her soon.' He bit into a salmon and cucumber sandwich and chewed reflectively, leaning back at ease in the grey leather chair. 'You are looking forward to tonight, aren't you, dear?' he enquired, anxiously. It was always difficult to tell what Una was feeling about anything. She kept her emotions under firm control and only looked happy when she smiled. Her face, rather sulky in repose, was then transformed. He courted those elusive smiles, like a lizard seeks the sun, to bask inert beneath the warmth and forget the long chill that had preceded it.

12

'Of course I am,' she answered, irritated that he should need to ask, after all the discussion and planning they had shared towards it. If she had been the mother of his children, would he have doubted?

'I don't know what I would have done without you all these years, Una,' he said, sensing that he had said the wrong thing and wanting to put it right.

She leaned across and placed her hand lightly on his knee. 'It was the same for me. We were lucky to meet when we did. At least you had your children. I had no one.' She smiled, only slightly, it is true, but enough to encourage him to think she was content.

He placed his hand over hers. 'I love you,' he said softly.

'I know,' she answered, slipping her hand away, 'and I am very fortunate.'

He did not ask her if she loved him. He knew the answer she would give. 'Of course,' she would say comfortably. Once a woman had lovingly whispered in his ear, 'I love you, Bart.' A woman who had demanded the constant petting and attention that it was in his nature to bestow upon the first object of his life. Una demanded nothing except loyalty.

She poured herself another cup of tea. 'I'll tell you something, Bartholomew Pascall,' she said lightly, lifting her cup and holding it before her as if she were about to toast him, 'you are a handsome old devil at seventy-five. Lean old men are definitely the most attractive.' She drank her tea, her dark eyes still upon him, wondering. Would Neil have been a lean old man? He would be sixty-seven now, if he had lived; three years older than herself. How different would her life have been, if she had remained a member of his ill-fated family?

Chapter Two

The spring sunshine, glistening upon the raindrops of the heavy shower that had ceased a few minutes earlier, was bathing the crowd around the font in a dappling of jewel colours through the rinsed stained glass.

In the semi-circular alcove at the side of the village church, with small, deep-set windows high in its grey stone walls, Una gazed down with tenderness into the pondering blue eyes of the infant in her arms and experimentally pressed the tiny form a little closer to her breast. The fine lawn gown, generously adorned with Swiss lace, hung in starched magnificence over her green suited arms, almost to the flagged floor. The precious family gown, worn by all the Favorys at their respective christenings for the past sixty-seven years. They were all there, the privileged wearers of that white robe, eighteen of them, counting this newest one. For once, Una stood prominently amongst them, holding the most important member of the congregation. She looked up from the inscrutable baby face, the tender half-smile still on her lips, to meet the eyes of the woman who was standing immediately opposite her on the other side of the font. Flora Macfarlane Brown's expression was unreadable. Una's hold on the baby relaxed and the corners of her full mouth resumed their customary droop, slightly sulky, yet not unattractive.

'How very gratifying to see the family here in full force,' the plump vicar declared, beaming round at them, pink skin taut over bulging cheeks and chins, his head tilted back slightly to enable him to see over his reading lenses, prayer book at the ready against a surplice which matched the robe in folds of white-laced purity.

The adults smiled back at him with righteous warmth. The children stared at him solemnly, waiting for the mystery to begin. Una alone was anxious. Unlike the rest of the gathering, she was ill at ease in church; her religious upbringing had been practically non-existent. She had drifted haphazardly between churches, chapels and meeting houses according to the convictions of her current school friends, broken by long periods of absenteeism and friendlessness—not without friends entirely, just temporarily without the bosom pal every little girl desires, someone to love, to envy and to share giggly secrets with. Her parents, open-minded and trusting, with no religious convictions of their own, were quite happy to allow their two daughters to be subjected to the religious ideas of others, no matter how unorthodox, well aware that Christianity in one form or another might rub off on them in the process. Somehow it never did. They had remained unconcerned, presuming that being healthy in body and mind, the girls would be naturally healthy in spirit.

Una was grateful to her maternal grandmother for insisting that she and her sister should be christened. Their easy-going parents had complied rather than distress the old lady. Neil's family was scandalised enough by the fact that his wife had never been confirmed. Occasionally, Una was reminded that it was never too late, but with each gentle hint she shrank further from the idea. It was not the Church she was resisting, so much as the influence of this family, gathered round her now in superior sanctity, members of a spiritual elite, which they were anxious for her to join. It was important to her that they should accept her for what she was, just as she had been obliged to accept them when she was brought among them as Neil's wife.

Una was standing between Marcia and Tom Hastings, the other two godparents. In such a position, with the precious object of the exercise in her arms, she could not help but feel the importance of the occasion and was reassured by her husband's presence behind her. Neil could be relied upon to tell her what was expected of her in any new situation. When the moment arrived to hand the well padded infant to the vicar and pronounce the name, her voice, habitually soft and low, was drowned by those of Marcia and Tom. 'Shirley Maria,' they stated, loudly and firmly. Una made an effort to speak up a little when she made the vows on the baby's behalf, but again her voice was almost unheard beneath the decisive utterances of the others, and she became convinced of something she had suspected all along, that her role as second godmother was a courtesy and would remain of little significance. The Favorys had a tradition of being godparents to their own offspring. Unlike Una's parents, they were averse to entrusting any part of their children's upbringing to other people, whether physical, emotional or spiritual. Their motto could have been, 'The family knows best'. They doubted whether Una would ever be a fully participating member of either the Church or the family, but for Neil's sake, they felt they ought to encourage her.

The baby was handed back to her proud mother and wrapped cosily within another heirloom, a wool shawl, cob-webby fine and cream with age. The group stirred into animation and, in a voluble mass confined narrowly between the rows of polished pews, made its corporate way, with occasional jams and gentle urgings forward, through the cool funnel of the arched stone porch. It surged out buoyantly and spread onto the grass-green, daffodil and forsythia yellow of the sloping churchyard, studded with worn and sunken head-stones, tilting with the land.

'Will you come back for tea, Mr Laston?'

'I should be delighted, dear lady,' the vicar answered genially, shaking the hand of the very tall, fur-coated personage who had extended the invitation.

Flora Macfarlane Brown turned from him to address her sister, who was in her required position, one step behind her. 'Go on ahead, Vin, and put the kettle on.'

Lavinia Favory scurried down the path towards the lich-gate, with yet another important task to accomplish.

'I'll come with you, Auntie Vin,' Sibyl, her youngest niece called, hurrying after her with a small boy in tow. 'Bruce is dying to get to the house.'

All three of them disappeared from view along the steep banked country road, moving past the Black Bull at a slight trot. The others began to dawdle after them in twos and threes around the imposing figure of Mrs Macfarlane Brown. Drawing on her long, black leather gloves, she stepped out majestically in the manner of one who has every intention of effecting an arrival when all is ready for her reception.

'Are you going to have a baby soon, Auntie Una?' a small girl asked pertly, running back to join Una and Neil as they brought up the rear.

'I don't know, Kate. Perhaps!' Una said, smiling at the child and avoiding the curious eyes, as heads turned.

'Don't ask personal questions,' Marcia told her daughter severely, pulling the shawl closer about her baby's face.

'That's all right,' Una said, but of course it was not. Personal questions were taboo in the family. It was one of the reasons they all managed to keep their distance in spite of constant socialising. Consequently, Una's childlessness, after eight years of marriage, remained a subject for private conjecture. Nobody knew if it was by design or chance and nobody would ever ask. Nevertheless, opinions had been formed on the subject and it was generally considered that Una was childless by intent—hers, not her husband's. The family disapproved.

'Have you decided where you want to go on holiday this year, Auntie Flora?' Ella Fielding asked her. 'I have a few more brochures for you in the car. Some of them are proving very popular. It would be advisable to make up your mind as soon as possible, wouldn't it, Ronald?' Her husband, a coach tour operator, agreed with a nod.

'It will probably be Torquay again,' Flora Macfarlane Brown said, comfortable in the knowledge that however late she left the decision, Ronald would manage to find places for her and her sister.

'Auntie Vin found it a bit too hilly last year, didn't she?' Ella remarked.

'Lavinia always complains about something,' Flora replied. 'She has a sickly constitution.' She had no patience with her sister's aches and pains, which she suspected were a ruse to draw attention to herself and add colour to a dull existence. If Lavinia's mental attitude were more robust, she would not need her sick fancies. It was really most annoying for someone so strong mentally and physically to have a sister who was neither and, for exacerbation, was impoverished. It was Flora's opinion that only the well-off can afford the whimsy of chronic ailing without ever being really ill.

Una, trailing along in the wake of the hydra's progress, holding Neil's hand to give herself a sense of being part of it, neared the lane leading to the Macfarlane Brown residence with a familiar sinking of the spirits, in the manner of a heretic about to face the inquisition—which was strange, because of course no direct questions would be asked; yet the trial that had begun on her introduction to these people would continue relentlessly, a pleasant, civilised verbal probing, to which they constantly subjected each other and to which Una could never become accustomed.

A car was heard approaching. As it swept round the bend into the village, the young ones were hastily shepherded onto the grassy bank. Tom Hastings stepped quickly to the side of his wife and baby.

'Don't go into the ditch, Peter,' Ella warned her six-year-old. 'It's very muddy.'

The car sped past. There was a yell, followed by loud accusations. 'You pushed me, Tina!' 'I did not!' 'Yes, you did! It wasn't my fault, honestly, Mum.'

The hydra observed the antics within its corporeal midst with calm detachment. Ella descended upon the muddied half of her twelve-year-old twin girls with vexation. Tina received a hard slap on her legs and, just to be fair, Sylvia got one as well. Sylvia's shoes were wiped in the long, damp grass. Her cousin Imelda produced a neatly folded white handkerchief, edged with lace, from her jacket pocket to complete the cleaning up.

'We'll have to hurry,' someone remarked. 'It's going to rain again. I told you we should have brought the cars.'

The offending black cloud was universally observed and rapidly assessed. The loose-limbed monster rolled forward at a quickened pace and in fifty yards turned along a lane on one side of which was a thatched Purbeck stone farm house, surrounded by an ugly assortment of outbuildings in need of repair. Further along, on the opposite side of the lane, was a large, sprawling house of cream brick beneath weathered brown pantiles, squatting in well-tended grounds of fresh April beauty. Four black cars were parked before it.

'The children can go in through the conservatory,' the mistress of the house ordered as they neared it, waving a long glove towards the side entrance.

'I don't need to,' Kate told her boldly. 'My shoes aren't muddy.'

'Do as you are told!' her father commanded.

Her great-aunt extended an ungloved hand. Kate took it and, with a triumphant glance towards her father, entered the house by the front door. Tom and Marcia exchanged looks of annoyance, but said not a word.

The Favorys were tall, well-proportioned people and, generally speaking, good-looking. The four girls, Jessica, Ella, Marcia and Sibyl, had managed to find themselves husbands even taller than they were, so that when the adults were assembled together they appeared quite intimidating to smaller fry. Una was five feet three inches and very slim, some would say thin. She passed amongst them at Neil's side, feeling insignificant.

The head of the clan, by self-promotion and not primo-geniture, was Flora Macfarlane Brown—Mrs Brown, actually, but she considered that common surname too ordinary and used her late husband's unusual Christian name to give it distinction. He had been dead so long, since the second year of their marriage, that only those closest to her recalled the connection and Macfarlane Brown was accepted. Flora was large and bony, with hands and feet to match. The latter she could disguise in sensible shoes. Her hands remained on show, ugly and masculine. She had a strong-featured face, handsome rather than beautiful, and her hair, which was dyed jet black, was swept off her face and neck in a thick roll around a loop of brown stockinette, from which it kept escaping. The black hair was not becoming to a woman in her middle sixties and made her face appear harsh. She went straight upstairs to put her black fur coat in the wardrobe. Everyone else did their best to hang their coats and jackets on the pegs in the hall and, failing that, threw them across the two chairs either side of the mirrored oak hall stand.

Tea was set out ready for them in the dining-room. The children had got no further than the conservatory, which ran the length of the side of the house and led into the dining-room by way of wide french windows. The black cloud was now releasing the first fat drops of a downpour. They pattered on the glass roof of the conservatory with a loud intensity, which satisfied the children and spurred them into excited activity. Their shrill voices brought Lavinia Favory, Flora's elder sister, from the kitchen. She hovered in the dining-room doorway, peering over the heads of the assembly towards the noise. She had the dubious advantage of being the tallest woman in the family, half an inch under six foot to be precise, and stooped slightly, as if in abject apology for it.

'It's all right, Auntie Vin. Imelda's keeping an eye on them,' Jessica Close, Imelda's mother, said.

Lavinia hurried back to the kitchen to pour the tea.

'Has the vicar arrived yet?' Flora Macfarlane Brown asked, coming into the room. 'Where is the tiresome man? We can hardly start without him. Pour the sherry, Hugh.'

Hugh Close, Jessica's husband, had no sooner picked up the

sherry bottle when the door bell rang and the next minute the 'tiresome man' was in the room, smiling benevolently around at everybody between frequent glances towards the mahogany table, its white linen cloth smothered with heaped plates, filled dishes and piles of shining cutlery. The family had pooled their rationed resources for this celebration, it was only fair. The chickens, ham and jug of cream had come to Flora from a local farmer friend. The sandwiches were spread with margarine, with the butter reserved for the scones. Jessica, whose husband Hugh was the general manager of a large department store in the town, had brought three large tins of peaches. Each woman had baked something. Una's contribution was the tinned salmon vol-au-vents. The christening cake, the centrepiece of the table, had taken their combined contributions of sugar and dried fruit. The eggs were no problem: Lavinia kept hens in a corner of the garden behind the greenhouse. The icing sugar had been procured by Ella, no questions asked, but a few eyebrows had been raised behind her back. Flora had made the cake. If anything was to be envied and admired, then Flora would expend time and energy upon it; the mundane she left to Lavinia.

The Favorys loved their food. Mr Laston, a bachelor, was correspondingly fond of the Favorys. After a surprisingly short time, when the baby's head had been toasted in mediocre sweet sherry, most of the food had been transferred from the table onto plates balanced on laps. Lavinia was handing round cups of tea and directing the children towards jugs of lemonade and orange squash in the kitchen.

Una, squeezed on the sofa between Neil and his third sister, Ella and her husband Ronald, was endeavouring to keep a low profile, but every time one of the other three rose to replenish their plates, they kindly enquired if they could fetch her anything and, eventually, it was noticed that she was not doing justice to the feast.

'Won't you try a pork pie?' Flora Macfarlane Brown urged her. 'There is some home-made pickle.'

'No, thank you,' Una replied, refraining from reminding her that she did not eat meat.

'Oh, I forgot,' Flora said although of course she had not. You don't eat meat.' She stood over Una, looking down with distaste at the lone buttered fruit scone gracing her plate. 'You cannot afford to be faddy, Una, you are too thin, my dear. You must see she eats properly, Neil. She isn't on a diet, I hope?'

'Of course not, Auntie,' he said, defensively. When meat was rationed it was not fashionable to give it up, and dieting merely for the sake of one's figure was considered by many, especially country dwellers, to be downright unhealthy. The only foods that were not good for you were those which happened to be in the shortest supply.

'You will never become pregnant if you starve yourself, Una,' Ella told her cheerfully.

Immediately, the talk amongst the women turned upon food, babies and health, with Una at the passive centre of the discussion; the very thing she had hoped to avoid. After all, she never objected to watching them tuck into succulent slices of ham, chunks of grosvenor pie, sausage rolls, roast beef sandwiches, tongue, chicken and other carnivorous delights; why should they take exception to her salmon vol-au-vents and scones?

'You can fill up on cake,' Hugh Close told her sympathetically. 'Have one of these,' and he handed her a plate of pastries, which were of an unappetising yellowish tinge filled with a dubious white substance.

Una blushed and took one, wondering what she would do with it, because she did not eat cream, either, not even this substitute for it. The term 'mock cream' was used to describe many revolting concoctions.

'Give it to me when no one is looking,' Neil said, quietly, 'or put it on old Laston's plate. He would never notice the addition.'

The new baby, in whose honour everyone was eating and drinking, set up a wailing from her carry-cot in the corner.

'Mummy, the baby is crying,' Kate said officiously, running to her mother's side.

Marcia rose hastily to carry the infant off to be fed, the milk already oozing through her blue silky blouse, which was gaping unbecomingly between stretched button-holes.

Neil left the sofa to fill his plate once more. He stood next to his eldest sister, Jessica, while he made his selection from the ravaged table.

'And how is my little brother?' she asked him fondly, unmindful of his lofty six foot two inches. To his four sisters, Neil was still the baby of the family.

'Fine,' he answered, picking up a sausage roll and two chocolate biscuits.

'I was going to have a chocolate biscuit, Uncle Neil,' a little boy said accusingly, glaring at the empty dish.

'You can have one of these, Bruce,' Neil offered. 'The other one is for Auntie Una.'

'I have never met anyone who doesn't like chocolate biscuits,' Jessica laughed, insinuating that even faddy people could stomach the delicacies of life.

Una kept her eyes on her husband, willing him back to her side. Within his family circle she felt defenceless without him. It was because she knew that they did not value her highly. Only one thing would change that—a baby. The fact that she had a good job in local government, as a secretary, meant nothing to them. They never enquired about her work; it was irrelevant to her role as Neil's wife. She did not yearn to be a mother; on the other hand, she was taking no precautions against becoming one. Neil expected them to have children and she adored Neil; also, she felt under an obligation to the rest. Neil was the last of the line and their only hope of a continuance of the family name.

There was a sudden flash of light, which brought her out of her reverie. Stuart Ferguson, Sibyl's husband, was taking photographs to mark the happy occasion. His first one, natur-ally, had been of Flora, who was posing, knife poised, in the act of cutting the first slice of the christening cake. She happened to be standing next to Mr Laston, the vicar, so he was in the photograph, too, holding his plate against his rotund stomach, his pink face radiant with glistening bliss. Flora towered over him by a head.

'Come on, Auntie Vin, your turn now,' Stuart insisted and Lavinia was urged forward from partial obscurity by the door to sit between Sibyl and Imelda.

She protested half-heartedly, assuring them that they did not want a photograph of her, yet soon allowing herself to be convinced otherwise, bending her head to smooth her iron-grey hair, which was short and straight, cut in a severe fringe to form a square frame for her round, blobby features that were in marked contrast to her sister's strong bone structure.

'How is your rheumatism, Auntie Vin?' Sibyl asked, as she sat beside her.

'She has put that behind her for the winter, haven't you, Vin?' Flora stated, daring her to disagree.

Lavinia smiled the smile of the long-suffering and said feebly that she hoped so.

'Of course you have!' Flora declared, in a cross confident, manner. 'For heaven's sake, don't be such a long skein of misery!'

'Move away, Imelda. Your uncle will be taking the children's photographs afterwards,' Ella said to her niece.

'I am not a child,' Imelda protested, coldly. 'I am twenty years old.' But she moved away just the same.

'I'm not a child either,' her seventeen-year-old brother, Marcus, drawled, leaning against the wall next to the french windows and watching the antics with a supercilious smile upon his handsome face.

'You are both children as far as this family is concerned,' their father, Hugh Close, told them.

'We can all see that you are grown up, dear,' Sibyl said to Imelda, in her patronising manner. 'We just mean that you and Marcus are members of the younger generation, that's all.

You will be getting your hair permed next and then we shan't recognise you.'

Imelda and Una exchanged glances of sympathy. Imelda was plain, with abundant fair hair as straight as a yard of pump water and, for some reason, they held this lack of curl against her. She did not yearn for curls, any more than Una yearned for a baby, but there was a subtle difference in their characters, which made Imelda determined to eschew curls to the last breath in her body, in order to spite them, and Una disposed to accept motherhood, in order to please them.

When all the fuss and bother of the photography was over—culminating in the most important one of the occasion, that of Marcia, now wearing a cardigan to cover the stains on her blouse, with baby Shirley in her arms and surrounded by Tom and their two other children, Kate, nine and Ian, thirteen —it was time to enjoy the cake, along with another glass of sherry. Not one adult, after the first bite and almost before it had been tasted, failed to praise the cake and exclaim over its richness and the expertise of its cook. Imelda decided, perversely, that she would claim the privilege of being one of the children and decline to fawn over her Great-Aunt Flora, by saying nothing at all about the positively disgusting cake, which had emerged from the oven a little on the dry side and had been moistened, surreptitiously, with a liberal dose of brandy. Most palatable for those who liked brandy and burnt currants.

After the demolition of the cake, the leave-taking began.

Sibyl's husband, Stuart, put his precious camera into its brown leather case and promised them all copies of the photographs. He intended to be the first to depart. He offered Una and Neil a lift, which was gratefully accepted.

Ella and Ronald Fielding left at the same time with Peter, the quarrelsome twins, Sylvia and Tina, who had to be coaxed away from belabouring the piano keys in the drawing-room, and their morose, spotty and bespectacled brother, fifteen-year-old Donald, who was clever.

Mr Laston was the last to go. He hung back, waiting for a

word with Mrs Macfarlane Brown on a church matter. He ate a second slice of cake while he was waiting for her to return from waving goodbye to Jessica, Hugh, Imelda and Marcus, in the last carload.

'It's about the fête, Mrs Macfarlane Brown,' he said, hastily swallowing the last mouthful as she entered the room, followed by Lavinia. 'Mrs Pope-Wessington has kindly given permission for it to be held in the manor grounds as usual. Last year, if you recall, after that little unpleasantness, she said never again, but I am glad to say she has relented.' He coughed apologetically before continuing. 'That means she will head the committee again, I'm afraid.'

Flora, who had been expecting to be boss for the first time, with the fête about to change its venue to the village sports field, took the news well, much to Mr Laston's relief. If he had mentioned anyone else as usurper she would have been affronted, but Jane Pope-Wessington, lady of the manor, was undeniably first lady not only in the community but also in the organisation of the annual fête. Flora felt not the least slighted; disappointed, yes, but not slighted. The fête would not have been the same on the sports field; it did not have the ambience of the grounds of Lapcombe Manor, where it had been held time out of mind. Nowadays the village had little to do with the manor. The Pope-Wessingtons were seen at church most Sundays and, if one managed to catch their eye, they smiled and nodded affably. The fête was the main contact between most of the villagers and the people up at the manor, and the fête committee the only close contact between Flora Macfarlane Brown and Jane Pope-Wessington. Flora was gratified that the *status quo* remained unimpaired.

'Shall we finish the sherry, Mr Laston? I think there is just about enough left for two glasses.' She picked up the bottle from the sideboard and shook it playfully in his direction.

Mr Laston quailed before the sight of this formidable woman being skittish. Although, from many years of accepting hospitality wherever it was offered, he ate indiscriminately, he had a fine palate for wine. Nevertheless, he bravely smiled his acceptance.

Lavinia poured the two glasses quite happily, although there was none for her.

Chapter Three

A terrible thing had happened to the Favory children when the eldest, Jessica, was nineteen. Their mother, who had been widowed three years earlier, disappeared. She left home without a word and never came back. Jessica had recently become engaged to Hugh Close, a shop assistant in the furniture department of a large store in the town centre. Overnight, her dreams and plans for her wedding had been crushed beneath the responsibilities of having three younger sisters and a little brother of nine, all of them, including Jessica herself, very much in need of a mother's love and support. At first they had waited expectantly for her return, but as sad days turned into weeks and weeks into long months, the hopes of even the youngest had faded and the times they saw her walking down the street had diminished in number; finally only an aching loneliness was left, and secret feelings of guilt: they should have been good children and not caused their mother annoyance and pain.

Into their lives for the first time came their two aunts, Flora and Lavinia; neither of them used to children, both of them still grieving for the brother they had worshipped and lost many years before his death. His wife, Emily, had cold-shouldered Flora and Lavinia from the moment she knew she possessed him utterly. They had watched her beguile him away from family and friends, powerless to fight the influence of her jealous seduction. After his marriage, he had visited his sisters occasionally, but his wife had gone berserk when she found out, accusing him of no longer loving her and preferring the company of his sisters to her own. Unable to reason with such irrational jealousy, his surreptitious visits had grown rarer and briefer. Emily Favory, strangely diminished in spirit without the love she had held in thrall, had even resented their presence at her husband's funeral, and the five children had remained strangers to their aunts. Very sad for the two well-meaning ladies—and the little boy so like his darling father!

It had been many weeks before Flora and Lavinia heard of Emily's sudden disappearance. It had never entered Jessica's head to turn to them for help. The information reached them in a roundabout way through a neighbour, whose sister lived in the same town as the family. Flora wrote to Jessica, asking if there was anything that she could do to help, and received such a forlorn, bewildered reply that she and Lavinia lost no time in paying them a visit.

The children had discovered two middle-aged, slightly eccentric protectors, who had undetected reserves of love waiting to be drawn upon. One of them also had undisclosed reserves of wealth, not intended to be drawn upon. Flora was mean, or, more charitably, careful with her money and Lavinia, poorer in comparison, was even meaner.

Still, love is a bottomless well and children canny diviners of it. They grew accustomed to their odd-looking aunts. The mellow brick house in the village of Lapcombe became their home and, eighteen months after their mother's inexplicable disappearance, Jessica left it as a bride.

Their mother's fiercely loving possessiveness, which had been a puzzling burden on their young shoulders, had been replaced by a less demanding, rather flustered fondness, as Flora and Lavinia valiantly coped with a species they knew very little about—children. The rules and regulations of a strict up-bringing had vanished and the five young people had to find a new security, based on a *laissez-faire* attitude which was the result of ignorance and a pathetic gratitude for their presence, even though that presence was disruptive of habit and routine: two things supposed to be dear to the hearts of the settled middle-aged. Only their religious observance continued without interruption, with the difference that their aunts were church and their mother had been very definitely chapel.

By the time the Second World War started, Ella was also married, to Ronald Fielding. When Ronald had to leave their small semi-detached house to join the navy, they had a child of three, called Donald and the one-year-old twins, Sylvia and Tina. Marcia and Sibyl married Tom Hastings and Stuart Ferguson, who were great friends and had joined the RAF together. Hugh Close, Jessica's husband, had been pronounced unfit for active service because he had a dodgy heart, so he remained at home to mind the shop and minded it so well that in 1946, when many of the staff returned to claim their old jobs, he was allowed to step into the place of one who did not, as Assistant Manager. Neil became a soldier. He met Una, who was a driver in the ATS, and married her in 1943. So, by the end of the war, the old house at Lapcombe once more held only Lavinia and Flora. Its heyday as a family home was over.

Unfortunately, the fondness felt by the adult Favorys for their aunts was not matched by their marriage partners. Oddness in one's in-laws is apt to be irksome rather than endearing and stinginess with money is seldom offset against generosity of intent. So it transpired that after the christening the occupants of the four black cars journeyed away from Lapcombe with alacrity, most of them relieved that the visit was over and none more so than Una.

There was little room in the back of Stuart Ferguson's elderly Austin, which meant that Bruce has to sit on Una's lap, with Julian, who was twelve, in the middle between her and Neil.

'I wonder what the next Royal Command will be?' Stuart said, glancing sideways at his wife.

'I wonder,' Sibyl echoed, smiling over her shoulder at Una and Neil in a meaningful way.

'Perhaps somebody will die,' Julian suggested expressionlessly, staring straight ahead between his parents' heads.

Bruce wriggled round to look at him, scrumpling Una's skirt beneath his plump bottom, which was snugly encased in grey flannel shorts.

'Auntie Vin?' he hazarded. At his age one always theoretically disposes of one's relatives in strict chronological order.

'Who knows?' his brother said darkly, without unfixing his stare. 'It might be Auntie Flora.'

'Then we'll be rich,' Bruce stated with satisfaction. He had heard his father mention this as a natural corollary on many occasions.

'You mercenary little devil,' Stuart remarked cheerfully.

'That is very unkind, Bruce,' his mother rebuked him. 'It is much nicer to have Auntie Flora than her money, isn't it?'

Her husband shot her a sideways glance. 'Well it is!' she said, with indignation.

'I feel sick,' Julian informed them flatly. 'I would have been all right by the window.'

Immediately, Stuart drew up by the grass verge and they all hastily piled out. Sibyl ministered to her son next to the hedgerow until he felt better. When they returned to the car, Neil got in beside Stuart and Una found herself between Sibyl and Julian, still with Bruce on her knees and enduring the occasional fidgety kick from his substantial black school shoes.

'Why does Auntie Vin keep making faces behind Auntie Flora's back?' Bruce asked, his red hair blowing in the breeze from the open window, out of which Julian had stuck his head.

'Of course she doesn't,' his mother said.

Julian brought his head in for a moment. 'She does,' he declared.

'It's because she hasn't the courage to make them to her face,' Stuart said.

It was true that Lavinia sometimes tried to mitigate the effect of her sister's sarcastic observations by making a dumb show of sympathy and reassurance behind her back. It was a disconcerting habit. The person being offended by the younger sister was so occupied trying not to stare over her shoulder at the grimacing encouragement being proffered by the older, that there was no option but to retreat from the ludicrous situation without the comfort of retaliation; consequently, Flora's remarks grew more daringly cutting and poor Lavinia's shakes and nods more grotesque.

The two sisters had received only a rudimentary education, both having left school at thirteen. Reading was too laborious a pastime to give them much pleasure, but after tea Lavinia read snippets out loud from the local evening newspaper and kept her sister informed of the marriages and deaths of acquaintances and any new additions to their families. The Favorys sprang from good yeoman stock and knew neither want nor extravagance, for wealth had been in land and beasts, and family pride set firmly in country traditions. Over the last hundred years or so both family and land had dwindled, until all that remained was Lavinia, Flora, their four nieces and one nephew and the old house at Lapcombe. Flora's money had come to her from Macfarlane Brown. A few distant relatives of the Favorys were scattered throughout the county and beyond, unknown and unconcerned.

What the family once had been was evident now in the sisters' home and possessions: furniture, china, silver and linen handed down through the generations; evident also in their innate sense of continuity. The long family history, which gave them their present secure place in the order of society, enabled them to look back through the centuries with comfortable pride and induced them to look forward with unease. All their hopes for posterity rested on Neil, yet Una persistently remained childless. Not that Lavinia, Flora and the rest ever consciously considered posterity. They merely shared an instinct for survival that in their ancestors had survived plagues, civil wars, bad harvests and two world wars. That instinct was still strong, but the family had inexorably diminished in each succeeding struggle.

Una, feeling a little car-sick herself now in the confines of the back seat, with Bruce leaning heavily against her, near to sleep, gazed at the back of her husband's head of tight, fair curls and prayed to God for a child for him and a position of consequence for herself within his family. She had no one else. One of the bombs dropped on Plymouth had demolished her home, killing her parents, her younger sister and her maternal grandmother.

Chapter Four

'You shouldn't try so hard to please them. It's not worth it,' Imelda said. 'They see it as a weakness and will end up despising you for it. There are two kinds of people in this world: the chameleons, who endeavour to be all things to all men, and the leopards, who won't change a spot for a stripe for anyone. You are a chameleon, Una, and I am a leopard. Which one of us has the better chance of survival, do you think?'

Una looked into the cool green eyes of her niece, nine years her junior yet taller by five inches, and felt inclined to award survival to her. Imelda was her ally in the family. Neil would have been, had he seen the necessity, but he was of an uncritical disposition, accepting people as they presented themselves and not looking behind their actions for motives, nor behind their words for malice.

Una, on the other hand, was sensitive to every nuance of expression in looks and speech, forever putting herself into other people's shoes to find excuses for their behaviour. It was true what Imelda had said, that if the world were to be divided into chameleons and leopards, she would definitely belong in the former group. She did not think that she had always been so willing to please, so hungry for approval. The bomb—the one beside which all other bombs had paled into relative insignificance for her—as well as wiping out her family, had destroyed part of herself. Beneath the rubble, the foundations of her home had remained more or less intact; conversely, the secure foundation of Una's life had disintegrated, while outwardly she appeared unscathed. She had been fortunate to have Neil at that time and she was able to re-establish herself upon the firm basis of their love. Now she needed to feel an established part of his family. Perhaps Imelda was right and she was trying too hard.

The two young women were standing in a cinema queue, waiting to see Doris Day in *Tea for Two*. They had slowly progressed from standing on the pavement outside the Odeon to half-way along the narrow foyer. From the walls on either side of them large head-and-shoulder portraits of the great stars stared with remote arrogance, or smiled with triumphant conceit, in black and white perfection behind shiny framed glass. The pay desk was now drawing tantalisingly near and the cheaper seats were full. The dimly lit foyer ended in double glass doors, beyond which was the sweet kiosk and two wide rows of red-carpeted stairs, leading upwards to the darkened realms of fantasy and the commanding brightness of the vast screen. Torches, disembodied lights in the sudden blackness, were waiting to beckon them into the warmth of that fantasy world. Visualising those torches, Una thought of Neil. He was away on the Isle of Wight for two weeks at his annual Territorial Army camp. She missed him very much. She wrote to him every day and received a reply to every second or third letter. Like many men who find it difficult to put their romantic feelings into words, Neil expressed his sentiments eloquently in writing, even dredging up from his unappreciative schooldays quotes from sketchily remembered Shakespearian sonnets. Una's own letters were mundane in comparison, just a record of how she was spending the long days until his return. She had never visited the Isle of Wight, but was forming a set of imaginative pictures of it, based on Neil's descriptions. One letter in particular had conjured up a vivid scene. He had described walking back to camp late one night along the moonlit cliff-top path, with glow-worms, pin-points of tiny lights in the dark patches of scrub at his feet, and, far below, the sea glimmering on the edge of the sand as it crept inland. He had wished she was there, he wrote to her, walking by his side within the curve of his arm.

'Where's your money, Una?' Imelda asked impatiently.

With a start, Una left the balmy cliff-top in order to return to reality.

She took her purse from her handbag and handed the woman in the ticket kiosk a ten shilling note.

Towards the end of the main film, in which Una was utterly absorbed to the exclusion of her surroundings, she was once more jogged back to awareness of the present, this time by a loud yelp of pain. She looked across Imelda towards the sound and saw a man lurching to his feet and then causing further commotion as he made his way along the row of hastily withdrawn legs and feet towards the gangway.

'What happened?' Una whispered, as the glow-worm torches flickered into spasmodic light across the smoke haze of the projection lights.

'I pinched him,' Imelda whispered back.

The seedy looking man who had been sitting next to her, under cover of a brown raincoat which he was holding over his lap, had surreptitiously moved his sweaty hand across to clasp Imelda's. Staring unconcernedly at the screen, she had passively allowed him to direct her hand to his unbuttoned trousers and then pinched him strategically with all the power of spite that she could muster.

'I shall have to wash my hands as soon as this film is over,' she added. 'Filthy little man!'

Anxiously, Una glanced sideways at her own neighbour, but as he was looking as shocked as she was, she relaxed a little. The merest touch from a stranger, male or female, was enough to make her draw away. She supposed the fact that Imelda was a nurse had hardened her to random human contact.

After the cinema, they took a bus as far as Imelda's home. The Closes lived in a handsome bungalow. It was secluded within a large garden, which was well screened by shrubs and trees and marauded by three large cats with fine hunting instincts. On most mornings the back doorstep bore witness of their prowess, in offerings to their doting mistress. Imelda, who was not fond of cats, nor furred or feathered corpses, always used the front door when she left early.

Imelda's mother, Jessica, was waiting for them in the kitchen with the cocoa already mixed in the cups. They went into the living-room, while she boiled the pan of milk. Hugh Close and Marcus were sprawled either side of the fireplace in armchairs, their long legs stretched out before them, reading. Hugh was smoking a cigarette. They barely acknowledged the young women's entrance.

Imelda and Una took off their coats and put them on the back of the sofa before sitting down. Jessica came in with the cocoa and a wooden biscuit barrel with a brass lid and handle.

'Did you enjoy the film?' she asked brightly.

They said they had.

Hugh folded his newspaper, placed it on the carpet beside him and took a cup of cocoa from his wife's outstretched hand, without a word. Marcus continued to read his book.

'When will Neil be back, Una?' Jessica asked, sitting down in an upright wooden chair next to the window, which was obscured by floor-length floral curtains.

'Saturday,' Una told her, smiling at the thought.

'It is Imelda's twenty-first birthday next month,' Jessica continued. 'You will both be coming, won't you? Marcus has to start his National Service in October, so it will probably be a long time before we can all be together again.'

At the mention of his impending National Service, Marcus scowled at his mother as if it were a notion of her own to get rid of him for a couple of years.

'I'm trying to persuade Imelda to have something done to her hair for the occasion,' Jessica said nervously.

'What do you suggest?' Imelda enquired icily, giving her mother's corrugated perm a glance of disparagement.

'A few curls, perhaps?' Jessica ventured.

'Curls wouldn't suit her,' Marcus scoffed from behind his book.

Imelda wore her thick fair hair drawn back from her large oval face into thick plaits, which were wound into a halo

37

around her head. She had a pale, matt complexion, with heavy-lidded green eyes, a short, straight nose, a small, well-shaped mouth and a round, very firm chin. She resembled a substantial Botticelli angel in a bad mood.

'I thought perhaps I would buy you a pretty dress for the occasion,' Jessica offered tentatively, trying to get it right.

'Oh, Mother!' Imelda sighed with exasperation, wrinkling her nose in disgust at the word 'pretty'.

Jessica drooped. She wished Imelda would not call her 'mother', it kept a distance between them of at least an arm's length.

'A nun's habit would suit her better,' Marcus observed, 'except she doesn't believe in God.'

Hugh, who had been unconcernedly drinking his cocoa and munching a rich tea biscuit, suddenly came to life, 'That is not amusing, Marcus!' he snapped.

Jessica turned anxious eyes from one of her incomprehensible children to the other and asked in a puzzled voice, 'Why would a nun's habit suit her?'

'I meant the austerity of it would suit her, that's all,' Marcus explained in his bored manner; then to his father, who was still glowering at him, he said, 'Ask Imelda, if you think I'm wrong.'

All eyes turned to that young woman.

'I have as much belief in God as Marcus has,' she answered imperturbably, fixing her brother with cold, pale eyes which were so like his own.

Jessica, who had embraced religion with great fervour after Marcus' birth as a means of blotting out problems in her marriage, shied away from the light of sympathy shining in Una's dark, expressive eyes and gazed instead into her cocoa, fighting down the feeling of panic which always assailed her during family conflict. Both her children resembled their father in looks and intractability. They seemed to have no need for anyone but themselves. She was not surprised to learn that they thought they had no need of God. Hugh pretended he had, of course, and went through all the rituals of religious observance. At least the children were not so hypocritical and did so occasionally only under pressure. She consoled herself with the thought that tomorrow morning, as soon as she had cleared away the breakfast dishes and fed the cats, she would hurry across to church. In the quiet vestry, surrounded by an assortment of jars and vases filled with faded flowers awaiting her attention, the smell of green, stagnant water and slimy stalks acrid in the still, cool air, she would sing quietly and happily as she fetched fresh water and set about the pleasant task of snipping and arranging a mass of fresh blooms. Most of the flowers would come from her garden, but a few special ones would be bought from the florists on the way, paid for out of the generous housekeeping. Jessica never sang in her comfortable, dust-laden home, but occasionally the cats caught a hummed refrain while she wandered round their territory, raiding it for greenery and blossom.

As soon as she had finished her cocoa, Una said she must be going.

'Marcus will walk you home,' Hugh said, lighting another cigarette and settling back in his armchair.

'No, really, there's no need,' Una protested. 'It isn't far.'

'It's all right,' Marcus assured her gracelessly, getting to his feet, resenting his father's offer on his behalf. 'I could do with some fresh air.' He yawned and stretched to his full height. Actually, he did not mind very much. His aunt Una was all right; he quite liked her. She had a tantalising air of sadness about her. It made a chap want to cheer her up. The trouble was that Marcus did not know how. He had no fund of funny stories, no sense of the ridiculous. His humour was wry, heavy with sarcasm, aimed at other people's discomfiture, even annoyance. When his mother looked near to tears, his father grew red with anger, or his sister glared with disdain, Marcus laughed inwardly at the joke and felt superior to them all. He did not want to feel superior to Una. When she regarded him with her slanted, warm brown eyes, an expression of wonder in them, as if she were asking why he enjoyed

39

making people unhappy, he was ashamed and, to make himself feel even more of a heel, said something cruel to his long-suffering mother, who did not know how to retaliate. Now, hands in trouser pockets, padding along in his crêpe soles by Una's side, with her high heels clicking quickly and rhythmically, staccatto in the quietness of the night, he felt extremely tall and protective towards her. He began racking his brains for something cheerful to say.

'Are you looking forward to going in the army, Marcus?' she asked, saving him the trouble.

'I am looking forward to leaving home,' he admitted, assiduously taking his place on the edge of the pavement again, after they had crossed the road. 'Dad keeps telling everyone that it will make a man of me, but he doesn't say how. I don't suppose he knows, never having had to go himself. I sometimes wonder what made a man of him.'

'Perhaps *not* being able to go,' Una suggested, quietly.

He turned his head to look down at her. The street-light was shining on her dark, wavy hair and long eyelashes. He thought she looked too pretty to be clever. Brains should be a compensation for ugliness, as in the case of his cousin Donald. Marcus was not too clever himself, but he reckoned his good looks would take him further than Donald's swotting. One aspect of joining up which he was looking forward to was the uniform. He would look super in uniform.

'You will look handsome in your uniform,' Una said, well aware of his vanity and speaking the truth. His large, heavy-featured face, so like his sister's, was more attractive in a young man. He had the same thick, fair hair, but it was slicked back with Brylcreem into a DA, with a quiff over one eyebrow, and appeared a few shades darker.

Marcus gave the dark waves another admiring glance.

They were within a few steps of their destination, which was midway along a Victorian terrace. Each house had a small, square front garden, three steps up to the front door, two long bay windows one above the other, and was topped by a dormer window. Una and Neil had bought the house three

40

years ago for a relatively modest sum, because it had been in a sad state of disrepair, neglected over many years by the elderly couple who had been its previous owners. Behind the house was a narrow, walled garden, which had been allowed to return to the wild, but which Neil was gradually taming.

Marcus opened the gate and watched patiently while Una walked along the path, up the steps and let herself into the house. She waved briefly before the door closed behind her. Immediately, a light came on and he saw her head bob down behind the coloured glass panel in the upper part of the door and a moment later come into view again and move away along the passage. He turned and sauntered homewards, hoping that the others would have gone to bed by the time he returned, so that he could raid the larder in peace, have a swig of the old man's sherry and pinch one of his fags. He thought of Una getting ready to sleep alone in the double bed and considered that his Uncle Neil was a lucky dog to have such a pretty wife. He allowed himself some lascivious thoughts, even imagining what it would be like to make love to her, or any other woman for that matter. He had no doubt that Una would be gently submissive, even grateful, for his fierce, manly embraces.

As soon as she had opened the front door Una saw that there was a letter from Neil on the mat and swooped to pick it up. She had met Imelda straight from the office and they had visited a restaurant for a pot of tea and buttered scones before going on to the pictures. The letter must have arrived by second post. She did not immediately tear it open, even though she was dying to read it, but made herself wait until she was in bed. Then she skimmed through the contents quickly before reading it again very slowly, making the most of every word. She slept with the letter under her pillow and re-read it next morning, while she was eating toast and marmalade and drinking two cups of tea. Afterwards she slipped it into her handbag and took it to work. Three more days to get through before Neil returned.

Late on Saturday night, Neil came home to a rapturous

welcome, which would have astonished, even slightly shocked, the cool, unshockable Marcus and which delighted, even slightly shocked, his uncle Neil, who had experienced many such tempestuous greetings after much briefer absences.

When the tumult of loving was over and they lay quietly in one another's arms, was Una happy then? Neil did not think so. The more intense their ardour, the more bleakly she gazed into the obscurity of the future, anticipating the next parting. Perhaps it was as well they had no children. Love is anguish where there is such fear of loss. Neil, whose presence brought her joy, had no words to bring her comfort. He held her close and did not ask why her face was wet with tears.

Chapter Five

Some families seemed to be marked out by the Fates for downfall. The process of gradual elimination, which goes on continuously in the natural course of events, accelerates as if by some malignant whim and centuries of breeding are brought to an end. History concludes in tragedy and all that went before of struggle and triumph, with no memory to mark it, is blankness.

Jessica Close was wrong in supposing that after her daughter's twenty-first birthday it would be a long time before the Favorys reassembled. The occasion was to be the last time they would all be together.

It was not the happy event it should have been, which was sad, in retrospect.

During the weeks leading up to it, Una gave the question of a suitable gift for Imelda much thought. It was not easy. Imelda only really appreciated something she needed and, when asked, professed to need nothing.

'Save your money. There's nothing I want,' she told Una.

'There must be something,' Una protested.

Imelda thought for a few moments, then shook her head. 'Nothing!' she stated, but at Una's look of dismay she amended this to, 'If I think of something, I'll tell you. I don't want to deprive you of the pleasure of being generous.'

'Thank you very much. That's very kind of you,' Una answered, nettled.

'No, really, I mean it. I shall try very hard to think of

something. It's easy to accept from you and Neil, because you love to give and one doesn't have to be grovellingly grateful.'

Two days later she telephoned Una at the office to say that she would like an anthology of modern English poetry.

'But do you really need it?' Una teased her.

'Yes,' was Imelda's serious reply. 'Poetry is essential food for the soul. I devour it secretly, like an ashamed glutton, mostly on night shift, to the musical accompaniment of sniffs and snores and the occasional frantic call for the bedpan.'

On the Saturday of the party, Una and Neil spent the afternoon gardening. It was a warm, still day in late August and the garden was untidy with the dying back of summer luxuriance. There was a heavy crop of apples on the James Grieve trees and long, pendulous runner beans, enough for at least two more meals, on the twining mass of vermilion flowers and bedraggled leaves tangled around a row of cane wigwams in a sheltered corner near the stone wall.

Everything produces in due season, why don't I? Una wondered. While Neil was cutting the grass and weeding the vegetable patch, she dead-headed the roses and tightened the string around the tall crimson hollyhocks, in an effort to pull them upright after their battering by the wind two nights ago. A full, over-blown flowerlet, dry and darkening almost to black with decay, resembling a closely furled paper rosette, dropped from the woody stalk to the ground, dislodging an earwig which landed on Una's shoe. She shook it off and trod upon it, but its hard body was protected by the damp earth and it survived her quick stamp of revulsion.

Later, lying in the bath, soaking away the soil from beneath her finger nails, feeling the smart of the scratches on her forearms inflicted by the spiteful thorns of the rose bushes, Una experienced the onset of the familiar mild depression which always attacked her at the thought of Neil's estimable family *en masse*. All those good deeds, all that goodwill, all those indulged children! How could they be so depressing? Sometimes she suspected that it was jealousy that lay so leaden within her, because Neil was devoted to them all and they to him. If only they would love me too, she sighed, placing a hand beneath the surface of the warm, soapy water onto her flat stomach. As individuals, his four sisters seem to like me well enough, but his aunts, who cannot be separated even in imagination, treat me like a family dependant, who must be endured with pleasantries, because no amount of animosity will make me disappear and Neil would be alienated in the attempt. Of course, they still hope that I will fulfil my obligations to them all. While there is that hope, there will remain an awful, kindly tolerance. Flora is the only one who could be accused of tolerance without kindness and she takes care to be nice enough when Neil is present.

When she returned to the bedroom, Neil was stooping before the mirror on the chest of drawers, adjusting his tie. He told her to hurry. Sibyl and Stuart would be arriving soon to pick them up. Then he went downstairs to wait for them.

Una sat before her dressing-table in her new nylon slip, edged with coffee-coloured lace, and began brushing her short dark hair vigorously, thinking, Brush it until it shines and your scalp tingles. Her mother's words, her mother's brush, her mother's brown eyes in the mirror, watching her sadly. She stopped the swift backward action and held the prickly bristles to her breast, her fingers caressing the warm silver back of embossed roses. It was the only possession she had of her mother's, one of the few objects that had escaped intact the flattening blast. A stranger, an elderly man with a lined face, grey with dust and misery, had handed it to her without a word. She had been standing on the pavement in her ATS uniform, gazing across the road in horror and wild disbelief at the site of her non-existent home. He had emerged from the rubble of the house next door and approached her slowly, one hand held before him like a figure in a dream. It was as if he and she were the only people left in the squalid desolation of that once well-known street. Then he had vanished. The brush was in her own hand. At her feet was a dirty scrap of faded regency stripe wallpaper from her parents' bedroom.

Rubbing her thumbs lovingly against the bristles, Una

recalled that bedroom. There was her mother, sitting before the walnut dressing-table on the square stool with the *petit point* seat, brushing her long hair with a rhythmic, sweeping motion.

'Mum?' and she would stop brushing and turn her head, her hair hanging over one shoulder like a glossy curtain of dark brown silk, gleaming with gold highlights; as she listened to the childish problem, she would hold the brush thus, the silver back against one warm cheek, considering . . .

'Una, hurry up! They are here.'

'Here we go again,' Stuart Ferguson said, loudly and cheerfully, as Una and Neil squeezed into the back of the car with the boys. 'And to think Tom and I could have been playing in a golf tournament.'

Sibyl ignored this remark, so Una and Neil did as well. From the venomous look which Sibyl gave her husband, they presumed that plenty had already been said on the subject. Sibyl and her sister, Marcia, were martyrs to their husbands' golfing addiction and had grown even closer since their marriages from numerous weekends spent together in grass widowhood, entertaining the children.

Advised by his wife beforehand that on no account did she want her best dress crumpled, Neil pulled Bruce onto his lap. Julian grudgingly squeezed into the corner and looked fixedly out of the window.

'Must you smoke in the car?' Sibyl enquired acidly, as Stuart reached for a packet of Players in the glove compartment. 'You know it makes Julian feel sick.'

'Everything makes the little brat feel sick,' he said, still determinedly cheerful, but he refrained from lighting up.

Una felt as relieved as Julian. She would be glad when they had a car of their own and no longer had to rely on lifts. They should have enough money saved in another year, providing that she did not have to give up work to have a baby. Neil was cautious with money and had a horror of being in debt. If he had a fault, it was a reliance on inheriting his share of the

46

Macfarlane Brown wealth. It was a reliance he shared with his brothers-in-law. One day, he often assured Una, they would have enough money to provide them with security and comfort in their old age; in the meantime they must conserve their resources. He was not anxious to inherit, far from it, he just knew that in the natural course of events he and his four sisters would share the proceeds from the grand old house and, lacking ambition to rise to great heights in the insurance world in which he worked, he was content to wait.

The evenings were drawing in and the afternoon's warmth had been replaced by a distinctly autumnal chill by the time they pulled into the lane at Lapcombe just before six o'clock. They were the first to arrive. Flora appeared in the porch before the open front door to greet them, large and upright, almost filling the dimly lit space. Lavinia, taller, hovered behind, her small, smooth head bobbing from one side to the other, as she peered over her ponderous sister's shoulders in a flutter of excited greeting. Once inside the spacious hall everyone embraced. It was part of the ritual. Lavinia lowered her head to kiss with quick, jerky movements, smiling and nervous. She had to bend almost double to reach Bruce's pink cheek. Flora allowed herself to be kissed, inclining her head with condescension, not approving of the hearty smack of Stuart's lips and barely acknowledging the light touch of Una's lipstick, which left a faint pink smudge on the white powdered cheek. Una wondered, not for the first time, if Flora doused herself all over with talcum powder. Perhaps she was too mean to buy a box of tinted face powder, or perhaps she enjoyed the effect on people of the dramatic contrast between white skin, jet black hair and red lips. On a small woman, the drama would have been reduced to farce, on an elderly one like Flora it was not far removed from it.

It was over four months since Flora and Lavinia had seen Una. They glanced at her from top to toe, hoping to discern a change in her slim outline. Una caught the surreptitious glance. Lavinia quickly said, 'What a pretty dress, Una. Is it a circular skirt? It's Flora's favourite colour.'

'I didn't know that,' Una said, supposing that Flora had always worn black and white with dramatic accessories in violent contrast.

'Yes, I used to wear it quite a lot when it was fashionable, years ago,' Flora admitted. 'Did you make it yourself?'

Una recognised this for subtle criticism, implying that it looked amateurishly put together. It was an insult whether she answered yes or no, so she chose to do neither, just smile; but Neil, proud of his wife's expertise with her sewing machine and the saving she made in its employment, put his arm about her waist and said, with a fond squeeze, 'Yes, she did. Isn't she clever?'

'Very,' was Flora's brief answer, while her sister went into raptures about it.

Flora was dressed in a black skirt and a handsome silver-striped blouse, with frills at the high neck and cuffs and tiny darns under the arms, where the material had weakened with extreme age. Over her ample bosom was an enormous floppy bow of bright orange silk. It clashed with her red lipstick.

Lavinia was wearing an olive green woollen dress, which clung to her long, lean form, emphasising the chasms. Her chronic stoop caused the hemline to droop at the front and curve up over her stringy calves. With her anxious round eyes in her small round face, set above an attenuated greenness, her thin hands fluttering about on the ends of her stiff arms, she resembled an agitated stick insect. Watching her and her younger sister together, it was not difficult for Una to see the more dominant one as a natural predator of stick insects.

'Is there anything I can do to help?' Una asked, following the rest along the hall and already feeling a little left out, as Sibyl walked between her fond aunts, answering their questions about her children.

'Everything's done,' Flora told her over her shoulder. 'Jessica and Ella have been here all the afternoon, preparing. You'll find them in the kitchen.'

Una found them in the kitchen. She once more offered her services and once more they were declined. She did not know

48

whether to go or stay. Her entrance had interrupted a low-voiced *tête-à-tête* between the two sisters and she felt like an interloper. They had both greeted her warmly enough, giving her the visual once-over that she had come to expect from them all, simultaneously asking her the expected question, 'How's Neil?'

She decided to go back to Neil's side, but her retreat was thwarted by the arrival of Sibyl and Marcia, with baby Shirley fast asleep in the carry-cot, which Marcia dumped on the table.

'Where are you going to put her?' Ella asked, 'She can't stay there, directly under the light bulb.'

'I'll put her upstairs in the green room, but first I want you to see her rash.'

The four sisters inspected the sleeping baby, all in turn poking a finger down the neck of her vest and up the leg of her nappy and each one giving an opinion. Una watched and listened and wondered how severe a rash would have to be before medical advice was sought. When a diagnosis and remedy were decided upon, a relieved Marcia took her baby upstairs. She had no sooner gone than there was the sound of new arrivals in the hall.

'The birthday girl has arrived,' Lavinia called excitedly in her high voice, putting her head round the kitchen door.

'At last,' Jessica said with relief. Only she knew how reluctant the birthday girl was to attend her own party. Everyone crammed into the hall to embrace Imelda and congratulate her, handing her their presents with kisses. The young males hung back, but were pushed into the fray by their mothers. They dutifully kissed their cousin's cheek and muttered their 'happy birthdays', thrusting their presents at her and retreating as quickly as they could.

Imelda's birthday had actually been the day before. It had passed by unrecognised at the hospital, because no one had known, not even her best friend and fellow nurse.

When it was the turn of six-year-old Peter Fielding to kiss Imelda, he put one hand to the back of her neck as she leant down to him and, drawing her closer, whispered in her ear,

'I'm coming to have my tonsils out, but I don't like ice-cream.'

'Then you shan't have any,' Imelda told him firmly.

Satisfied, he handed over a square box wrapped in mauve tissue paper. He could believe Imelda, she never told fibs. He darted his twin sisters a look of triumph. They had lost their tonsils five years ago and had been adamant that eating ice-cream was an essential part of the experience.

Imelda suffered the homage of the family stoically, smiling her thanks, secretly exultant to be free of them all at last; an adult, whether they liked it or not.

'Bring your presents into the drawing-room, Imelda. Help her carry them, someone. Don't let's stand in the hall any longer,' and Flora swept off, while Lavinia scrabbled at the parcels on the chair, trying to carry them all at once.

'Let me help you, Auntie Vin,' Sibyl said, frightened that she was going to drop something. Una gathered up the few things they could not manage and followed Imelda into the drawing-room. The presents were deposited on a round table by the window.

'I haven't even taken my jacket off yet,' Imelda said, doing so and handing it to Lavinia, who scurried off with it.

The parcels were opened and exclaimed over by everyone, but most enthusiastically by Jessica, who detected a lack of warmth in her daughter's spoken gratitude.

Most of the gifts had been bought with a total lack of understanding of the recipient, but Una thought it was Imelda's own fault. If she had desired only useful things, she should have helped people by hinting at the kind of things she put in that category. After all, what one person considered useful, another person might have no use for whatsoever, such as a book of poetry. Jessica and Hugh had given their daughter a beautiful gold watch, which she had chosen herself, so it was to her taste, very plain. Marcus, on the other hand, had kept his gift a secret and Imelda was touched to discover that he had bought her a brass table lamp to stand beside her bed. She had complained at the breakfast table a couple of months ago how difficult it was to read by the light of the one she had already.

Marcus, leaning up against the wall on the far side of the room, met her delighted look of thanks with a nonchalant shrug, as if he were given to such acts of thoughtfulness and could not imagine why this one should be considered exceptional.

From her two great-aunts, Imelda received an envelope, in which was a cheque. She opened it last, to a hushed gathering, with everyone wondering how much a twenty-first birthday merited, when the going rate for ordinary ones was half-a-crown.

'Thank you very much,' she told Flora and Lavinia. It was impossible to tell from her tone whether she was pleased or disappointed.

'Buy yourself something nice, dear,' Flora told her.

'Yes, something nice,' Lavinia echoed.

'It is better than being given something you don't want,' Flora said. 'When people give me chocolates or soap, I always give them away again.'

Una blushed. She was guilty of having given both.

Imelda replaced the cheque in the envelope and put it in her skirt pocket. The combined generosity of her great-aunts amounted to £5.00.

That was that. Imelda's importance gave way to the importance of the supper table in the dining-room. She thankfully resumed her customary place in the pecking order, determined that the next time she visited Lapcombe it would be on her own, because she felt like it, not brought in the family car as part of her mother's fond duty and her father's fond expectations.

The evening now progressed in the same way as many similar evenings. Flora's home-made barley wine was produced from the sideboard cupboard and under it's benign influence—and that of the whisky she secretly used to fortify it—she began to indulge in arch raillery towards the men and tell embarrassing tales about her nieces and nephew, when they were young. At least, the tales used to be embarrassing, but they had been told so often that the victims were now able to listen without squirming and would laugh with as much hidden tedium as the rest. Marcia had wet her knickers in church; Neil had fallen into a dung heap on his way to school, the sun-baked outer surface cracking beneath his weight when he misjudged his jump over it; Ella had told a big fib and been caught out through her own naïveté; Sibyl had described a hat worn by Jane Pope-Wessington in uncomplimentary terms and been overheard by the wearer; Jessica had made herself a dress for a dance, but had forgotten to replace the tacking stitches round the waist with machine ones; consequently, when her partner trod upon the hem, it had ripped apart. There were other stories. No one escaped, no one expected to do so. The mention of Jane Pope-Wessington reminded Flora to regale them all with the latest meeting between her and that lady, which happened to be two weeks ago at the village fête, which had been a great success.

'You weren't there, were you, dear?' Flora said to Una.

Una shook her head. She had wanted to go—well, not exactly wanted to, but knew she ought, because Neil's aunts and his sisters would be there and would be expecting her support on Flora's big day. Neil, forgetting the fête, or so he said, had planned a paddle steamer trip with some of their friends and he knew where he would rather be. So they had gone to Swanage on the steamer and only Una had earned disapproval for doing so.

'Louise was there, with her husband and three children. Claude Pope-Wessington is so proud of them. He took them round all the side shows and gave them money for goes on everything.'

Louise was the Pope-Wessington daughter. Una had never met her, but had been introduced to her parents once in the Lapcombe church porch. She had felt uncomfortable at the honour Flora supposed she should feel at meeting the middle-aged, inoffensive couple, who were rather shabbily dressed and whose accent alone betrayed their breeding—that and the quality of their well-worn clothes. They had no wealth to be mean with, in fact, they were what the Favorys once had been, rich only in land and livestock. What they had needed was for

Louise to marry into money. Instead, she had married a man with a good career, which was some consolation. He was the Deputy Clerk of the County Council. Una knew him by sight and reputation, although she worked in a different department at County Hall.

While she was listening to Flora recounting what she had said to Mrs Pope-Wessington and what that lady had said to her in reply—mainly congratulations on the work Flora had put in on the fête and the excellence of her stall, on which was displayed a variety of local handiwork—Una, sitting beside Ella and Ronald Fielding, became aware that they were distinctly frosty with one another. Ronald was a pipe smoker, the kind of man who habitually sits in a corner, contentedly smoking, busy with his thoughts and letting the women get on with it all. This evening, he was not happy. He grunted with derision a couple of times at some of the inane conversation he was forced to overhear and drew hostile glances of reproof from his wife, who was having surprisingly little to say for herself.

Una liked Ronald. He was her favourite brother-in-law. Something had jarred him from his usual mild humour and she wondered what it was. When Flora began to tell them about the trials and tribulations of her holiday in Torquay, she thought she knew the answer. Every year since the war, Flora and Lavinia had taken one of Ronald's coaches to a seaside resort in England or Wales and spent a fortnight going on day trips to local beauty spots and places of interest. Every year without fail she complained about some aspect of the holiday, assuring Ronald that it was not his fault. As it was usually the hotel or the weather she complained about, or Lavinia's insistence on being poorly while they were away, he could agree with her. This year, she was telling them, their friendly coach driver had been vulgar and over-familiar. Ronald would have to do something about it, Flora told him, otherwise the driver's suggestive remarks would mean that no respectable female would take one of his coach holidays again. 'He had something smutty to say about everything,' she concluded, 'even the sticks of rock Lavinia bought for the children, didn't he, Vin?'

Lavinia agreed with her, but looked a little puzzled. She probably did not recognise a smutty remark when she heard one.

'I'll look into it, Aunt,' Ronald promised in a resigned tone, getting to his feet with difficulty. He limped badly from a wound sustained on a Russian convoy during the war. There were deep lines either side of his mouth and a strained look in his mild, grey eyes, which told of incessant pain.

'Where are you going?' Ella asked him sharply, as he made for the door.

'To see what the kids are up to.'

She watched him leave the room, biting her lip with anxiety.

There was no need to ask what Sylvia and Tina were up to. The crashing of the piano keys in the room next door told its own story. He discovered his clever son, Donald, humiliating Ian Hastings at chess. Ella was extremely proud of this prodigy of theirs, but Ronald, who had once been very sporty, was disappointed in him. He would have liked to enjoy his sporting activities all over again, by watching his son compete; instead Donald only enjoyed intellectual pursuits. Having no common interests, father and son had little conversation. Ian, who was being wiped off the chess board for the third time that evening, would much rather have been outside kicking a football about. Ronald envied Tom this very normal boy and, unfortunately, Donald knew it.

Julian was found in the kitchen, eating things guaranteed to make him sick. Tonsilitis-prone Peter was upstairs, just looking at the baby; at least, that was what he told his father he was doing. Bruce and Kate were nowhere to be seen.

They were snuggled together in the warm half-darkness of the linen cupboard. With solemn eyes and furtive whispers, they were being naughty and enjoying it. When Marcia came upstairs ten minutes later to feed the baby, who was crying, and smacked Peter hard, which made him cry, the guilty pair crept out from hiding and appeared in moments in the dining-room, looking demure. When Sibyl demanded to know where they had been, Kate promptly answered, 'Playing hide and seek, Auntie,' and Bruce returned his mother's enquiring glance with a look of wide-eyed innocence.

Marcia had discovered crisps upon Shirley's pillow and, horror of horrors, in her mouth. At her entrance, Peter had backed away towards the door, surreptitiously stuffing a packet into the pocket of his short trousers and denying that he had done anything. A blue twist of paper containing salt, which fell from his pocket, proved his guilt.

'I didn't know she didn't have any teeth,' he sobbed, running downstairs to his mother, with the red imprint of Marcia's hand on his plump leg.

Ella was annoyed with her sister for the smack. It was not Marcia's place to punish other people's children. Ella would not have been so annoyed had she not already been upset. The trouble was that Ronald had recently become suspicious about the relationship between Ella and their local grocer, when there was no longer anything to be suspicious about. How maddening it was for her to have gone through all the bother of rejecting everything, well, almost everything, that the grocer had to offer and then, this morning, to be accused of still accepting more than the occasional half-pound of butter or tin of salmon. She had been confiding in her sister, Jessica, when Una walked into the kitchen, but she had not been completely honest with her. Ella's grocer had been a joke to her sisters all through the war, while Ronald was away in the navy. They had referred to him as Ella's fancy man, because he was so obviously smitten with her charms and always treated her as a privileged customer. In those days, who would not smile and flutter their eyelashes for a few extra rations? What her sisters did not know, was that he delivered her groceries personally, more than once a week; which was unusual, to say the least, in times of shortages, when one cardboard box was more than sufficient to take the week's groceries of an average family. Ella's neighbours could have told them how often the cumbersome delivery bicycle was wheeled along the side path, but no one ever asked them, so they only discussed it between themselves.

After Imelda's party, driving homewards in silence beside Ronald, with the four sleepy children in the back, Ella could have wept with vexation. The affair between the young, lonely housewife and the middle-aged widower had never been a passionate one. There had been kisses and cuddles after the unpacking of the comestibles and, occasionally, unsatisfactory couplings in the back bedroom, with the curtains partly drawn against the intrusive daylight which fell upon the dust on the furniture and the blackheads on the grocer's fleshy nose with equal dispassion, and robbed their hurried embraces of any romance.

Ella was still getting her groceries from the same shop, even though, since Ronald's homecoming and resumption of his wife's favours, the grocer had found another lonely housewife to ply with cardboard boxes of goodies. However, Ella still exercised her considerable charm over the bacon counter, sure of an extra rasher. Now, she supposed, with Ronald accusing her of encouraging the grocer's sly winks, she must shop elsewhere. It would be most inconvenient, not to say unprofitable.

Ella had no sense of shame. She had a curious morality, no doubt fashioned in the period when she was painfully coming to terms with her mother's devastating disappearance. She must never deprive her children of her presence. When they were at home, so must she be. When they needed her, it was imperative to respond promptly to that need. On the other hand, by some strange quirk in her reasoning, she considered that it was permissible to please herself in her own time. While the children were at school, she felt answerable to no one. Consequently, her war-time affair with the amiable grocer had been conducted strictly according to the school timetable. During the long school holidays, the tell-tale bicycle was never once propped against the side of the house. It was shoved into the privet hedge beside the pavement every

Thursday by the gangly youth whose job it was to make deliveries. He had struggled along the path, puffing and blowing, carrying the unsupplemented rations. A time of plenty began again with the new school term.

For seven years now Ella had been a faithful wife. If Ronald had not gone away, she supposed she would never have been unfaithful. She blamed the war.

Chapter Six

The sterile months slipped past. Every week-day morning, Una and Neil walked together to the station. Una caught the 8.30 train to the small county town eight miles away. Neil walked along the sea-front to his office in the centre of the slightly larger seaside resort where they lived. Every week-day evening, Una arrived home twenty minutes after Neil and they prepared the meal together. They worked the same three out of every four Saturday mornings. One evening a week, usually on a Monday, they went to the cinema and one evening a month, on their free Saturday, they went dancing. They were very fond of dancing. It was in a dance hall that they had met, when they were both in uniform.

They had occasional contact with the various members of Neil's family. The only one they saw regularly was Imelda, who dropped in about once a week and, with Una's encouragement, kept them informed of the happenings within the family circle.

With any marriage, one acquires relations who are comparative strangers. Usually it is possible to get to know those strangers through one's mother-in-law. A shrewd person takes care to like her, to side with her on domestic issues, to seek her advice, not necessarily to take it, and to aid her in championing her child against the world. Neil had neither mother for Una to befriend, nor father for her to bewitch; but four older sisters and two peculiar aunts, who were more possessive than any parent would need to be. They were not only jealous of his present but they hogged his past, that period between his mother's disappearance and Una's unwelcome arrival.

Una was in an ambivalent position: wanting to be close to them all, yet resenting them because they would not love her. How simple life would be if she could present them with another mortal to cherish, someone who was part of herself and to whom she was of paramount importance.

'They are all fond of you, darling,' Neil would often assure her. It was not true. They did not dislike her and she was thankful for that. She would hardly know anything about them if it were not for Imelda and, being merely one of the children, her information was fragmentary. She knew what she saw, understanding more as she grew older; she half understood what she overheard and, now that she was old enough to understand fully, overheard precious little.

The four sisters and their offspring met frequently, casual meetings involving dropping in on each other unannounced and sending the children with messages between their respective homes. Una and Neil lived apart from this constant intercommunication. Neil was content to see his sisters and his aunts once in a blue moon. Una's occasional visits to their respective homes had shown her that Jessica and Ella were not good housewives, their hearts were not in it; the former would rather dust and make beautiful the church than her bungalow, and the latter was inclined to indolence and novel-reading. Marcia struggled on as best she could. Between coping with the demands of her three children and an exacting husband, she kept the house tolerably clean and tidy. Sibyl was positively houseproud and had little time for anything else but polishing, cleaning and redecorating—a passion she shared with her brother.

They were all obsessive: Jessica was obsessed with the church; Ella and Marcia with their children; Sibyl and Neil with their homes.

A month after her twenty-first birthday, Imelda imparted the news that Ella had changed her grocer of long standing, to one in the centre of the town. As far as Imelda could make out,

Ronald had grown suspicious about the preferential treatment his wife had been getting at their local shop and claimed to have heard rumours that it was in return for goings-on during his absence in the navy. Imelda had questioned her mother about the nature of those goings-on, but Jessica had scoffed at the very idea, saying that Ella had been far too busy bringing up the children on her own to have time for philandering. The grocer was old enough to be her father, for goodness sake!

Peter had his tonsils out. Imelda visited him in her nurse's uniform and made sure that no one mentioned ice-cream. He had been immensely relieved to see his big cousin as soon as he had recovered from the anaesthetic and his eyes had spoken volumes of gratitude as she put his scruffy teddy bear in bed with him. The twins and Donald were not allowed into the ward, so, during the visiting hours, he had his parents all to himself, which was a rare privilege. They were careful not to let him see the growing estrangement between them, but Imelda noticed, in the few minutes she could spare to look in on him. She also noticed what an anxious state Ella was in, sitting beside the child's bed in the alien environment, his welfare out of her own hands for the first time. Imelda did her best to reassure her, but it was useless. Ella's agitation would not cease until Peter was once more restored to her maternal power.

Marcus left home to join the army. He had chosen the Royal Artillery and was sent to Oswestry. After a fortnight there he was moved to a training regiment in North Wales. Una saw him on Christmas Day at the gathering at Lapcombe. He looked thinner and older and somehow more wary, as if he were frightened to relax in case he was subjected to another haircut.

Marcia and family were not there, because Kate had the measles. Imelda had to work in her festively decorated hospital ward, singing carols and being briskly cheerful. Their absence had a curious affect upon the others. They were spoken about incessantly as if their loss was felt more keenly than their

presence would have been, in the manner of someone enduring a constant irritation on a missing limb. The food was not
consumed with so much relish. Nobody tried to press Una
into eating things she hated. She was left to be faddy in peace.
Flora's playful teasing was half-hearted, which meant that
Lavinia did not have to make so many placatory faces behind
her back. Even the children were subdued. Donald missed Ian
to thrash at a newly acquired board game and Bruce missed
Kate, the instigator of their clandestine cupboard love. The
piano stood with upright dignity against the drawing-room
wall, its yellowing keys passive beneath the wormy, hinged
lid, the stool underneath it unburdened by the bouncy bot-
toms of the girl twins, who, for once, had no desire to give
their all to music, but preferred to quarrel with one another
and be spiteful to their little brother, Peter. Even Julian seemed
out of sorts and did not once mention feeling sick.

Una missed her god-daughter. Shirley was now ten months
old. She was a contented child, who allowed herself to be
passed from lap to lap with equanimity. With Shirley in her
arms, Una had some idea of what it would be like to have a
baby of her own and when someone else coaxed her away, she
was left to consider how fortunate Marcia was to have so
desirable an object.

Ronald sat in a corner most of the time, smoking his pipe,
which was not unusual, but he was allowed to do so without
constant application by Ella for his opinion or support in every
discussion. Stuart sat next to him, smoking cigarettes, giving
his opinion on absolutely everything and seeking no one's
support in the arguments that he provoked.

Hugh Close, who could be relied upon to put himself
forward, with good humour, as a candidate for Flora's roguish
banter, did so that evening from habit, without enthusiasm.
Flora teased him about his bald patch, his thickening waist, his
short sight, his position as General Manager in the depart-
mental store, which she thought he gave more consequence to
than it deserved. She even teased him about his weak heart. He
bore it all stoically enough, giving her bland replies, which

robbed her of the verbal ammunition to hurl back at him Lavinia smiled at him anxiously, in case he should take offence, and did her best to alleviate the worst of the insults which were lurking beneath the thick veil of jest. He was not bald, she assured him, just a little thin on top; he was nowhere near so fat as Mr Laston, the vicar; he looked very distinguished in his spectacles; he was just like the captain of a great liner in that vast shop. Even she could think of nothing comforting to say about a weak heart, apart from confiding in him that the doctor had informed her that her own heart was in pretty poor shape and advising him that he would live longer if he gave up smoking. As there did not seem any part of her which was not in poor shape and he found it impossible to give up smoking, Hugh was not mollified.

Flora had something uncomplimentary to say about everyone. She told Sibyl that she looked awful in her new dress. 'That's a pretty dress, dear, but not quite your usual style, is it?' was what she actually said. She disliked the shoes that Una had bought Neil for Christmas, asking, 'Did Una choose those for you? Yes, I thought perhaps she did. Very nice, dear.'

Una thought how unfair it was that they must all suffer her remarks with brave smiles and were not supposed to retaliate. One day, when she is fishing for a compliment, instead of saying, 'Most becoming, Auntie,' copying all the others, who are adept at giving her the flattery she craves, I shall shake her rigid by telling her the truth. It was just a fantasy, she knew she never would.

Flora's nieces flattered her out of fond kindness, her nephews-in-law did it tongue-in-cheek, Una did so to conform; only her nephew told her she looked marvellous and spoke from fond blindness. Una loved Neil for that blinkered devotion.

Una and Neil travelled home with the Close family. Neil sat beside Hugh. Una between Jessica and Marcus. It seemed to be her lot to travel in the back of other people's cars. At least this was a large one and there was ample room on the seat for the three of them, which was as well for, had she but known it, the occasional pressure of her thigh against his own when they cornered was causing Marcus pleasurable unease.

Travelling in Hugh's pre-war Humber, with its distinctive smell of leather upholstery, reminded Una of travelling in similar cars during the war, as a chauffeur. She wondered what Hugh's reaction would be if she offered to drive. Not favourable, she suspected, mindful that Jessica was always relegated to the back when another male was present, even her own son.

'You should be sitting in the front,' Una said to her, testing her theory.

'Oh no,' Jessica replied quickly, casting a swift glance at her husband's face in the rear-view mirror. 'I like riding in the back.'

'She's used to it, aren't you, Mum?'Marcus drawled, shifting his leg with care in case Una should sense the heated acuteness of their nearness.

'Have you never wanted to drive, Jessica?' Una asked.

Hugh laughed unkindly.

'I don't go anywhere on my own,' Jessica explained, 'only to church and it's not very far. Imelda is taking lessons, but Hugh won't let her have a go in the Humber,' and she shot another look at his image.

'She has never asked,' he said shortly.

'You have never offered,' his wife retorted.

'We should be getting a car soon,' Neil said. 'Then Una will be able to drive to work instead of having to rely on trains. By the time she gets home on a Saturday, the afternoon is half over.'

How soon was soon? Una wondered, excited at the prospect.

'Poor Marcia,' Jessica said, determined to change the subject. 'How miserable for her to have one of the children ill at Christmas. Measles is such a nasty thing. I can remember when Imelda had it. She was very poorly and kept having nose-bleeds. We were sleeping in the Morrison in the dining-room, all huddled together, and Imelda was running a temperature and having nightmares, as if the raids weren't bad enough.'

Sitting on her daughter's bed that afternoon, reading *Winnie-the-Pooh*, Marcia was feeling depressed. For one thing, she did not enjoy being left out of family celebrations; for another, Tom's parents were descending upon them in two days' time for the New Year period. Shirley was fractious, which probably meant she, too, was going down with measles. Thank goodness Ian had had them when he started school.

She stopped reading and placed a hand on Kate's hot forehead. Kate shifted uncomfortably and grumbled without opening her eyes. She had dozed off. Marcia shut the book, but remained sitting where she was, staring out of the window at the bleak December sky, thinking of them all getting ready to go to Lapcombe. Tom, of course, was relieved that they did not have to go. She had overheard him talking to Stuart on the telephone. Julian and Bruce had caught the measles at the same time as Ian, so Stuart had no hope of being released by an epidemic.

Marcia no longer liked her husband. She was cleverer than he was and he resented it, therefore he made her pay for it. Sometimes, looking at him when he was unaware of her hostile scrutiny, she had the urge to say to him, 'I am not going to have any more sex,' but the words never came, she was too nervous of provoking a violent reaction. She knew it was not right for one person to dominate another, either mentally or physically, yet she remained powerless even to discuss it with him. Perhaps if their minds were in accord, if their love transcended both his need for her body and her need—which, she miserably acknowledged, existed—to satisfy him, then their physical love would be placed in a healthier perspective. As it was, she wondered dismally what old age would bring. When he was no longer able to brutally revenge himself upon her for her mental supremacy and she no longer had the children near to solace her for all the nights of shameful, sometimes pleasurable, yet always distasteful, subjugation,

64

what then? Did Tom really think he loved her? He mentioned love frequently, but always when she was in his power. There must be more to human love for a woman than a constant giving in to a man's demands; yet, on the rare occasions when she nerved herself to say no, he accused her of not loving him enough and became bad-tempered and aggressive towards the children. The accusation that she did not love him had been unjust in the early years; now it was all too true, but she hid her dislike, not wanting to be responsible for the smacks and bullying which the children would suffer as a result of his frustration.

Marcia sighed heavily and got to her feet, gazing down tenderly upon her little daughter. She wondered what other women suffered in the secret side of their marriages. One could not discuss it, not even with a sister. Everyone assumed that she and Tom were happy, because they seldom argued. She had realised soon after they were married—no, even before that, let's face it—that she could always get the better of Tom in an intellectual argument and that he would always make her pay for it later, when they were alone.

'Mum, Shirley's crying and Grandma's on the 'phone,' Ian whispered, creeping into the room.

'I'm coming,' Marcia told him quietly, following him out.

'Is Kate a bit better?' he asked anxiously, as they went downstairs.

'A little bit,' Marcia said, touched by his concern. She put an arm around his sturdy shoulders and gave him a quick hug. Was it possible that this tender-hearted son of hers would grow up to be like his father and channel the aggression, which he now expended upon the sports field, into his marriage bed? Marcia's depression deepened.

Chapter Seven

In April, Marcus was killed in Korea.

In July, while on holiday with Flora in Scarborough, Lavinia choked to death on a chicken bone.

There was no funeral for Marcus, just a memorial service. At Lavinia's funeral, Jessica, distressed into total confusion, thought she was burying her son.

Still without a car, Una and Neil accompanied Sibyl and Stuart to Lapcombe. They were late and went straight to the church. They joined a knot of mourners on the village green, waiting in the warm summer sunshine. Within five minutes of their arrival, the hearse appeared around the corner at the end of the village, closely and sedately followed by two cars, the first bearing Flora Macfarlane Brown, Jessica and Hugh, and the second Ella, Ronald, Marcia and Tom.

Mr Laston, the vicar, was waiting by the lich-gate, his plump face benign even in sympathetic sorrow. The villagers, who had known the deceased all their lives, stood at a respectful distance from the family, murmuring to each other the identification of the principal mourners, such facts about them that were common knowledge and such rumours about them that were common gossip. Miss Lavinia Favory herself, it was generally agreed, had led a blameless life, which was enough to make her unusual. 'Poor soul,' they sighed, 'she was harmless. A bit dotty, but harmless.'

When Mrs Macfarlane Brown stepped from Hugh Close's car, dressed in unrelieved black, her face whiter than ever, looking not quite so straight and arrogantly tall as she normally did, it was remarked that no doubt she had had the stuffing knocked out of her, losing her reliable dog's-body, and that she was wearing the felt hat that she practically lived in from 1st October to 31st March every winter. Mr Laston spoke some kind words to her, but she appeared not to heed them. She sought and soon found her handsome nephew's arm and, leaning gratefully upon it, not to be budged, followed the coffin up the steep incline of the churchyard path, followed by her nieces. Together with their brother, they were all well known in the locality from the years they had lived in the village. Neil's wife, the pretty, dark-haired young woman, standing a little apart, small in comparison with the rest of them, was not known, except by sight.

Jessica was on her husband Hugh's arm, Ella was on her husband Ronald's arm, Marcia was on her husband Tom's arm and Sibyl was on her husband Stuart's arm, and they proceeded towards the church in that order behind Flora. Imelda was at home, minding the young children.

Una, left standing among strangers, glanced around at a loss for a moment, not anxious to face the ordeal in church without the comfort of Neil's closeness. Someone stepped to her side and a quiet voice said kindly, 'Allow me, my dear.'

Her hand was taken and gently drawn through the arm of Claude Pope-Wessington. They stepped after the small procession, with the intention of becoming part of it. Una knew they failed.

The Favorys were rooted in the community as deeply as the family from the manor and that fact was acknowledged by the presence of the Pope-Wessingtons. Jane was there with her daughter and son-in-law. After them came many acquaintances and neighbours of the deceased—no close friends, for the sisters possessed none. Eccentricity relates only to self and makes it difficult for others to reach the essential person beneath its veneer.

During the service only Jessica and Una wept, and neither of them was shedding tears for poor Lavinia. Jessica was crying for her boy. Una, sitting isolated at the end of the family pew, where Claude Pope-Wessington had handed her before rejoining his own family, and next to Tom whom she always found unsympathetic, was crying for both Jessica and Marcus and for herself and everybody, that they should have to bear such grief.

After Lavinia had been laid to moulder in the churchyard where so many Favory bones were buried, and Jessica had been persuaded to leave the grave wherein her sick fancy had lowered the body of her son, people stood around in bemused groups, wondering what there was left to stay for, yet not anxious to leave.

Una, standing patiently on the edge of the family circle, waiting while Jane and Claude Pope-Wessington spoke a few words of condolence to Mrs Macfarlane Brown, was surprised to see that Neil was standing a little way off, talking to Louise, the Pope-Wessingtons' daughter. They were conversing with ease, like old friends, and, with sudden insight, Una realised they were just that. It had never occurred to her before. Her expression, as she watched them, must have been one of mild surprise, it was certainly one of interest. Louise suddenly glanced towards her and Una quickly looked away, only to encounter the intent regard of Louise's husband. He smiled and she smiled back, in mutual recognition of the fact that they worked in the same building. Una's eyes went back to Neil. He was leading Louise across the grass towards her.

'I've brought an old friend of mine to meet you,' he said, looking—what? Embarrassed, pleased, shy, uncomfortable? It was difficult for Una to guess.

There was an air of sudden watchfulness around them. People were waiting for her reaction. She smiled politely as she shook the other woman's outstretched hand, while Neil was saying, 'This is Una, my wife. I don't think you two have ever met.'

He knows damn well we haven't, Una thought.

'This is Louise,' he said.

'I am delighted to meet you at last,' the woman said in a clear, well-bred voice. She was a few years older than Una, tall and slender, with fair hair and smiling grey eyes. 'I have heard so much about you,' she added cordially.

Una could not say the same thing about her.

'We are staying with Mummy for a few days and I couldn't miss the opportunity of paying my last respects to dear Miss Favory. You will all miss her dreadfully, I'm sure. I wonder how Mrs Macfarlane Brown will manage without her. They were so devoted. The village won't be the same now.' She lowered her voice and took a step nearer Una. 'When I was little, I used to meet Miss Favory quite often when she was doing the shopping. She always had a basket and an umbrella, even on a day like this, and would be clutching a list which she consulted frequently with sighs and tut-tuts. Do you remember, Neil? We followed her once from the sweet shop, imitating her, I'm ashamed to say. Isn't it dreadful. Children are so cruel. My husband tells me you work at County Hall, Mrs Favory. Lucky you! I miss my job awfully, but the children keep me busy. I couldn't possibly return to it. Oh, I must dash! Daddy's beckoning. He's anxious to get back to see a man about a dog, or something. Lovely to have met you at last. Goodbye, goodbye, Neil.' She left them and went across to have a word with Flora and her nieces. She told Jessica how very sorry she was to hear about Marcus. Jessica, holding tightly to Hugh's hand, did not respond at all to the softly spoken sympathy and it was left to Hugh to say what was required. Then Louise hurried across the green to the car, where her husband and parents were waiting for her with fond resignation.

Una watched her go.

'She's not very healthy,' Ella said to Una.

'She seemed full of vitality,' Una answered in surprise.

'She burns herself out quickly. She never recovered properly from the birth of her third child. She has relapses of some sort and has to spend weeks in bed. She was always a favourite with our aunts, although they never really understood her humour and didn't know whether to be amused or scandalised. They rather hoped that Neil would marry her. Yes, they did, Neil, admit it! Then he met you and that was that.

'You know how Auntie Flora feels about the people up at the manor,' Neil said lightly. 'She's an awful old snob.' He spoke affectionately.

'Heavens, don't let her hear you,' Sibyl said, grinning.

'It's the truth,' Stuart stated. 'I can't see what she sees in them to admire. No money and they are a dowdy lot.'

'Not Louise,' Sibyl protested. 'She has always made the best of herself. She has a lovely face—' then something, no doubt the listening expression on Una's face, prompted her to add, 'but she lacks Una's colouring. Dark eyes and hair are very striking.'

The cars filled up with the same personages as before. The casual mourners drifted homewards, back to the tasks of the living, with a sense of temporary reprieve.

In the course of the short journey back to the house, Flora broke down and began sniffing loudly into her handkerchief. 'Lavinia could sew beautifully,' she said brokenly. Who would do the mending now? Someone would have to put the kettle on when they returned, and pour the tea. Lavinia was going to be greatly missed.

As they turned into the lane, she told Jessica, who was sitting pitiably alone on the back seat, 'I shall have to get someone in from the village. I'm not used to being on my own.'

Jessica looked at the back of her head uncomprehendingly. What on earth was she talking about? She wasn't on her own. Auntie Vin would—then, fleetingly, Jessica remembered, Auntie Vin was dead. It was Auntie Vin, not Marcus, thank God! No, that was not right. It was Auntie Vin *and* Marcus. How odd! How terrible! The tears, which had ceased for a few minutes while she sorted out her thoughts, began coursing down her wasted cheeks again.

Flora turned round. 'You must pull yourself together, dear.

You shouldn't have come today. It has been too much for you.'

Not come to her darling's funeral? What kind of mother did Auntie Flora think she was?

'Lavinia would have understood.'

What did Auntie Vin have to do with it? It was all totally confusing and Jessica was very unhappy.

The car pulled up before the house. Flora got out and waited while Hugh, haggard with grief and looking much older than his forty-six years, took his wife indoors. Another car turned into the lane. Oh good, here was Sibyl. She would make the tea. Una could help her.

Una questioned Neil about Louise Pope-Wessington at the first opportunity, which was while they were undressing that night. She was not very subtle.

'Why didn't you marry her?' she asked.

Neil was standing behind her, obligingly undoing the long zip on her grey dress. 'Marry who?' he asked, as if he did not know.

'Louise Pope-Wessington.'

'There!' he said, task accomplished.

'Well?' Una demanded, swinging round to face him.

'Let me see,' he said, frowning with affected concentration. 'There are so many reasons, I don't know which one to give first. I suppose the main one is that she never asked me.'

'She never asked you?' Una repeated slowly, with emphasis.

Neil laughed. 'The thought never entered my head to ask her. She was a good friend, that's all. She went about with Sibyl and Marcia and, occasionally, I tagged along. She's nearly two years older than I am and that's quite a lot when you're young, especially when the difference is that way round. She was very high-spirited—still is, I suppose—and used to persuade the girls to do forbidden things behind my aunts' backs.'

'Such as?' Una asked, intrigued.

71

'Oh, I don't know. Fishing for tadpoles and things, and getting muddy. Swimming in the river starkers, that kind of thing.'

'With you?'

'Not to their knowledge,' and he grinned, having the grace to blush.

Una, who had been brought up in the middle of a big town, had no knowledge of swimming in streams in water meadows, with only disinterested cows and skylarks and curious little boys amongst the tall rushes, with the half-seen vividness of dragonflies darting through the shining summer air above the still grasses.

'You must have known her quite well,' she observed stiffly.

'That was the trouble,' he agreed, smiling. 'I was looking for a woman of mystery to marry, not a bossy older girl with a mole on her back under her liberty bodice.'

'I used to wear a liberty bodice,' Una said defensively.

'I would never have guessed it,' Neil assured her, taking her into his arms.

Chapter Eight

Neil bought a second-hand car, eagerly encouraged by his wife.

Lavinia Favory had left £500 to each of her nieces and her nephew, and £50 to each of their children. Whatever else she had possessed was left to her dear younger sister, Flora, in whose service, apart from two bleak years between Flora's wedding and widowhood, she had spent her life.

Every morning, Una dropped Neil off opposite the statue of King George III on the sea front and drove the eight miles to work. She was at home in the evenings almost as soon as he was. At the weekends, they went for long drives along the coast or into the country. Once or twice a month they went to Lapcombe. When they went dancing, they no longer had to rely on friends for a lift and were in the position to offer lifts themselves. Una was thrilled to bits with the car and with the sense of freedom it gave her. Neil soon learned to drive, helped by her enthusiasm and patient instruction.

Flora made it plain the first time they drove over to see her that she thought they had their priorities wrong. A car was no substitute for a baby, and a woman behind a steering wheel was not so becoming as a woman behind the handle of a pram. She sniffed at their feeble excuses. It was no good blaming nature. If Una wanted a baby badly enough, no doubt she would get one. Neil hinted, tactfully, that her own marriage had been barren. That was different. Macfarlane had died too soon and, anyway, he had had a condition. She never explained what that condition had been and no one dared ask. It was none of their business.

Flora had found herself a woman from a neighbouring village to take her sister's place. Mrs Standish came every morning from Monday to Friday. She was unlike Lavinia Favory in almost every respect. For a start, she was short and rounded, with narrow eyes which shrewdly missed nothing, and a quick, breezy manner. She was full of her own importance and considered her way the best way in everything. She went to great lengths to practise small economies, which was something of which her employer approved, and was a great saver of brown paper, string, cardboard, milk-bottle tops, butter wrappings, small balls of left-over wool—she was an industrious knitter and pom-pom maker—and many other items too numerous to list, for all of which she found a use. Lavinia's dithery and anxious domesticity had been superseded by a relentless efficiency.

Flora needed Mrs Standish, but could barely tolerate her. Flora's nieces detested her and even her nephew expressed a mild dislike. She was suspected of encouraging Auntie Flora's idiosyncrasies. Somebody was spreading an ugly rumour around the rural community that Mrs Macfarlane Brown was becoming positively unhinged since the death of her sister. Who could be saying such a thing? Not Mrs Standish, surely? She was always very quick to deny that there was anything peculiar about her employer, almost before the accusation had been made, and put the little oddities, such as Flora's bizarre appearance and partiality for home-made barley wine, down to an amusing eccentricity.

In the mornings, Flora sat about in dyed and powdered, massive splendour, addressing Mrs Standish as little as possible and then only about domestic matters. Mrs Standish listened, balancing on one leg, ready for the off, begrudging the minutes away from her self-inflicted busyness. In the afternoons, Flora sallied forth to a bridge party or a committee meeting about church or village affairs; sometimes she spent an hour or two in the kitchen, baking and making a mess for

Mrs Standish to clean up the next morning. A guerilla war was waged between the two women, with Flora sabotaging and resisting every effort by Mrs Standish to organise, supply and sanitise her home environment. A month before the Coronation in 1953, Flora had bought herself a television with a small screen, enhanced by a huge, free-standing magnifying glass, and she spent her evenings dozing before it, planning counter-attacks.

Una and Neil became the most frequent visitors to Lapcombe. The rest were always making excuses for not going. Occasionally, Flora was persuaded to visit one of the families for tea and was taken for a drive beforehand, but these outings were not so enjoyable as they once had been, when Auntie Lavinia had also been in the car, exclaiming happily at the views from the back seat and obligingly translating her sister's scowls at an alarming turn of speed into words of mild caution.

Gradually, Una's prayers for a baby to satisfy them all became less fervent, except in the aftermath of a quarrel with Neil. Then it seemed hard to be alone and unloved. A baby to cry over and kiss into shared laughter was a short-lived day-dream. Between those rare quarrels, she had sufficient to make her happy: Neil, a home of her own, a job she enjoyed and some good friends. With no large family gatherings from which to feel set apart, she grew reconciled to her position as a mere sister-in-law, who would not—they would never accept could not—fulfil her function. Neil no longer expressed a wish to have children, nor disappointment at their inability to produce one. Una began to feel contented, which is always a mistake.

Since the death of Marcus, she had seen very little of Imelda. Jessica was spending more and more time on church activities, which meant that Imelda was doing most of the housework and cooking, to compensate for her mother's neglect of the home. She had been doing her own washing and ironing for years; now she was doing it for all three of them.

The army, which Hugh had so confidently predicted would make a man of his son, had killed him. Hugh's wife, who should have turned to him for comfort and by whom he should have been comforted, was lost to him, drifting in and out of the bungalow as silently and mysteriously as the cats; like them, a stranger who came indoors to feed and sleep, making use of the shelter and selfishly ignoring the other inmates. Hugh had estranged himself from his daughter years ago. Now, prosaic and practical, the young woman was doing her best to make life tolerable for him during her brief off-duty hours. He was grateful to her, but found it difficult to tell her so. The rift between them was of his own making. He could never forgive himself.

When Imelda had been about ten, she had got up late one morning during the Easter holiday and gone into the bathroom in her white cotton vest and knickers in order to clean her teeth. She had been scrubbing away at them happily, with her back to the door, when her father came in. He had over-slept as well and was still in his crumpled striped pyjamas. He apologised for his intrusion, explaining that he had not realised she was there, yet he did not go away. He sat on the edge of the bath, watching her. When she had rinsed her mouth twice, conscientiously, and replaced her brush in the red beaker, she turned to leave. He surprised her by catching her to him, pulling her between his knees, muttering about what a big girl she was becoming and feeling all over her firm young body with big, clumsy hands. Imelda had squirmed beneath his indelicate touch, not liking the unnatural way he was speaking, in jerky, silly phrases, one of which, 'good girl', was repeated over and over in a pleading tone utterly unlike the way he usually spoke to her. She was alarmed by this strange behaviour, his funny voice, his hands on parts of her body no one ever touched, only herself, fleetingly; but most of all she was frightened by the feel of his own body, where it pressed hard against hers, warmly throbbing and oddly shaped. She had wriggled frantically in his rough grip and her shrill 'Daddy?', cried as if she was appealing to a stranger, was

76

the release mechanism for them both. She had fled through the empty bungalow into the chill garden, to crouch shivering in the shrubbery with the somnolent cats, waiting for her mother to come home from church.

Hugh had been left sitting on the edge of the bath, head hanging, his trembling, sweaty hands between his knees, his heart pounding in his chest as if it desired to burst free from his treacherous body.

Although bewildered, Imelda understood enough to avoid being left alone with her father again. It was not until years later, when maturity brought insight and with it pity, that she realised a similar avoidance had been scrupulously practised by him. In the weeks that followed that shameful episode, Imelda had tried to speak to her mother about it, to warn her that something was the matter with Hugh, which perhaps she could do something about. Jessica had deliberately misunderstood every awkward word the child had muttered. It gradually dawned upon Imelda that her mother did not want to know. Strangely, this put a bigger distance between them than between Imelda and her father and she never learned to forgive her.

On a wintry Saturday morning, shrouded with fog, the boom of the fog horn a persistent lament across the oily waters of the harbour and the obscured chimneys of the town, Una had finished shopping and was on her way back to the car park, when she spotted Imelda coming out of the bank. She stood still in amazement. The fog was not playing tricks, it was definitely Imelda, but her hair was hanging loosely to her shoulders, permed.

'Imelda!'

Imelda smiled at the incredulous tone of the greeting. 'Do you like it?' she asked, turning her head from one side to the other.

'You said they would never persuade you to have curls,' Una reminded her, a little reproachfully.

'They didn't,' Imelda said, 'but someone else did. I'm glad

77

we've met, because I want to bring that someone to meet you. Would tomorrow evening be convenient?'

'Yes, of course,' Una answered with enthusiasm. 'Who is it?'

'Wait and see,' Imelda told her. 'How's Neil?'

'Imagine!' Una said to her husband over lunch. 'Imelda has curls. I can't get over the difference it has made to her. She looks softer, less severe. I'm sure her patients must approve. She is bringing someone to meet us tomorrow evening. He must be really special. I wonder how long she has known him?'

The answer was, two years. He was a doctor at the hospital, dedicated to his profession and attracted to the serious young woman in the crisp white uniform, in whom he thought he detected a dedication to match his own. He had never seen her flustered in a crisis, nor visibly upset by a calamity, only sympathetic and practical at all times. She got on with the job in hand, utterly dependable, and kept her emotions to herself. Unemotional himself, he approved of that.

Neil opened the door to them that evening. Una hurried from the kitchen to welcome them in the narrow hallway. The man standing next to Imelda was about forty, thin and round-shouldered, with a sardonic expression upon his large-nosed face.

'I think you should know,' Imelda said in a matter of fact way, immediately after the introductions, 'that Felix is married.'

'I see,' Una said feebly, regarding Felix in a new, hostile light.

'Let me take your coats,' Neil offered, to cover an awkward silence.

'It's no good pretending that he isn't,' Imelda said, shrugging out of her coat and handing it to Neil. 'You would soon learn otherwise, so what's the point?'

Una looked at the man, disappointed for her young niece.

He held her look with composure. She wondered if he were waiting for a divorce.

'There is no question of a divorce. We just have to make the best of the situation,' Imelda stated, in a deliberately off-hand manner. 'Something smells delicious, Una. Have you been baking?'

'Yes. Come into the dining-room. I thought we would have supper straight away. I hope you are both hungry.'

'I am,' the man said. His voice had a lowland Scots accent and Una thought it was the most attractive thing about him.

During the course of the evening, she watched the couple for signs of their being head over heels in love. Felix had little to say. He listened attentively when others spoke and occasionally contributed a wry, humorous observation, which was accompanied by a slight smile. There was a warmth between him and Imelda generated by mutual admiration, and they both spoke in praise of the other's professional expertise. Felix was a fine surgeon, Imelda informed them with pride. Imelda was an excellent nurse, Felix declared. Love was there, certainly, but not the headiness of first, delectable desire.

Una recalled how she had felt about Neil in the early, rapturous days and how they had been continually gazing deep into one another's eyes and touching at the slightest opportunity. These self-possessed people were behaving more like a married couple. Yet later, when Una and Imelda were alone in the kitchen at the back of the house, washing-up—hardly speaking, because Una did not know how to say what she wanted to say and Imelda had nothing more to add to what she had already said—the latter suddenly stated quietly, 'He is everything to me, Una.'

'What about the future?' Una asked hesitantly. 'His wife?'

'Neither of us think we have much future. It's no good deluding ourselves. We must be satisfied with the present.'

'But that's awful, Imelda. You are only twenty-four.'

'Age doesn't come into it,' Imelda sighed, sorting out the dried cutlery into the dresser drawer. 'I brought Felix to meet you, hoping you would be able to understand. Nobody else in the family knows about him. Mother would never approve and, anyway, with the way she has been since Marcus died I could hardly leave home now, even if I wanted to. Felix has a small flat on the other side of town. His wife lives in Portsmouth. We are going to make the most of the time we have together, no matter what the opposition. It would be nice if we could count on you and Neil as friends. You aren't obliged to react like an aunt and uncle, you know.'

'We'll always be your friends,' Una told her warmly. 'I'm so frightened that you will be unhappy.'

'Everyone is unhappy sooner or later. The people to pity are those who have never been anything else.'

When their guests had left, Una and Neil sat either side of the dying coal fire in the living-room, listening to the wireless. Una was weighing up the affair between Imelda and the quiet, sardonic man who was old enough to be her father, and trying not to think of his wife, somewhere in Portsmouth. She came to the conclusion that it was not the curls which had softened Imelda's face, indeed on closer observation the new hairstyle did not suit her broad features. Love was making the transformation. Una had difficulty in imagining Felix coaxing Imelda into something so frivolous as curls.

'Have you ever wanted me to change the way I do my hair?' she asked her husband, after a long thoughtful silence, while Dickie Valentine was singing 'Someone crept into my heart and stole a beat or two'.

Neil shifted his gaze from the crumbling red embers to her dark waves, regarding them as if he had never really looked at them before. 'No,' he said, puzzled. 'Why should I?'

'Good,' she answered, smiling, 'because I hate going to the hairdresser, even to get it cut.' A few minutes later she observed, 'They don't seem very amorous, do they?'

'Probably because they have passed the initial stages of their affair.'

'I suppose you're right,' Una admitted. She uncurled her legs from the big armchair and got up to turn off the wireless

80

and place the dull gold metal spark guard in the fireplace; then she sat on the hearthrug at her husband's feet, her back against his legs, her cheek against his hand where it lay on the chair arm.

Neil placed his free hand on her neck, fondling her hair, which curled silkily around his fingers.

'I love you,' she said, snuggling nearer and turning her head to look up at him.

He smiled into her adoring brown eyes, leaned forward and kissed her tenderly. 'Don't worry about Imelda,' he whispered, his arms around her shoulders. 'She knows what she's doing.'

Neil was right. Imelda had a mind of her own and nobody had ever been able to influence her, even as a young child. She had been twelve years old when Una first met her, detached and level-headed, firmly, even cruelly, rejecting her mother's affectionate advances and resisting with childish sarcasm her brother's efforts to torment her into a temper. Then Una remembered the curls and felt uneasy. Imelda had found someone with the power to influence her, because her love for Felix transcended self-love. Una pressed her lips against Neil's hand, sympathising with her.

Chapter Nine

Donald, the scientist, was at Cambridge. Sylvia and Tina were in their last year at school and Peter was ten. Ella was working every morning in the office of Ronald's coach tour company. He had hit on this idea of keeping her occupied under his benevolent surveillance. It pleased her very much. She had always disliked housework; now she could feel less guilty about not doing it. Ronald considered an untidy house and un-ironed shirts a small price to pay for such a suitable arrangement. Ella had some money of her own each week, for the first time since she was married, and he saved on the wages of a secretary, who would expect much more. The grocer episode was not mentioned again. In mitigation, Ella had pleaded an innocent desire to feed her family on forbidden extras by the insignificant expenditure of a few come-hither looks and go-thither hand-offs. Ronald had accepted her explanation, influenced by his brothers-in-law who, in their turn, had been heavily influenced by their wives. The grocer was portrayed by them as a lascivious old beast, who had used his power over the coupons and points to prey upon the emotions of susceptible, lonely young wives. Ronald came round to this line of reasoning; it was easiest and, in the manner of so many frail and erring human beings, of which his wife was one, he blamed the war.

After work each lunch time, Ella shopped in the town, passing the emporium of the lascivious beast on the way home in the bus, without so much as turning her head. She then spent an hour or so with her feet up, with a sandwich, a cup of tea and her latest novel. Eventually, the novel had to be abandoned for the chores, mainly the washing, which could not be ignored with a grubby boy and two clothes-conscious teenagers in the house. Then it was time to cook the evening meal. By this time, Peter, Sylvia and Tina were home from school and Ella ceased to be a romantic dreamer and became just Mum, a person to be shredded between their conflicting needs, until she wondered if the pieces would ever fit together again. She was fortunate, she had her fiction to creep about in until she felt whole. She was relieved to think that her sisters had their own means of self-repair. Jessica had religion, Sibyl had her home, expending time and energy upon its constant cleaning and refurbishment, but, come to think of it, what did Marcia have? Ella wondered about Marcia. Was she like their mother had been, unable to gather up the pieces of her personality when it was fragmented by the many demands made upon it? And then there was Una. She had no children to fret about and no constant claims on her attention, no mounds of washing and ironing, no dirty finger-marks on the paint-work. If anybody had an easy life, it was Una. Neil was an exceptional husband, kind and loving; all his sisters agreed about that. He would have made a good father. Ella would like to see Una shredded just a little. What right had anyone to be so happily married without their fair share of labour pains, nappy washing, sleepless nights and aggravation? Love was there as well, of course; it was the reason one endured the worry and the sleepless nights. Ella supposed, enviously, that Una would go on looking youthful and romantically dewy-eyed until old age robbed her of the bliss of long, slumberous nights.

'Mum, have you seen my new nylons? Sylvia must have taken them, then. I'm fed up with her taking my things. I wish you would have a word with her about it. Can I move into Donald's room? I'm sick of sharing with her. I'll move out when he's here at Christmas. Is that my nightie? You've melted a hole in it? I told you not to iron it. It doesn't need it. Honestly, I thought you hated ironing!'

83

'Are these what you are looking for?' Sylvia asked Tina sweetly, coming into the kitchen with a packet of stockings in her hand. 'You shouldn't accuse people before you look properly.' Then, seeing the nylon nightdress on the table, 'Oh, no, you've ruined it, Mum!'

'It's not yours, it's mine,' Tina said, snatching it up.

'Thank goodness for that,' her sister replied, throwing the packet onto the table and flouncing out.

'Have you washed any socks today? I need a clean pair for school tomorrow,' Tina said. White socks were still worn with school uniform until the weather became cold enough for black lisle stockings and the discomfort of a suspender belt, with sixpences replacing the lost studs behind the stocking welt.

'No,' Ella admitted. 'I'll be washing tomorrow. You'll have to rub them through yourself. Most of them need mending.'

'But I've got my maths homework to do.'

'It won't take you long,' Ella told her, starting to fry the sausages.

'Not sausages again! I've gone off them. Can I have an egg instead?'

'Dad's home!' Peter yelled from the living-room. His father's arrival meant it was time to eat and he was hungry.

'Wash your hands,' Ella shouted back, then, speaking to Tina, she said, 'Set the table, please.'

Tina went into the hall and shouted upstairs, 'Time to set the table, Sylvia.' If they did not share anything else, the twins made sure they shared the irksome things in life.

Now that Julian was sixteen and Bruce twelve, Sybil would have liked to return to teaching. Ella was working every morning and seemed to be managing quite well, in her own slap-dash fashion. Sibyl, who counted herself more efficient than her lazy older sister, had no doubts about coping with the extra school hours. She mentioned it to Stuart. He had very working-class attitudes about married women and thought their place was in the home. He reminded Sibyl that the house was her domain, to do with as she pleased. He never interfered with her ideas for its alteration and glorification, nor hindered her by lifting an incompetent finger to help her achieve those ideas. She could paint, strip wallpaper, tile and colour-scheme to her heart's delight. She could even dig up the garden and rearrange the flower-beds in her leisure moments. Surely, with all this, she could find enough to occupy herself? They could manage on his teaching salary and he was not having people say that his wife had to go out to work to make ends meet. Why wasn't she satisfied?

Sibyl turned to her sisters for support. Jessica gave her none. She agreed with Stuart, his wife's place was in the home. Sibyl should thank God that she still had both her children and not look to deprive them of one moment of her time and attention.

'But what shall I have when they leave home?' Sibyl asked her.

'The satisfaction of having done the right thing,' said Jessica sanctimoniously. 'If you have time on your hands, you should devote more of it to God. This life will take care of itself.'

'Like your house and poor Hugh, I suppose,' Sibyl snapped.

Jessica did not take offence. She had travelled too far along the road of the spirit to be drawn into a conflict of the mind. People were becoming unreal, even those closest to her. She was inured to pain and could feel no sympathy. Like her mother, she had run away; unlike her mother, her body remained as evidence of her suffering. She often wondered what miracle had enabled her mother to disappear so entirely.

Sibyl appealed to Ella, expecting support. Ella was dubious. Things were different for her. Giving a few hours every morning to the family business was not such a commitment as giving whole days to the local education department. If one of her children was ill, Ella could stay at home. Who would look after Bruce or Julian if they became poorly? She would not be able to help, with her own job to do and it would be no good asking Jessica, she was just about capable of looking after her horrid cats. Marcia lived too far away for convenience and, anyway, she had enough to do with her own three children.

Una was not worth considering. She had never been available in an emergency. That was what happened when women went into full-time work: you could not depend on them.

'I want to do something with my life before it's too late,' Sibyl explained. 'I shall be forty in three years' time. Nobody will want to employ me then.'

'Well, I am forty-one and someone employed me.'

'Yes, Ronald! That's different. You didn't have to impress him with your typing speed after years of not typing a word.'

'I soon picked it up again,' Ella said defensively.

'I would soon pick up teaching again, given the chance,' Sibyl answered with bitterness.

When she approached Marcia, she received an unexpected response.

'I think you should give it a try,' Marcia said. 'Why should Stuart dictate to you? Men have it all their own way.' With Shirley only four, Marcia had no option but to stay at home herself, but there were times when Kate, now thirteen and wilful, and Ian, seventeen and downright difficult, made the thought of life beyond the home seem infinitely desirable. The periodic bouts of depression, to which she had become increasingly prone since her third pregnancy, were becoming more prolonged. While suffering them, her misery centred upon her growing dislike of her husband and she revelled in dark fantasies of revenge, in which the broad-bladed bread knife, familiar to her hand, played an hypnotic part. 'How is my little sweetheart?' Tom would say to Shirley when he arrived home each evening, kissing the little girl as she sat at the kitchen table, eating her tea. His wife, watching him dispassionately, noticed how handsome he was, how conceited and sure of himself, how very sure of her. Her hand, lying beside the saw-toothed blade, which she had used to cut the bread and butter for the egg soldiers, would itch to pick it up by its wooden handle and plunge it between his shoulder blades, while he was bending dotingly over Shirley's head. How surprised he would be! Standing over his inert body, she would say into his wide, blank eyes, 'Make me pay for that, if you can!' and laugh.

Unsuspecting, Tom would turn from his little daughter and ask his passive wife if she had enjoyed her day. Marcia, staring into his unclouded eyes, always replied quite calmly that she had, thank you, while Kate rushed in to say hello to her daddy and ask him for some favour or other, which was rarely refused.

The mornings after her total surrender to his lust, which she had gone to bed half-dreading, half-anticipating, Marcia was consumed with self-disgust and, lying in the bath indulging in a ritual cleansing, would ease the humiliation of it with lurid scenes of reckoning. While she listened endlessly to his boastful talk about his achievements on the golf course or at work, where he seemed to be constantly putting down his well-meaning colleagues, Marcia comforted herself with thoughts of his destruction. She imagined herself drawing the bread knife from under her writhen pillow to attack him while at his most vulnerable. Sometimes she plotted going on a picnic with Tom and the children to a favourite spot of theirs in Portland, high above the curving expanse of the Chesil Beach bay and, when nobody was looking, pushing him off the cliff onto the unyielding, sea-cleansed rocks. Why couldn't he go off with another woman? Other men, far less attractive, did. She supposed, miserably, that he needed to be married. A sense of full ownership was necessary for him to achieve his satisfaction. It was not enough for her to say no to him, in fact, her nervous pleading only made him more anxious to subdue her and make her prove that her refusal was not an utter rejection of his egotistical male supremacy. The answer was to leave him—or kill him. The first would be complicated, the second far more satisfying.

Each morning, Marcia watched him from the dining-room window as he left for work, waiting until the car eventually pulled out to join the constant stream of traffic on the wide coast road. She thought how amazing it was that nobody guessed how much she disliked him, not even Tom himself. It made one wonder what dreadful thoughts were harboured by others behind the bland masks we call faces. Even her children, the only precious things to result from the years of sordid abnegation and the reason she found it impossible to contemplate flight, were guilty of deception. Ian had a life with his school friends, from which she was excluded. Her anxious questions about where he was going and what he was going to do, were met with evasions and lies, if he thought she would disapprove. Kate's winsome smiles were aimed at getting her own way and disguised a scheming brain, which had already worked out that men were her easiest victims. Marcia wished her well in the role of female predator; she hoped it would save her from a similar fate to her own. Little Shirley was the only true innocent. Sometimes, Marcia wondered dully if it was fair to let her become deceitful like the rest, only to grow up to be misused by what the world calls love.

Marcia's only comfort was that Tom was growing older and was spending more time and energy upon the golf course, which meant his nights of excess were becoming less frequent. During the short periods of respite her colourful fantasies faded, leaving only an obscure, sad vision of the future: an elderly couple sitting opposite one another, his passion burnt out, her dislike transmuted to apathy, both with nothing kind to say and no tenderness to remember.

'Go back to work,' Marcia urged Sibyl with surprising energy. 'It's too late for me. Even my mind isn't my own any longer.'

But Sibyl never made it back to work, Stuart's opposition to it was too unreasonable. She decided that a spurious independence was not worth all the quarrelling and bad feeling, so she gave her services to the Citizens' Advice Bureau instead and spent three mornings a week helping to sort out other people's problems. She was in her element. She had an outlet for her energy and organising ability, not to mention information galore on which to feed her enquiring mind. She liked particularly the cases where an individual was pitted against bureaucracy, usually the town hall, and her officious, patronising manner won her many small victories over petty officialdom—she saw them as her victories, rather than the clients'.

Chapter Ten

Gazing across the typewriter out of her office window on the first floor of the modern County Hall, her hands lying idly in her lap, Una watched a car pull into a row of parking spaces beside the Weights and Measures Department. Out of it stepped Jane and Claude Pope-Wessington and their grand-children, two girls and a boy. The eldest girl looked to be in her early teens, the boy was about eight. They must be going to visit their father in his office. They walked across the park towards the corner entrance in the main block by the library, keeping close to their grandmother like three little waifs who, having been brutally cast adrift, were in desperate need of warmth and protection. Their mother was dead. She had died a year ago, after five agonising months in hospital.

Una fed a sheet of paper into her machine and began typing furiously, trying not to think about Louise. She made a mistake, corrected it, made another mistake and corrected that. She finished the letter, read it through, grabbed it from the typewriter and tore it up. She placed another sheet of paper behind the roller and started again. Fifteen minutes later, the children reappeared with their grandparents. Una watched them get into the car and drive away from the flat-roofed complex of red brick offices, out past the statue of Thomas Hardy into the traffic of the busy market town.

Two months later, Una saw the children again, this time accompanied by their father as well as their grandparents. It was Christmas Day. Una was standing outside the church at

Lapcombe, waiting while Flora and Neil exchanged the compliments of the season with some acquaintances. It was a raw day; the cold was the cold of the churchyard beneath the muddied turf, damp and bone-aching. It had been chilly enough inside, but the joyous energy of the carol service, attended by a congregation thrice the size of a Sunday turnout and almost filling the polished wooden pews, had taken people's minds off their frozen feet.

Una stepped backwards off the cracked and sunken path onto the grass, in order to let someone pass, her high heels sinking into the rain-sodden earth. A light, bitter wind from the East swept round the corner of the church and sliced across the nape of her neck, between her short hair and her coat collar. She shivered, pulling the collar up about her ears. Mr Laston was saying a cheerful farewell to the last knot of villagers in the porch. His snub nose and bulging cheeks were shiny-red with the cold. Claude Pope-Wessington walked past Una. He lifted his hat and wished her a happy Christmas. His wife smiled absently. The children regarded Una with solemn unconcern. Their father appeared to notice nobody. Una watched them walk down the sloping path, through the lich-gate and turn towards their car which was parked across the road in front of the Black Bull. While he was holding the car door open for his children, Bart Pascall looked back and acknowledged Una with a brief nod of his head.

'Do you want a lift back, Flora?' a big, bluff, elderly man asked, his skin ruddy and toughened by a lifetime of outdoor work, the veins on his nose showing blue with the cold.

'No, thank you, Arnold. I'm going to Neil's,' Flora informed him, putting her arm through her nephew's and giving it a fond squeeze.

The farmer wished them both a happy Christmas and shepherded his very ordinary and dumpy little wife towards home. He felt under a constant obligation to Flora Macfarlane Brown and often gave her a lift to and from church on Sundays. She had once had the good sense to turn down his proposal of marriage, given in a moment of mad impulse when he was a mere lad of twenty, needing his brains tested, and she was a magnificent woman of twenty-three, her oddities not yet manifest. He often wondered what she would have been like if Macfarlane Brown had lived longer. There was no doubt she had grown increasingly peculiar during the years she had lived with her dotty sister. To his knowledge, no one had ever asked Lavinia for her hand in marriage, not even in a moment of aberration brought on by rough cider.

'Arnold Slinger always smells of milk to me,' Flora said to Neil. 'When I first knew him, he used to do a milk round for his father, ladling the milk from a huge churn into our jugs. It was a sickly, stale smell, which hung about his clothes and I smell it every time he comes near me. I find him quite revolting.' She began easing herself into the front seat of the Morris Minor, then she had a sudden, arresting thought. 'Are you going to drive?' she asked Una, one foot still on the pavement.

'No, Neil can,' Una said, hiding a smile.

Flora settled herself comfortably into the passenger seat, looking smug.

Sitting behind her, Una fixed her eyes upon two grubby spots on the brim of her horrible, mustard yellow hat, which was perching like a demented bird upon its messy nest of hair. Flora's coat, gloves and shoes were the customary black. Una wondered why Flora, in her early seventies, still continued to dye her hair. She did it herself at home and nobody was supposed to know. It was ludicrous. Lavinia had kept a loyal silence, but had been known to blush and stammer when denying all knowledge of the delicate subject. 'You must ask Flora herself about it, dear,' she had once said to an inquisitive Kate, getting in a fluster, adding when pressed by Julian, 'She had black hair when she was young, you know,' as if that were answer enough.

Neil put his foot down, mindful that Una was anxious to get back to the slowly cooking turkey, although by now Imelda should have arrived and be busy in the kitchen.

Flora shifted uncomfortably in her seat and cast Neil a look of pained annoyance. She did not appreciate speed. Her look was ignored. There was no Lavinia sitting on the edge of the back seat, wringing her hands at Flora's transmitted agitation and, slipping into dialect with nervousness, asking tentatively, 'What we be doin'? Flyin'?' Flora clutched her massive black handbag to her equally massive bosom, minute lines of aggravation radiating out from the compressed smudge of her holly-red lips.

'I can't think why Jessica had to go to St George's this morning,' she complained to Neil. 'She always used to come to Lapcombe at Christmas.' Hugh always drove at a sedate speed.

Una had also invited Jessica, Hugh and Imelda for Christmas dinner. She had discussed the arrangements with Imelda three weeks ago, after Neil's other sisters had declared their plans. Ella was entertaining Ronald's sister and her family for the day. Marcia had her in-laws for a whole week, up to the New Year, and Sibyl and family were in Cornwall, staying with Stuart's mother. As Imelda would not be working over the holiday for once and Felix had declared his intention of spending the time with his wife in Portsmouth, it had been decided—by Sibyl, actually—that Imelda should invite Auntie Flora to the bungalow, otherwise the poor old soul would be all alone.

'Honestly, Auntie Sibyl is the limit!' Imelda protested to Una. 'She is always having schemes of do-gooding that involve other people. Can you imagine the fun we shall all have? Mother coming back from church in the morning, praying over the food and going on about the starving until it gets cold, Auntie Flora getting tiddly on the port, removing her teeth to dislodge a bit of nut when she thinks no one is looking and baiting Dad about his bald patch and his paunch. You and Neil wouldn't like to come, would you? It will be awful if you don't.'

'I have a better idea,' Una had told her. 'Why don't you come to us?'

'I don't like that bossy woman,' Flora said. 'I'm going to get rid of her.'

Jessica, who had just finished listening to the Queen's speech on the wireless, turned to regard her elderly aunt with an expression of dismay. Ella had warned her that this might happen and spelled out the consequences. Mrs Standish would be difficult to replace, perhaps impossible. Flora could not live on her own. Ella had no room, neither had Marcia. Sibyl could not have her; Stuart would not hear of it, he was not very fond of Auntie Flora—even Jessica recognised this as a considerable understatement. Jessica was the only one with a spare room, Marcus's. There was no way Auntie Flora was getting that!

'She took the curtains down in the green room and washed them until they fell to bits,' Flora complained. 'Now I have to buy new ones, at my time of life!' She picked up a pretty box from the carpet beside her chair and stared inside it. 'Who gave me this?' she asked incredulously.

'Neil did,' Una said, with a wink at Imelda.

'Very nice,' Flora said, replacing it. 'I don't want to be late back, Neil,' she told him, thinking with regret of the programmes she was missing on the television.

'Are you quite sure you won't stay the night?' he asked her. It would be so much more convenient.

'Quite sure,' she said firmly.

'I shall be leaving soon after tea for Evensong,' Jessica said.

Imelda and Hugh exchanged looks of resignation.

'I'll take you home when I take Jessica to church, Auntie Flora,' Hugh told her. 'It will save you turning out, Neil. I'll come back for Imelda later.'

'There's no need,' said his daughter. 'I can walk home from here, it's not far.' She had a car of her own, but the three of them had arrived in her father's.

'I'll come back. I may as well,' Hugh said.

'Yes, do come back,' Una urged him, thinking of the lonely Christmas evening waiting on his own for Jessica to return from church and then sitting with her afterwards in non-communicating silence.

'Christmas is a time for children,' Flora stated, selecting a piece of turkish delight from a box being proffered by Neil. 'It's dull without them. I wonder what Santa Claus brought Shirley this morning?'

Una, remembering the fun and excitement that she and her younger sister had experienced emptying their stockings, agreed with Flora. While small fingers fumbled eagerly to tear open each packet, her mother and father had waited with as much suspense as if they had not known what each one contained. There was always an orange, some nuts and a packet of gold-covered chocolate money right at the bottom. Whatever happened to her sister's cherished rabbit? A white, luminous-painted pottery rabbit, that had appeared from her stocking one year and was placed beside her bed to keep her company in the black-out. No doubt it had still been there when the bomb dropped. Why had they not gone to the Anderson shelter in the garden? They might have survived if they had and Una and Neil would now be celebrating Christmas with her own dear family, being gently teased by her father and told to take no notice by her laughing mother, while her sister and grandmother looked on, contented and safe.

'Don't look so sad, darling,' Neil whispered in her ear. He felt so helpless when she was miserable and only knew one way to comfort her, by taking her in his arms and loving her. Words were inadequate at such times, her sadness was too deep to be touched by them.

Imelda decided that the time was right to tell them of a funny incident that had occurred at the hospital a few days ago. They enjoyed the story and laughed and commented upon it. Imelda smiled, hiding her own unhappiness. Talking about the hospital brought Felix prominently to mind. Was he thinking about her as well? She wondered what he and his wife were doing, what were they talking about. Why had he felt obliged to spend Christmas with her? He had never explained adequately. It was four years since Imelda had generously given him the largest slice of her life and she was only too well aware that in return he fed her own hunger with crumbs.

'Christmases aren't what they used to be,' Flora sighed lugubriously. 'Do you remember, Jessica, when . . . ?'

Oh no, Una thought, not another trip along the road she could not follow; but in fact Flora was thinking back only so far as the last Christmas they had all spent at Lapcombe, two years before Lavinia and Marcus had died, when Una had been well grafted onto the scene. Lavinia's death had, inexplicably, signalled the falling away of family visits. Admittedly, the children were getting older and had their own interests to pursue, yet it was not only that. Auntie Vin was missed more than anyone would have supposed probable and, without her, Flora had become even more unlovable to everybody but the five whose devotion sprang from gratitude.

'I miss Lavinia,' Flora was telling a sympathetic Jessica. 'The house has become uncomfortable without her.'

They all missed Lavinia, the thin shadow that had swayed and dipped about Flora in an anxious effort to be of some use. She was the one who had dried childish tears, stuck on sticking plasters and buttered bumps, made sure there was lemonade to drink, thrown out crusts for the birds and boiled potato peelings for the chickens' bran mash; she was the silly one, often gently ridiculed behind her back and patronised to her face. If it had been Lavinia left and not Flora, Una wondered if the visits to Lapcombe would have been more frequent. She suspected they would, simply because they would have felt a responsibility for the poor old thing, assuming she could not exist without being supervised and browbeaten. In the event, it was Flora who was having difficulty in existing without someone to fetch and carry for her and darn the weaknesses in the lavishly embroidered myth of her ego.

'I miss Marcus,' Jessica confessed in a tearful voice.

'Of course you do, dear,' Flora said. 'We all do. Louise's husband and children were at church this morning with the Pope-Wessingtons. Jane looked very tired. Let's play cards, shall we? Fetch the cards, Neil.'

Una and Imelda declined to play. They sat together on the settee and talked in low voices until it was time to get the tea.

Flora played cards with grim enjoyment, not missing a trick. Neil played with good-natured enthusiasm, generously applauding his opponents' cute play. Jessica was not thinking about what she was doing and remained completely disinterested, which drew disapproval from her aunt and encouragement, edged with repressed impatience, from Hugh.

'How do you feel about Felix spending Christmas with his wife?' Una asked Imelda, very quietly.

'How do you think I feel?' was the quick rejoinder, followed by, 'Perhaps it's just as well. We could hardly have spent it together. I couldn't ask him home and there's no way I would leave Mother and Dad on their own. They have no pleasure in one another's company any more.'

'How awful!' Una exclaimed, glancing across the room first at Jessica and Hugh and then at Neil, who sensed her look and smiled back at her, unconsciously proving that they were still on the same, warmly pulsing wave-length.

'It's kind of you to have us today, Una,' Imelda said.

'Neil's family is the only one I have,' Una reminded her. 'Shall we get the tea? Don't laugh at my attempt to ice the Christmas cake.'

'I promise,' Imelda said, following her into the kitchen. 'Sometimes I think the only really enjoyable pastime is eating. Everything else is over-rated.'

'You don't mean that!' Una protested.

'I did say, sometimes,' Imelda grinned.

Chapter Eleven

Una was thirty-four in January.

'What would you like to do to celebrate?' Neil asked her, a week before the date. 'Go out to dinner?'

'No, let's go to a dance. It's on a Saturday, so it shouldn't be difficult to find somewhere different to go.'

'Why can't we go to the Royal, as usual?' Neil asked. 'We would be sure to see some of our friends there.'

'I would rather go somewhere where we aren't known. It would be more romantic. It's not very exciting going to the same place all the time.'

Una looked in the *Echo* that evening and found that there was a special dinner and dance to celebrate the New Year at an exclusive hotel in Bournemouth. Neil said it was too far to travel just to dance.

'It's only about forty miles,' Una protested.

'It's stupid to go so far,' he insisted. 'We should be so late getting back.'

'Please, Neil,' Una pleaded. 'It is my birthday treat, after all. I don't mind driving back, I quite like driving in the dark. I shall be able to wear my new dress.'

He gave in eventually. He usually did, but he did it with a bad grace. The tickets were three times as much as the ones for the Royal Hotel. He could only hope the event would be worth the expense and the inconvenience of the travelling.

However, by the time her birthday arrived, Una's enthusiasm had rubbed off on him and he was looking forward to it almost as much as she was, but he still had misgivings about the distance.

'I used to drive much further than that at night during the war,' Una told him at breakfast on the day, 'often going to places I hadn't been before. I never had any difficulty finding them, well, not much, and don't forget it was in the black-out, with no sign-posts.'

'I'm not worried about finding the place,' he laughed. 'It's just the thought of driving back so late. I only hope it isn't foggy.'

'Oh, don't be such an old Jonah!' she teased him. 'Look, I've had a card from Imelda and one from Jessica.'

Neil's relations did not usually remember his wife's birthday, much to his chagrin. This year Imelda, who was the only exception, had prompted her mother by buying a card, placing it in front of her to be written and, subsequently, posting it along with her own.

It fell to Una to remember all their birthdays on Neil's behalf and to buy gifts for the children. She readily accepted this as a natural part of a wife's duties, but each year she was hurt, just a little, that his sisters and aunt could ignore her own special day. Two of Una's friends in the office had also sent cards. On Monday she would be buying all her colleagues chocolate biscuits with their coffee. Her boss would look up from the papers on his desk and say, 'Somebody's birthday? Good show!' and never ask whose. Every August she collected the money from him for his own birthday offering to the staff and he had been known to make the same remark when receiving his coffee. 'Yours,' she would remind him. 'By George, so it is!' he would answer, looking immensely pleased with himself.

January is a month of anticlimax, during which the festivities of Christmas and the exciting promise of the New Year resolve into the actuality of deeper frosts and a bleak, long-drawn-out wait for Spring. That year was no exception. The dampness of December gradually gave way to colder, brighter weather, interspersed with days of flurrying light snow that did not pitch.

A first peek through the bedroom window that morning had revealed to Una dry pavements sifted over with patches of white frost. By mid-morning all traces of the frost had disappeared beneath a benevolent sunshine. The sea in the wide bay only a few streets from the house glinted with a wintry white-capped blueness, reflecting the cool blue of the sky, which was decorated with a few white clouds with furry edges, drifting very high up.

Both Una and Neil were off work that morning and altogether the day appeared an auspicious one. They shopped together in the morning and had coffee, accompanied by sugary jam doughnuts, above a cake shop opposite Woolworth in the busy shopping street running parallel to the sea front.

In the afternoon Una pressed her evening dress. It was a pink silk taffeta, shot with metallic grey, shoulderless and with a very full skirt. She had made it herself and was pleased with it.

'What a pity my present hasn't arrived yet,' Neil said later, when she had it on. 'It would have looked perfect with that dress.'

'When did you order it?' Una asked, disappointed since breakfast, when he had explained its absence.

'Ages ago,' he said.

'What is it?'

Instead of answering, he said, 'I won't be a minute,' and left the bedroom.

Una opened the wardrobe and took out her black coat. She was just about to put it on, when Neil returned. 'You won't need that,' he declared, throwing it on the bed and covering her bare shoulders with a honey-coloured fur jacket.

'Oh, Neil, thank you,' she exclaimed, delighted with it. 'It came after all. I thought it would be a necklace.'

He and Imelda had gone shopping for it a fortnight ago, during his lunch hour, and it had been in a suitcase under the spare bed ever since.

So they set off for the evening, she in her new fur jacket over her pretty gown and he in his smart evening suit; a splendid young couple, sure in their love for one another, anticipating hours of perfect happiness in the kind of evening that comes rarely and remains forever shining like a jewel in the random clutter of memory.

Neil drove the car to Bournemouth and, as he had predicted, found the prestigious hotel without difficulty. After depositing their coats in the cloakroom, they walked hand in hand up the wide, sweeping staircase towards mirrored images of their own magnificence which, momentarily, they admired and failed to recognise. The chandelier-lit ballroom was awash with a kaleidoscope of colourful gowns against a background of white table-cloths and shining cutlery, on tables set near the far wall next to the band. They were shown to their own table to the strains of 'Some Enchanted Evening'. Una was enchanted.

The meal was delicious, the band was excellent, the company high-spirited and the dancing a well-balanced medley of old and new, which suited them perfectly. They fox-trotted, rocked and rolled, waltzed, and romped about the slippery oak boards performing the 'Dashing White Sergeant'. In fact, apart from while they were eating, they hardly sat down at all. By the time they were closely clasped together on the crowded floor in the last waltz, moving dreamily under a romantic candlelight, they had danced themselves into tired contentment. Five minutes later, while their arms were being vigorously pumped up and down by their neighbours in an exuberant rendering of 'Auld Lang Syne', once more under the brightness of the blazing chandeliers, uppermost in both their minds was the irksome thought of the long drive home before they could blissfully snuggle into bed.

'I'll drive,' Una said, as they emerged from the warmth and excitement into the icy cold of the car park, shining white beneath a clear sky which was sparkling with a host of tiny stars.

'No, it's all right, I will,' Neil told her. 'There's been a heavy frost, we'll have to take it easy.'

'I'm well aware of that,' she replied. 'I want to drive. I said I would.'

Neil began scraping the thin layer of rime from the outside of the windscreen. Una got into the driving seat.

'I wish you would let me,' he said crossly, getting in beside her.

'You had more wine than I did,' she reminded him, switching on the ignition.

'Just because you have been driving longer doesn't mean you are the better driver,' he remarked, though he suspected she was.

'I never said it did,' she answered, pulling out of the car park.

There was a long silence, while she concentrated on getting through the town and picking up the Poole road.

Eventually he said softly, in a mollifying tone, 'I just thought you would be more tired than I am.'

'Perhaps I am,' she admitted, with a smile. 'We'll swop over at Wareham.'

They never reached Wareham.

As they were approaching it along a tree-darkened road with many sharp bends, a car pulled out into the path of the one coming towards them. There was a blinding blaze of light in their horrified faces, a crashing impact and oblivion.

Una opened her eyes. What on earth was Imelda doing in her bedroom and why was she wearing her uniform? She shut her eyes again, sinking back through a sea of pain into dark depths of forgetfulness.

The nurse noticed the flickering eyes, accompanied by a slight motion of the head and notified the doctor that the patient had regained consciousness at last.

When Una opened her eyes once more, she was alarmed to find herself in a room she did not recognise, being closely regarded by a stranger who was smiling at her kindly.

'How are you feeling?' the man in the white coat asked

gently, picking up her arm by the wrist, his wise eyes looking intently into hers.

Una thought about the question. She answered in her head. I am frightened. I hurt all over. I am very tired. I want my husband.

The man replaced her arm on the white, unwrinkled counterpane and turned to speak to the woman in the nurse's uniform, who had appeared beside him as if from nowhere.

I am in hospital, Una thought dully. I must be very ill. Neil will be coming to see me soon. She closed her eyes and slipped into a drowsy, timeless world of shadows, in which she seemed suspended between painful dreams and half-wakeful physical pain, which nagged at her whole body but could be carefully isolated to her head, her chest, her left arm and both her lower legs. She decided to wake up to escape from it. She remembered the crash. Where was Neil? Was he badly injured as well? She turned her pleading eyes upon the nurse, who came to her side immediately.

'My husband?' she whispered, fear on her face.

'He isn't here, dear,' the nurse said, softly. 'You will be able to receive visitors this evening. They are all very anxious about you. Try and get some rest before then.' She watched the patient anxiously as she spoke, the concern in her eyes belying the cheerfulness of her tone.

Una turned her head from side to side in frustration and growing distress.

'You mustn't worry, Mrs Favory. You have to concentrate on getting better.'

'I'm very thirsty,' Una told her, sounding petulant like a sick child.

'I'll fetch you a cup of tea,' the nurse said, making her escape.

Una spent the remainder of that day, the succeeding night and the following day alternately sleeping and waking. Each time she woke it was like regaining consciousness all over again, but she stayed conscious a little longer and grew increasingly concerned about Neil.

When you are ill, you have little choice but to be a good patient. Una allowed her healing body to be administered to as if it belonged to someone else, for whom she was feeling the pain. She jealously guarded her mind from the kind strangers who were tending her, sensing their anxiety on her behalf and terrified to be told the cause of it. She had never felt so vulnerable in her life. She awoke from a ghastly dream, in which she had experienced the moments leading up to the crash all over again, with a palpitating heart and found someone sitting beside her bed. It was Imelda.

'Where's Neil?' she implored her.

Imelda's eyes filled with tears. She picked up Una's uninjured right hand and said, 'You are going to have to be brave, Una.'

Una did not feel well enough to be brave, she resented the request. She tried to release her hand in protest, but she was too feeble. What was Imelda asking of her? 'I want Neil,' she whispered pathetically.

Why must I be the one chosen to tell her? Imelda thought wretchedly.

'Una, Neil was killed in the crash.' What other words could she have used to make it sound less terrible?

Una stared at her as if she had not heard. It's the truth, she was thinking. Why else would he be absent from my side? —unless he was badly injured, of course, but Imelda had said he was killed and, like little Peter before her, Una knew that Imelda did not tell lies. Once before Una had refused to believe such dreadful news, once before she had miserably discovered that she had no option. Sooner or later she would have to accept this. It might just as well be now. Despairingly, with a horrid fervour, Una embraced the truth as if it were her husband's corpse. She was not meant to be happy. Neil was dead!

'Una?' Imelda was not sure whether she ought to repeat the difficult words, she was not even sure she could. Once had been bad enough.

'I heard you,' Una answered faintly. 'Neil is dead.' She

turned her head away and shut her eyes tightly, until her head throbbed. Tears trickled sideways across her face onto the starched pillow.

Imelda sat very still, in sympathetic sorrow. There was only ten minutes to go of visiting time. She had been told that she must stay no longer. How did one solace such grief in ten minutes? 'Everybody is anxious to visit you,' she said. It was not strictly true, but even Imelda had to prevaricate sometimes. Actually, everybody was dreading it. She had dreaded it herself, knowing what she had to tell her.

Una turned her head towards her. 'I knew he was dead,' she stated, without emotion in her voice, her eyes dull with pain.

'Did the doctor tell you?' Imelda asked in surprise, for it was the doctor who had thought it best that she should be the one to break the news. As a trained nurse, she would be well aware of the adverse affect it might have on the patient. He had asked her to tell Una that evening, because he did not believe in lying in order to postpone the inevitable, once the patient was strong enough to bear the news.

'He did not say that Neil was alive,' Una explained simply.

The nurse came in, smiling bravely, wheeling a trolley on which were five vases of flowers. She exchanged an understanding look with Imelda, before leaving again.

'See, we are all thinking about you,' Imelda said. 'The original flowers have died.'

'Original ones?'

'Yes, the flowers we sent when you were first admitted, with the cards.'

Una followed her glance towards the window-sill. Sure enough, there were about a dozen cards along its length.

'When was that?' she asked, apprehensively.

'Nine days ago.'

'Nine days!'

Imelda held the limp hand against her cheek, saying with compassion, 'Una, Neil was buried last Wednesday.'

The hand went rigid and icy cold. Una's brown eyes opened wide in distress and her lips quivered with the struggle between tears and speech. 'They took him from me,' she moaned. There was a long pause, while she pulled herself together. When she spoke again it was in a cold, distant tone. 'Tell them not to come. I don't want them now.' She tugged her hand weakly and, reluctantly, Imelda released it.

'I have to go now, Una. I'll come again tomorrow. I'm so sorry.'

Una watched her leave the room without regret. She wanted to suffer in solitude.

Chapter Twelve

Una wished to die. She had no one to live for, therefore she made no effort to get better. Nevertheless, get better she did. Each day there was an improvement in her physical condition and each day she submitted, apathetically, to the brisk administrations of the medical profession to further that improvement. Within another week, she was moved from the small single room next to the sister's office into a bright, long ward, which was full of characters who possessed the determination that she lacked to get shot of the place as quickly as possible.

Neil's sisters visited her regularly and each, in her own way, did her best to comfort her, despite her own sorrow. Jessica advised her to seek refuge in God's love as she had done, and assured Una that Neil and Marcus were keeping one another company until such time as they would all join them, reminding her, whimsically, that Louise Pascall was there as well, as if that made any difference. Jessica spoke about Heaven as if it were someone's front room, where people were sitting about waiting for late arrivals to join them for tea. The frivolous thought of Neil and Louise drinking tea together in some celestial drawing-room was scarcely comforting to Una.

Ella came, with her daughters for moral support. Sylvia and Tina were subdued for once and let their mother do most of the talking. Ella found it hard going: Una was totally unresponsive. Ella wondered if her brain had been permanently damaged. Nine days was a long time to remain unconscious and the death of one's husband a dreadful shock to face on waking. 'You must come and stay with us when you get out of here,' Ella suggested. 'You can have Donald's room until you feel well enough to cope on your own.'

I shall never feel well enough to cope on my own, thought Una, but she said nothing, she could not be bothered to talk; indeed, she could hardly bring herself to listen.

Marcia and Sibyl arrived together. Marcia reminded Una more than once that she was fortunate to have a job to take her mind off things and Sibyl exhorted her inert sister-in-law, in a firm, but gentle manner, to pull herself together and think positively about her future, assuring her that it would be Neil's dearest wish.

Flora did not come at all; apparently she was too upset. She sent a message, delivered by Ella, trusting that Una would soon recover her health and be out and about again.

Imelda visited that hospital as often as her work at the other one allowed her. She was the only person to whom Una responded, but it was a cautious response and Imelda felt as if she were talking to a stranger—which was odd, because Una looked upon her as a true friend, whereas she believed she no longer had a claim on the affection of the rest of them. They had been duty bound to regard her for Neil's sake, now they need trouble themselves no longer. One advantage of getting better in spite of herself, was that she would soon be out of hospital and their conscientious visits could cease. Self-pity was making Una churlish.

Una's two office friends, who had sent her birthday cards on that fateful day, visited her, so did her boss, Mr Truebody and his wife. To everyone she presented a still, closed countenance. They tried their best to find suitable words of comfort and encouragement, but she did not help them. The visiting hours were interminable to patient and visitors alike. It was not her unhappiness so much as her utter despair that so oppressed them all and sent them out into the wintry nights with uncomfortable thoughts about the terrible things the Fates might have in store for themselves.

Left alone, Una played the solitary game of 'if only'. If only she had not persuaded Neil to buy a car; if only she had not read the advertisement in the *Evening Echo*; if only she had listened to Neil and gone to the Royal Hotel as usual; if only she had let him drive, for he drove—used to drive—more quickly than she did and they would probably have been a mile or so further on when the oncoming car swerved across the road; she even thought, if only we had children, quickly dismissing the wish as selfish in the circumstances. She was being driven crazy with regrets, which would alter nothing. Neil was dead and she was not.

She slept only with the aid of two little pills. She regarded them lying in the nurse's palm and wondered how many she would need to swallow to postpone the waking until she, too, reached the comfort of eternity.

It was Imelda who collected Una from the hospital and took her home. It was Imelda who witnessed the flood of tears as Una stepped into the cold, empty house, collapsing into a paroxysm of grief.

'Don't stay here tonight,' Imelda pleaded with her, when Una had grown calm again. 'Come and sleep at our place for a few nights, until you feel a bit stronger.'

'No, thank you. I want to be here. I feel closer to Neil at home.'

Imelda understood.

Una caught at her arm and beseeched in a tone of desperation. 'Will you take me to his grave?'

'Tomorrow,' Imelda promised. 'I'll call for you about ten.'

Three weeks later, Una returned to her job, once more travelling by train. Her former travelling companions noticed that she was thinner and that the ready smile had left her eyes, which were lustreless with private tears; otherwise she looked much the same—a neat, quite pretty little thing, who acknowledged the greetings of acquaintances with a friendly 'Good morning', but sat in a corner seat of the compartment with eyes downcast upon an open book. A remarkably slow reader, a discerning passenger might have supposed, for during the twenty minutes between seaside town and county town, she seldom turned a page.

Una's job was her salvation. She had always enjoyed it and continued to do so, as much as she could derive pleasure from anything now. Neil had never been involved in that part of her life. In the office he had existed only in her mind, so in that respect little had changed, except the happy anticipation of seeing him again once work was over. It followed that she was not so eager to leave the office as she once had been and began catching the later train, which meant journeying with many people who were unknown to her. On the 5.30 p.m. she knew most of the passengers by sight and many by name. On the 6.15 p.m. she was the stranger. She preferred it that way. She was not obliged to concentrate on her book to repel conversation, but could gaze out of the window at the swiftly passing fields and brood without fear of interruption.

Her boss, Frank Truebody, was very kind to her in the weeks following her return. His wife enquired after Una's well-being on most evenings, reminding him to be considerate. Mrs Truebody valued her husband's secretary almost as much as he did. She had not liked the temporary replacement at all and had watched the after-shave being splashed on in the mornings with misgivings. Had he started to change his socks and underpants more often, she would have panicked. As far as she was concerned, Una had returned in the nick of time.

'We must do something to help her,' she told her husband. 'Poor little thing, she must be very lonely, living all on her own. How about asking her to baby-sit for Joan occasionally?'

'What a splendid idea!' Mr Truebody said admiringly. Their married daughter had two children under five and she was in constant need of the services of a baby-sitter.

How selfish we can be when we sorrow! It is as if the world closes in about us. Somewhere in the void beyond our tunnel vision, other people exist in shades of neutral grey.

Una was finding the weekends almost unbearable.

Occasionally, Imelda was free to do some shopping with her, eat with her, go to the pictures or theatre with her; but only occasionally. Besides her nursing, which required her to work many weekends, Imelda had her parents to consider. Hugh had been forced to take early retirement the previous Autumn, because of deteriorating health, as far as Una knew. Not every Saturday and Sunday away from home were spent at the hospital, for Imelda had to find time for Felix as well.

'I think you should get yourself another car,' she told Una firmly. 'Why not? Are you terrified of being involved in another accident?'

Una laughed scornfully, 'Of course not! What have I to lose?' Yet she did not buy herself one. It was as if she were inflicting the inconvenience of public transport upon herself as a punishment for surviving.

During the week she had lunch, usually a sandwich and coffee, with her two extrovert friends from the office. They were both younger than she was, married and leading busy social lives, in which there was no room for a woman without a partner. They both felt sorry, even guilty, about this and longed for the day when Una was ready to look about her for male company. In the meantime, they were keeping their own eyes open for a suitable candidate. They were not inhibited in their search by comparison with Neil Favory, because they had hardly known him—except through Una, of course, and she had been both reticent and extremely biased. Their own experience was that men were an imperfect bunch and women must weave their own romance out of the unpromising material. They found it very difficult to believe in Una's former contentment.

Out of the kindness of their Christian hearts Neil's sisters urged her to visit them more often, and she did, usually for Sunday tea, because Sundays were the loneliest days of all. She did not visit Jessica on Sundays. She only went to the bungalow on Imelda's invitation and would help her to prepare a meal and talk to faded and mostly forgotten Hugh, smiling every now and again in Jessica's direction, but getting little response. Jessica did not so much enter a room as drift into it and then she remained sitting in an attitude of listening, as if she were waiting to hear a summons to drift out again. It was most unsettling

Una had a livelier time when she visited Ella. Ronald fetched her in the car, usually accompanied by Peter, who entertained her all the way there with the latest schoolboy jokes, told so ineptly that his father often had to repeat them in order for Una to see the point. The twins were at an age to be clothes- and boy-mad. If they were at home, they were probably getting ready to go out. Sylvia was a keen knitter, Tina sewed. It was their way of adding to their fashionable wardrobes with economy.

'Do you fancy doing a bit of this rib?' Sylvia would ask Una. 'I hate doing rib, it takes so long.'

Una always obliged. Tina often asked her advice when she got into difficulties with a sewing pattern and appreciated help with the button-holes. Before long, both girls were calling at Una's home to leave or pick up pieces of work, and sometimes they were offered an item from Una's wardrobe, which she thought they might like and which they jealously guarded from one another. Their favourite adjective was 'super'. 'Thanks, Auntie Una,' they would say, holding the garment up against them and regarding the effect in the cheval mirror in Una's bedroom. 'It's super!' They were full of fun and chatter about their current boy-friends and their rock and roll music.

Una was not so comfortable with Marcia and Tom. There was a wild look in Marcia's eyes which had not been there before, and an edginess in her manner. Some of the remarks she made seemed ill-considered in the circumstances and almost made Una think that Marcia envied her the sorry state of widowhood, especially the cold double bed she had all to herself.

Shirley, who had been such a sweet, amenable baby, was now spoilt and petulant. Marcia behaved in a ridiculously over-protective manner towards her, which upset the rest of the family. Kate was now fifteen, extremely pretty, with a stormy, uncontrollable nature. She stamped her foot and cried with rage, she bit her lip and cried with vexation, she smiled and cried with joy. Una had never known a girl shed so many tears. She took every emotion to the limit and kept the household balanced on a tightrope of taut nerves. One moment she was tearfully convinced that nobody loved her, the next she was tearfully grateful for proof that they did.

'I don't understand her,' Marcia sighed to Una, adding with what seemed very like satisfaction, 'She's going to make some man's life absolute hell.'

Privately, Una suspected she was just going through a difficult period and would grow out of it.

Ian was in the army, training to be a physical education instructor.

It was Marcia who told Una that it was not ill health alone that had made Hugh give up his job at the early age of fifty-three. He had been forced to do so in order to avoid a scandal concerning his alleged molestation of young members of the female staff, some of them only fifteen years old. Una was almost as shocked and saddened by Marcia's gleeful venom as by Hugh's disgraceful conduct, if it were true.

The Sunday afternoons that Una spent with Sibyl and Stuart were instructive of the way a household should be run and children managed. Julian was in the lower sixth at school, thin and pasty faced; Bruce was fourteen, fresh-faced and robust. The former was outspoken and rude, like his father, only quieter and more subtle with his insults, which meant that he was rarely overheard by his parents and seldom rebuked. The latter was well-mannered and naïve. He drew derision from his brother and tender smiles of compassion from his mother, who was convinced that he would eventually be taken in by an unscrupulous woman or a confidence trickster—much the same thing, in her opinion. She did not know, of course, that he had already been in the role of docile victim, to his cousin Kate's experimental play. She had long since discarded him, still an innocent, for bolder, older boys, who could teach her a thing or two.

Sibyl lectured Una tactfully about taking herself in hand. Like Imelda, she urged her to get herself another car; she also urged her to eat more, smoke less and get rid of Neil's possessions that were of no use to her—such as the set of golf clubs he had scarcely used, which would only bring back sad memories for her every time she looked at them. Stuart agreed with his wife.

Una explained patiently that her memories were not sad, in fact they were the stuff her present was made of, but Sibyl considered that too morbid and thought she needed to be taught a more positive approach to the future.

The one person in the family Una had not seen since the accident was Flora. No one had offered to drive her over to Lapcombe and she would not ask to be taken. She was intensely hurt that Flora had neither visited her in hospital nor shown any interest in her since. Anyone else would have done so if only out of politeness, but Flora was never directed by good manners to do something against her inclination. Nevertheless, if the distance had been less, or the village easily accessible by bus, Una would have called in to see her, not only out of politeness but out of stifled affection which, if Flora only knew it, needed very little encouragement to blossom forth.

With the first definite signs of Spring, which for Una were the daffodils swaying in Neil's garden, her spirits lightened just a little, enough to make her company more of a pleasure and less of an endurance. One Saturday afternoon, she had just returned from the office when Imelda called at the house with a suggestion. 'How about coming over to Lapcombe to visit Auntie Flora?'

Una readily agreed.

When they arrived, she was surprised to see that the garden surrounding the house, in which it had settled over the centuries like a dilapidated and broody old hen, looked unkempt. It was evident that there had been no winter tidying-up by the odd-job man from the farm down the road, nor any essential pruning. The house itself was looking seedy: the paintwork was flaking, the guttering was coming adrift near the side porch and there were some pantiles missing from the gently sagging roof. Altogether, the place presented a sorry sight. It was as if the last winter had done for it more than the last fifty. They had to wait some while for Flora to answer the door and were coming to the conclusion that she was out when she appeared before them. Una could not believe her eyes: Flora's hair was an ugly, streaky grey, escaping from the brown stockinette roll in wild array, rather like the live locks of Medusa. The white powder caked on her face did not hide the unusual pinkness of her raddled cheeks. Her blue eyes were bright, but vacantly hostile as she stared at them. She was swaying in the doorway like an ancient goddess in a crumbling shrine and both women were in no doubt which deity she was impersonating. They were confronting a female version of Bacchus, not at his best. Flora had been tippling.

They followed her slow, very stately progress along the hall and into the dust-laden drawing-room.

'I thought you had forgotten where I live,' she remarked haughtily, carefully lowering her large frame into an armchair.

'Of course not, Auntie, I was here ten days ago,' Imelda reminded her.

'I meant the other one,' Flora stated coldly.

'I'm sorry,' Una said. 'It's difficult to get here without a car.'

'Humph!' was the reply. 'Where's Jessica?'

Imelda started to explain. Una was thinking, Good heavens, was Imelda here ten days ago? Has she taken on Auntie Flora as another of her lame ducks? Did she ever have any time for herself? Una felt ashamed, even more so when she heard Flora say:

'The weekends aren't the same since Lavinia died, and now that Neil has gone my life is very empty. Sometimes I can't even be bothered to go to church; then the vicar comes and makes a nuisance of himself, silly man. Is that why you are here? Has Mr Laston been telling tales? Well, in that case, would you like a drop of barley wine to warm you after the journey?'

'I'll make some tea instead, shall I?' Imelda suggested. She went into the kitchen and reeled at the state it was in. She returned to the drawing-room. 'Is Mrs Standish on holiday?' she asked.

'I got rid of her last week,' Flora said defiantly.

Imelda returned to the chaos, motioning with her head for Una to follow.

'Look at this!' she exclaimed in disgust.

Una was appalled. 'Has it got like this in only a week? How on earth will she manage on her own?'

'It's obvious she won't. All her life she has been waited upon and fawned over; she hasn't a clue about simple household chores and she's too old to start learning. Somebody will have to do something, instead of just waiting for the poor old girl to peg out and leave them her money.'

It was ironical that one of those people who had confidently counted upon her fortune had preceded her to eternity. Una wondered how many more she would outlive; not many if she wallowed in too much barley wine!

She helped Imelda to wash up the mounds of dirty dishes and return the kitchen to some kind of order. When, eventually, they took Flora her cup of tea, she had fallen asleep and was snoring heavily, her head at an uncomfortable angle on the back of the chair. They sipped their own tea and discussed her in whispers. It was sad to see how much she had aged since Neil's death; it had obviously affected her profoundly and robbed her of that indomitable will which had once manifested itself in pride and vanity.

'Poor old sod!' Imelda said compassionately.

'Imelda!'

'Sorry, Auntie Una,' Imelda grinned.

On the way home they took a detour and called at the cottage in the next village, where Mrs Standish lived. They were both angry with her for leaving Flora to her own inept devices without informing someone in the family. Imelda was going to tear her off a strip. It turned out to be unnecessary. Mrs Standish explained in an affronted manner that she had every intention of going back when her employer had been taught a much needed lesson in humility.

'She had no call to treat me like she did. I'm doing her a service and small thanks I get for it,' the woman said in tones of outrage, standing at her cottage door. 'She's so hoity-toity and not a bit grateful. It's not the first time she's told me to go, not by a long chalk, but it's the first time I've taken her at her word. I'm not to be spoken to as if I'm dirt.' She smoothed her spotless, paisley-patterned pinafore over her full stomach and straightened her back. 'She can't do without me. Perhaps when she's got through all the barley wine she'll realise that. There's only a few bottles to go and I'm not making any, I'm a good Methodist, I am. I'll be turning up on Monday, don't you fear, but I'll have to see if I can stay or not. It depends,' she ended ominously.

Imelda resolved to speak to her Aunt Sibyl about the situation. She should be able to sort out the difficulties between the elderly autocrat and her bossy daily and perhaps organise her sisters into doing something positive about Flora's loneliness, although, as far as Jessica was concerned, Imelda knew Sibyl would be wasting her time. Imelda did not suppose, as Mrs Standish seemed to, that the end of the barley wine would be the beginning of Flora's salvation; unfortunately, she was almost as partial to sherry.

The visit to Lapcombe had touched Una's conscience. For the first time since Neil's death, she was concerned about someone else's unhappiness as well as her own. Colour was insidiously returning to the grey world about her.

Chapter Thirteen

In April, Una began to baby-sit for Mr Truebody's daughter, Joan. She was so readily available that Joan soon dispensed with the services of the teenager who usually obliged and employed Una on a regular basis, which worked out about once a week. The only trouble was that Joan and Una lived so far apart; in fact, Joan lived very near Lapcombe. If she was required on a Friday, Mr Truebody gave Una a lift to his daughter's house straight from the office. She had been persuaded that it was more convenient for her to spend the night there and Joan's husband took her home soon after breakfast. If it was a Saturday, she travelled there by bus. After five weeks of this arrangement, Una came to the conclusion that she was being ridiculous. It was not in her nature to be dependent, except where she loved, and having to be fetched and carried like a parcel was becoming onerous. She lay in bed one night, curled up tight in her fleecy cotton nightdress in the manner of a tender grub in a cocoon, leaving three-quarters of the bed as cold and inhospitable as the arctic wastes, and made up her mind to buy a car. Not only would she be free to travel when and where she desired, but she would also be privileged to travel alone.

Within a week and with advice from her brother-in-law, Ronald, she had acquired another Morris Minor. She no longer had to sleep at Joan's house when she baby-sat, and when she was needed on a Saturday night she spent the afternoon at Lapcombe, driving over from the office if it was one of her working mornings.

Flora, who had never seen Una on her own, was surprised the first time she arrived, surprised and not exactly pleased. She desired no favours from Neil's widow who, presumably, had nothing better to do than bat about the countryside in her shiny new car.

'Where's Imelda?' were her first words.

'I came on my own,' Una told her.

'Oh, I see,' Flora said, in a tone that asked, what for?

For a moment, Una was unsure whether she would be invited into the house, then Flora stepped heavily to one side, saying ungraciously, 'You'd better come in.'

It had been an uncomfortable visit. Unlike Imelda, Una was not the type to take charge of other people's lives. She waited in vain for Flora to offer her a cup of tea and, eventually, when their stilted conversation ground to a halt, tentatively offered to make one.

'Don't bother on my account,' Flora said, then, relenting a little, 'No doubt you are thirsty, if you have come straight from work. Make yourself a sandwich as well.'

It was amazing what a mess Flora could make between Friday lunch-time, when Mrs Standish left, and the middle of Saturday afternoon. Una was glad she had bought herself a sandwich in town. At least the kitchen was basically clean beneath the clutter of dirty dishes and crumbs. Una did a quick tidy-up while she was waiting for the kettle to boil and stacked the dishes in the sink to be washed up later with their tea cups.

'You've been a long time,' Flora complained when Una arrived with the tea. 'I hope you haven't been doing anything out there. I want it all left for that woman. That's what I pay her for.'

Una did not stay long. When she left she said, 'I'll probably come again next Saturday,' but as there was no response, she wondered if she should bother. On Tuesday evening, she went to the cinema with Imelda and told her about the cool reception she had received at Lapcombe. 'I don't know whether to go again or not. I know she is lonely, but perhaps she would prefer to be. Now that Neil is dead, I thought she would have stopped resenting me.'

'Don't give up on her, Una,' Imelda urged. 'Mrs Standish is only hanging on there until Sibyl finds a replacement for her. Unfortunately, word has got around locally that Auntie Flora has grown even more peculiar and is impossible to work for, so nobody wants the job. Her money might have made the position more bearable, but she has always had a reputation for stinginess and nobody could hope to be adequately rewarded for putting up with her.'

Imelda was driving her own car. As they pulled into a side street near the Odeon to park, she said, 'Perhaps you and Auntie Flora should try sharing your loss.'

'How?' Una asked, sharply, feeling an immediate dislike of sharing even the briefest thought of Neil with anyone else.

Imelda shrugged, 'I don't know,' she answered wearily. 'I only know we have to try and make life bearable for each other.' She brought the car to a standstill next to the kerb. 'Come on, let's have a basinful of fantasy.'

They got out and walked past the shuttered shop of a seed merchant. The warm air of the June evening was redolent with the lingering smell of the sacks of seed and corn that had stood on the pavement during the day. Una was assailed by a sharp pang of nostalgia for her childhood. Her grandmother had owned a budgerigar for years and she had often been sent to a similar shop for millet. The little bird had also perished beneath the rubble of her home.

As they walked up the steps into the foyer to join the queue for the box office Una asked, 'How's Felix?'

Imelda smiled. 'Fine,' she said. 'May we come over to supper next week? It's nice to have someone in the family we can visit together. Dad knows about him now, but we keep it from Mother. She has become a dreadfully mirthless woman, not that she was ever much fun. She can tell you all about sin and nothing about love. Poor old Dad, he is so unhappy. If she were a true Christian, she would at least smile at him once in a while. I can't remember the last time she smiled.'

The next Saturday, Una drove over to Lapcombe again. Flora greeted her with the same lack of enthusiasm, but with no surprise. She had been anticipating her arrival and would have been disappointed if Una had not turned up. The visit followed the same pattern as before and the conversation remained careful and polite. Flora only once became voluble and that was in castigating Mrs Standish. 'She has the nerve to leave things off my grocery list,' Flora complained. 'When they are delivered, half the stuff is missing and the grocer swears blind that he has included everything on my list. He would, too, he doesn't want to lose the pennies.' She did not say what kind of things were missing, but Una guessed that Mrs Standish was deleting the bottles of cheap sherry and her guess was confirmed when Flora called, as she was leaving, 'Remind Hugh about the sherry.'

Neither woman had mentioned Neil. Una had tried to do so, but she was so reluctant that no suitable words came to mind.

'Would you like to come for a drive tomorrow afternoon?' she asked, standing by the car with the door open.

'Ella's coming,' Flora said.

'Then I'll see you next Saturday.'

'Are you sure you've got nothing better to do?' Flora asked in a churlish tone.

'I may have,' Una said, getting into the car and slamming the door. Flora Macfarlane Brown was an old woman who was difficult to like, who deserved to be lonely!

Nevertheless, Una persevered with her. On her fourth visit she asked quietly, into an extended silence, 'Would you care to visit Neil's grave with me?'

Flora was on the point of answering that she went alone every time she went to church, but she refrained. She steadily regarded the thin young woman sitting opposite her, with her hands clasped together in her lap as if she were keeping a tight rein on her emotions, her candid brown eyes appealing to Flora's better nature, and she said, 'Yes.'

'Now?' Una asked.

'My hair's in a mess. I cannot manage it any more.'

'I'll fetch your brush and see what I can do.' Una hurried upstairs to Flora's bedroom, with its small-paned bow window overlooking the side garden; the shrubs were hanging heavily beneath the weight of a sudden downpour. The bed was made, after a fashion: the cotton patchwork quilt, in numerous shades of washed-out blue, was pulled over the untidy heap of blankets and pillows. On the white-powdered oak of the dressing-table top, amidst a scatter of hair pins, scent bottles and small china ornaments, reposed the wooden-backed hairbrush, an unsavoury mess of accumulated grey hair. Una cleaned it up as best she could with the scruffy comb she found in the bathroom, then washed both in the hand-basin. The bathroom was old-fashioned, with bright yellow stains beneath the ugly taps on the white enamel of the cast iron bath, and the rim of the lavatory pan was cracked beneath the weighty mahogany seat, which had been dropped on it with a hefty thud over countless years. Una flushed away the bird's nest of matted grey hair.

'Couldn't you find it?' Flora asked irritably, eyeing the clean brush with disfavour.

'I went to the bathroom,' Una explained, positioning herself behind Flora and beginning to extricate the grips and stockinette circle. 'Would you like me to wash it? I expect you find it difficult to do on your own?'

'I manage,' Flora said, adding, after a long pause, 'Perhaps next time you come.' Actually, Sibyl had been doing it for her, when she remembered, but she was heavy handed and impatient compared with Una.

Una tidied the thinning, coarse hair and brushed it gently away from her face. Flora bridled a little beneath the brush, but remained silent.

'I'm not very clever with hair,' Una admitted. 'I'm afraid I can't manage to roll it up again.'

'I can't do it very well now,' Flora said, which was something that had been patently obvious to everyone for years. 'My arms are too stiff. Just leave it. Good heavens, did all those come out?' she exclaimed, looking at the pile of hair pins on the table beside her. 'No wonder my head felt so uncomfortable in bed.'

Half an hour later, they were walking side by side away from the car along the path behind the village church. The sun was rapidly drying the drenched green of the Summer landscape. Una was regretting the impulse that had prompted her to ask for Flora's company on this private pilgrimage. She was holding a bunch of flowers that she had picked, on Flora's instructions, from the garden. It was only the fourth time she had visited the grave in the six months since Neil's death. Her husband was in her heart and in her home; she did not feel closer to him here, where even the headstone had been a joint family offering, to which she had only contributed.

Una laid the flowers to wither at the foot of the handsome new headstone. It seemed more appropriate than putting them in a vase of water to give false hope of continuing life. Her eyes travelled over the deeply etched inscription, which recorded for uncaring posterity that Neil had been not only her beloved husband, but a beloved brother and nephew as well. She fought back the tears as she murmured, 'I never even said goodbye to him. I would have liked to tell him that it was my fault.'

Flora ignored the last bit. 'Goodbye means forever,' she said, in a voice softened by sorrow. 'I hope no one says it to me when I go.' She trudged across the grass to stand beside the grave of her devoted sister, leaving Una to commune alone.

They did not remain for many minutes, nor did they ever repeat the shared experience, yet they felt more at ease with one another from that day. Una kept up the regular visits to Lapcombe and, on the rare occasions when she had to miss a week, Flora was sorry. She pretended that it was annoyance at having to wait to have her hair washed and brushed and told herself that no doubt Una had found herself something better to do with her time, but she was growing reliant upon the younger woman's gentle ministrations.

The Summer wound on and Autumn arrived. Una kept herself busy and stayed in the house as little as possible, preferring the gardening to the housework. Outside, she was surrounded by signs of life: people, animals, birds, insects, even plants, and the clouds which moved across the sky with an animation she could not find inside, where the stillness made her dwell upon her lost love and the harshness of life's emptiness. She encouraged her nieces and nephews to call, but they had more interesting things to do most of the time and only visited her when they had a reason, usually at their mothers' behest. Only Sylvia and Tina came quite often, with their sewing and knitting problems, leaving bits and pieces for Una to finish off for them.

Una grew thinner and paler. How she got through the dark days of the succeeding Winter, when the garden became a hostile land, she did not know.

One day, she became aware that it was Spring again.

Chapter Fourteen

Three years after the car crash, little had changed in Una's life and the lives of those nearest to her. Then, one morning, an incident happened that was to change everything for her; just a small incident, but it marked the start of a series of more important events which were to effect her profoundly.

She drove into the County Hall car park one Thursday morning in May, behind the car belonging to Bart Pascall. This was not unusual. They often arrived about the same time, especially since September when Bart had started bringing his twelve-year-old son in with him. Luke was now attending the direct grant grammar school in the town. Una parked in the usual place, beside the tennis courts, and was on the point of leaving the car when she heard a shout, followed by the sound of heavy braking. Beside the cumbersome green mass of the travelling library lay a small figure and, a few yards from it, a school satchel. She leaped from the car and ran towards the young boy, arriving as he was struggling to his feet.

'It's all right,' he said shakily, to her and to the other people who had arrived with her, including the driver of the huge van. 'I'm just bumped.' Then, seeing his father running back towards him, a look of alarm on his face, Luke burst into tears.

Bart grabbed him and questioned him, feeling him all over with anxious care and causing him to wince a couple of times, while the van driver protested, to all who cared to listen, that he had not seen the lad.

'He must have walked straight into the side of it,' he stated on a note of pained incredulity.

Luke dried his tears and confirmed, with shame, that he had done just that. He had not realised that the van was backing into the library loading bay and had turned to wave goodbye to his father, but Bart had not been looking and Luke had continued to walk with his head turned, watching his father striding towards the office entrance, in a hurry as usual.

'Are you feeling well enough to go on to school, Luke?' Bart enquired with impatient concern.

'I don't think he should go yet,' Una said, and those spectators who had not already drifted away from the anti-climax agreed with her.

'Where's my satchel?' Luke asked, glancing round wildly for his precious Latin homework. Someone handed it to him and he breathed a tremulous sigh of relief. 'Here's your cap,' someone else said. 'Oh, that!' he muttered and stuffed it into his blazer pocket.

He had a large bump on the side of his head and a cut leg beneath a hole in his grey trousers. He complained that his shoulder hurt, but not badly, just enough to get him off rugby practice, he reckoned.

'It obviously wasn't your fault,' Bart consoled the van driver, who was recovering from his shock and showing signs of grievance.

'Blinkin' kids, should look where they're going,' he declared angrily, watching Bart leading his superficially damaged son away. 'Could've been nasty. Could've run right over him,' and he went back to his cab and the business of the day, beginning with the loading of the large chests of books destined for the far-flung readers of the county.

Una walked on the other side of Luke.

'Come and sit in the office until you've recovered, Luke,' Bart said. 'I have to rush off to London soon, but you can stay with Miss Robins until you feel like going on to school.'

'Let him come with me,' Una suggested. 'I'll make him something hot and sweet to drink to help him get over the shock, and then I can drive him to school.'

'That's very kind of you, Mrs Favory,' Bart said with gratitude.

Una was a familiar face to Luke, seen on and off for years in Lapcombe and, more recently, on many mornings outside County Hall. He had grown accustomed to greeting her, as his father did, with a nod and a smile from the car, or a brisk 'Good morning' when on foot. He favoured her over his father's younger, but severer, secretary.

'Will you come with me, Luke?' Una asked.

'All right,' he said unenthusiastically, regarding her with grey eyes so like his mother's, but without the smile which had lurked in Louise's eyes even when she was being serious. 'I don't drink tea,' he warned her.

Una did not fuss over him, for which he was thankful. The only person who was allowed to fuss was his grandmother, and she could not help it. His mother had been fun and made light of minor catastrophes, which had made them easier to bear. His father did his best to follow her example, but without much success. His father had told him that Mrs Favory's husband had died a year after his mother. He remembered Mr Favory, vaguely, very tall with curly hair. Not many men in his experience had curls. He wondered if someone missed a husband as much as a mother. He doubted it, but it was a kind of bond between him and this woman who was handing him a mug of hot chocolate and two bourbon biscuits.

'Will it matter if you are late for school,' Una asked him.

'I don't want to be late,' he informed her firmly. He did not think that his sarcastic form master would look with tolerance upon a little boy whose excuse was that he had been stupid enough to walk into the side of a damn great van.

'Then drink up,' she said, 'and I'll drive you over. I'll just let my boss know where I am going.'

The next morning Una was a few minutes later getting to work and arrived in her office to find Bart Pascall waiting for her.

'I want to thank you for looking after Luke yesterday,' he said.

'It was nothing. How is he?'

'Fine, I'm relieved to say. I hope it will teach him to be more careful in future.' He sighed, 'The children have become more of a responsibility than a pleasure since Louise died. I feel guilty at not being able to spend more time with them and dreadfully inadequate, especially where the girls are concerned. Louise had a very bright, sunny disposition. I make a sorry substitute,' and he smiled wryly. He wondered what kind of life Una was leading without her husband. He knew she was baby-sitting occasionally for Frank Truebody's daughter—Frank had told him—and that she was visiting the old lady at Lapcombe, because he had seen her there sometimes when the children were staying with their grandparents at the manor. Of course, she had Neil's large family to support her, she was fortunate in that. She was too young, mid-thirties he supposed, to be living on her own and too attractive for that to remain the case, surely. He had always considered her to be most attractive, despite, perhaps even because of, a wondering, serious expression in her eyes and a downward droop at the corners of her full lips, which presented a challenge to anyone who had once seen them smiling, as he had, years ago, when they had both possessed someone to smile about.

'You are lucky to have such fine children,' Una said.

'Yes, I don't know how I could carry on without them.' Then he remembered her childlessness and wished he had not said it. 'I must get back to the office,' he said quickly. 'Thank you again. Luke was full of praise for your hot chocolate. He said it was worth the bash on his head.'

Luke's carelessness had forged the first link between Una and his father. They began to greet one another as friends rather than acquaintances, and to exchange sentences rather than a couple of words when they met, which, strangely enough, was quite frequently. Una began timing her arrival every morning so that she would meet Luke. Bart watched for her to leave in the evening, often walking across the car park with her.

One morning, Una's car did not appear.

'Mrs Favory must be ill,' Luke said, 'or perhaps she's had another crash.'

His father did not answer. He threw his satchel at him and slammed the car door. Luke set off for school, expecting to pass Una's car on the way, but no such luck.

Within half an hour Bart had thought of a good reason to ring old Truebody. Una's voice answered the telephone.

'What happened to you this morning?' he asked her lightly.

'I had to come by train. My car needs a new clutch.'

'Then I'll drive you home this evening,' he offered on the spur of the moment. 'Will you be leaving at the same time as usual?'

Taken completely by surprise, Una said, 'Yes, but really, there's no need. I can easily catch the train.'

'I want to. It's my way of repaying your kindness to Luke.'

'Thank you,' she said, 'but I did very little for him.'

'Let me be the judge of that.'

There was an awkward silence, then she asked him, 'Shall I put you through to Mr Truebody?'

'Oh, yes, thank you.' Suddenly, he recalled his excuse for ringing.

That night, Una sat on the edge of the bed to kick off her slippers and experienced a strange emotion emerging through her weary despondency, as unexpected as clear, iridescent bubbles appearing miraculously on the surface of an over-shadowed pool: she was almost happy. Bart Pascall looked like being that rare find, a true friend, who knows without being told, sympathises without unnecessary words and is interested to hear one's opinions, even when they differ from his own. Also, Bart knew as she did the full meaning of that doleful word 'mourning'. It set them apart from those fortunate beings who had yet to learn it.

It is amazing the amount of conversation that can be exchanged during a twenty-minute journey, even by two people who hardly know one another and have reservations about revealing their bruised centres. Una did not think that she had given very much of herself away, but she had certainly learnt a lot about Bart Pascall. Her thoughts as she was drifting towards sleep were, as always, of Neil, and her faithful heart clung to the past with even greater fervour, as if, suddenly, she had been placed in danger of forgetting it.

Ten miles away, Bart shuffled together the typed foolscap pages he had been looking through for the planning meeting first thing the next morning. He was pleased that he had encouraged Una to talk about herself and satisfied that he had succeeded so well in drawing her out. She was utterly unlike Louise in looks and temperament, thank God. In his fond memory his wife would remain unique.

Chapter Fifteen

Over the following six months, the friendship between Una and Bart grew into a mutual dependency. One day, soon after Luke's collision with the library van, they met quite by chance—one of those fortuitous chances that occur between two people who have one another on their minds. It happened in the High Street at lunch-time and Bart seized the opportunity to suggest that they have a sandwich together. This was rather awkward, because Una was not alone. She was buying some apples on a stall outside Boots, while her two young friends were inside choosing a lipstick. She was explaining this to him when they reappeared, laughing and talking together. When they saw Bart they fell silent and drifted off a few yards in the opposite direction. One of them was in his department and did not want to draw attention to herself. Lunch-time is for escaping from the boss, who is just work personified. They were aware that he was a friend of Una's, of course. She had explained to them that he had married a friend of Neil's, but seeing them together, with Mr Pascall looking earnest and Una clutching a brown paper bag of apples and looking slightly embarrassed, made them wonder.

'Perhaps another time?' Bart suggested, disappointed.

'Yes, I should like that,' Una answered, feeling just the same.

A week went by before the invitation was repeated. One evening they emerged from the office together and, as they walked towards their cars, Bart asked if she would like to have lunch with him the next day.

So once a week, usually on a Thursday, depending on Bart's commitments, they travelled in his car to a small restaurant attached to a pub about a mile out of town and over a light meal talked and listened, growing to know one another and the circumstances of their respective lives, stretching back almost to their cradles yet leaving blank the important years of their marriages. It was as if the people they had been during those years had been buried with Louise and Neil. Bart heard about the very young Una and her immediate family, which had consisted of mother, father, younger sister and grandmother. She even found herself telling him about the tragic circumstances of their deaths. He was also getting to know Una the widow, and Neil's family, especially Imelda. The woman in between had vanished. Una meant never to resurrect her.

In a similar way, she heard about Bart's early years and the members of his family, who were still living in Newcastle upon Tyne. She was becoming familiar with his children, and with their grandparents at Lapcombe, for whom Bart obviously had a deep affection. As time went by, Bart allowed himself to talk a little about Louise, but Una kept Neil firmly and jealously locked within her mind. It was not surprising, therefore, that Bart was the first to acknowledge that his fondness was growing more complex than friendship. Once he did, he became anxious for Dolcis and Angela to get to know Una.

While he was planning how best to introduce Una into his home, without antagonising his already suspicious daughters, Una was preoccupied with troubles within her adopted family; the tremulous happiness which had been creeping into her life, like fitful sunshine between brooding cloud masses, was almost extinguished—almost, but not quite; Bart saw to that.

She arrived home one evening to find a note from Imelda on the doormat, which read, 'Dad is dead. Please come round'. Una hurried there straight away, to find Jessica alone and distraught, clasping a wild-eyed cat in her arms.

'Isn't Imelda here?' Una asked in dismay. She followed Jessica into the kitchen, where the cat made a frantic effort to get free. Jessica tried to calm it, but the animal was alarmed by the tension in the familiar embrace and stuck its claws viciously through the fine wool jumper into its mistress's arms. Jessica cried out and let it go. It streaked into the hall and Jessica collapsed against the draining board in tears.

Una placed an arm around her shaking shoulders. She was surprised that Hugh's wife was exhibiting so much distress at his loss, when she had shown so little pleasure in his company. She made soothing noises until Jessica's sobs subsided into a gulping control.

'He was only fifty-seven,' Jessica lamented, more in a tone of complaint than regret. 'He brought it on himself. He couldn't stand the shame. He hated being cooped up in the house, when he really wanted to go out walking to get it out of his system. He always used to go for a walk when he had something on his mind, but he hasn't been able to do that for years, not with his bad heart. He'd got as far as Turnbull Road. He was probably making for the sea. I think he wanted to drown himself! He used to love walking along the water's edge. We often used to walk along the prom together when the children were small and you couldn't go near the water, because of the barbed wire.'

Una led her into the living-room and gently pushed her down into the nearest chair, but she jumped out of it as if she had been scalded, crying, 'That's Hugh's!' and fled across the room to collapse upon the sofa.

Una was annoyed with herself for such a thoughtless mistake.

'First Marcus and now Hugh. I can't bear it,' Jessica moaned, a forlorn heap of crumpled handkerchief, well-washed botany jumper, baggy tweed skirt and pink furry slippers.

They heard the back door open. Immediately Jessica made

an effort to compose herself, wiping her eyes and stuffing the damp hankie up her sleeve.

Imelda appeared. 'I had to go out for a few minutes,' she said. 'Thanks for coming, Una. Have you eaten? Neither have I. Not that I feel like much, but I'll have to force down something, or I'll drop. Come and help me prepare it. We won't be long, Mother.' As soon as they were in the kitchen, she said, 'Dad was brought into the hospital yesterday afternoon, while I was at work. I rushed down to casualty but he was dead. He had died in the ambulance.'

'I'm very sorry, Imelda. Jessica's taking it very badly.'

'Yes, strange, isn't it? I suppose she cannot bear not having him here to ignore and despise. It will leave a big gap in her existence. Goodness knows what will become of her now.' Imelda sighed and began opening a tin of baked beans. 'Do some toast, will you, Una? I think there's plenty of bread.'

Una took a large loaf from the roll-top bread bin and began slicing it.

'I was telephoning Felix when you arrived,' Imelda explained. 'I did it from the box up the road, so that Mother wouldn't overhear. I had to tell him to forget about the week we were going to have together in Innsbruck. I won't be able to leave Mother for a while.'

'I could look after her,' Una offered.

'No, thanks all the same. We were going after Christmas and that is too soon. By the way, you weren't at Lapcombe at the weekend, were you? Mrs Standish has finally had enough. She told Sibyl and said she was very sorry, but nothing, absolutely nothing, would induce her to remain. She accused Auntie Flora of making nasty messes on purpose, just to annoy her.'

'I'll go over on Saturday,' Una promised, feeling guilty. She had been shopping in Poole with Bart on the previous Saturday, helping him to choose material for a new suit and a birthday present for Angela, while his children had been staying with the Pope-Wessingtons.

'Dad hated beans on toast,' Imelda said, wiping the tears from her eyes. 'Poor Dad!' She had hated watching him change over the last ten years from a man of firm convictions and responsibility to a pitiable mess, first rejected by his wife and then by his colleagues, his only comfort a weak heart which would not take him into an old age he dreaded.

'He is going to be cremated on Monday,' she told Una. 'I have a week off. When I go back to work, I shall be on nights. Do you think you could spend an occasional evening here with Mother? Just until she gets over the worst of it. Her sisters have asked her to sleep at one of their homes, but she won't leave the blasted cats.'

Una said of course she would. She was no longer baby-sitting for Joan, Mr Truebody's daughter, because they had recently moved to Salisbury; so she would be free any evening she was needed.

In the New Year, they were all recovering from the shock of Hugh's death when Marcia had a terrifying experience and had to spend some months in a mental hospital as a result. Shirley, the child she adored, over-protected and spoilt, quietly shut the door of the cupboard under the stairs on her way to school one morning, incarcerating her mother who was rummaging in its far depths for a pair of wellington boots. Marcia went berserk. She screamed in claustrophobic terror in the pitch dark, flinging herself from wall to wall in stark panic, her sense of direction lost. Nobody knew how long she was in there. Eventually, the latch on the door snapped beneath her hurled weight. She was found by Kate, when she returned home from school in the afternoon: a huddled heap in the corner of the hall, rocking herself backwards and forwards and moaning; with an emptiness in her eyes which was most alarming. She was bruised all over and her hands were bleeding.

Shirley was questioned closely about what had happened. She had been the last to leave the house that morning and the door could not be latched from the inside. She flatly denied any knowledge of how it had come to be fastened and was as amazed as everybody else at the chaotic state of the inside of the cupboard—shoes, boxes of games, shuttlecocks and other stored paraphernalia trampled and broken and coats torn down from the snapped wooden pegs.

'She must have shut herself in,' she insisted sullenly, 'or perhaps the dog knocked against the door.'

This last explanation was accepted as the only reasonable one.

When Marcia returned home from the hospital, it was to a husband who was as changed as she was. Tom could take no pleasure in subjugating a weakened intellect. He had only pity and physical revulsion for the woman whose astuteness had once made him feel inferior and inadequate. There was no point in proving his male superiority, where there was no will to resist it. He lay impotently beside her in the double bed, humiliated and defeated by the slack indifference of his adversary. If he rolled against her in insensible sleep, Marcia got up and bathed.

Their secret drama, enacted, as domestic drama often is, behind the closed bedroom door, was over. Nobody else had known of it. The world, Marcia's and Tom's world of friends and family, had merely glimpsed the scene changes. Superficially, they had turned from normal, happily married people, into a troubled couple who were doing their best to come to terms with the legacy of Marcia's inexplicable breakdown. Only Marcia knew how long it had taken her to reach the finale, that awful climax, which had taken place behind the cupboard door; only Marcia knew the refuge her illness now afforded her. Tom was frequently urged by Sibyl, who had already tried and failed, to coax his wife into better health. Tom was the last person who could do it. Whenever he seemed like succeeding, Marcia had a relapse and another long spell in hospital.

One afternoon on the golf course, Tom confided to his close friend and brother-in-law that it was his opinion the Favorys were an unbalanced lot—with the exception of Stuart's wife, Sibyl, of course, and Neil, who had been normal in everything except a lack of enthusiasm for golf.

Chapter Sixteen

'Something must be done about Auntie Flora,' Sibyl declared one evening in July, looking in turn at each sister with a no-nonsense expression on her face, as they sat around her in Marcia's living-room.

'What do you suggest?' Ella asked nervously.

'One of us will have to have her. She isn't capable of living on her own. I can't spend any more time at Lapcombe. I'm doing more than my fair share as it is. Una is going every weekend, which is all she can manage, what with working all week and going out and about with Bart Pascall. It's unkind leaving an elderly woman all alone in that big house. It's falling to bits around her ears and the garden has become a positive disgrace. Stuart's done what he could, but he has his own garden to do and, goodness knows, that takes second place to his precious golf. She shouldn't have another winter there, unless she can be persuaded to spend the money to keep it heated.'

'Can't you have her?' Jessica asked in a pleading tone.

'No, I can't!' Sibyl snapped. 'I have three grown men to look after.' Julian and Bruce were both working and still living at home. 'I would've thought you were the obvious choice, Jessica. You have an empty third bedroom. Auntie Flora would be company for you when Imelda is at the hospital, especially when she's on nights.'

'I couldn't,' Jessica said, stiffly. 'She doesn't like cats.'

'Don't be ridiculous,' Sibyl said. 'She could keep away from them.'

'Auntie Flora would be very difficult to live with,' said Ella, coming to the rescue of her favourite sister. 'She would be forever complaining and criticising. Anyway, I don't think she would leave Lapcombe. That old house means everything to her. It's been in the family for generations.'

'I agree,' Jessica said quickly.

'Then it's a pity she won't spend some of her money on it,' Sibyl remarked.

Marcia was just sitting, dull-eyed, nodding or shaking her head, seemingly at random. No one was going to suggest that Marcia should take care of Flora. Neither did they suggest that Una should have her. Una was only an in-law and her work gave her an excuse for getting out of most things.

'Well, she's going to have to leave it, whether she wants to or not, unless one of you is prepared to go there more often and help me keep an eye on her,' Sibyl told them.

'I don't drive,' Jessica reminded her, 'so I can't. I have to rely on Imelda to take me, or Una.'

'You could come with me sometimes,' Sibyl suggested. 'Two of us could get through twice as much cleaning.'

'Very well,' Jessica conceded in a weary manner. Anything was preferable to having Auntie Flora living with her, making demands on the time she devoted to the church and the cats.

'I think she should go into a home,' Ella decided. 'She doesn't eat properly now. She stuffs herself with bread and jam. I always take her something, a cake or a meat pie, and the next time I go I have to throw most of it away. Her kitchen is disgusting. I wonder she hasn't died of food poisoning. I'm not surprised that Mrs Standish left. Auntie Flora can reduce the place to a pig-sty in a couple of days. I couldn't have her at home. The girls are always bringing back their boy-friends. It would be extremely awkward.' She shuddered inwardly at the thought.

'She shows no sign of ill health,' Jessica observed.

'Unless you go when she's been at the sherry,' Sibyl remarked drily. 'What are we going to do about her, then? Just leave her to get dirtier and smellier?' Sibyl's true god was

Personal Cleanliness. She had a bath and washed her hair before going to the doctor with a septic finger. She had a horror of dying dirty. She did not want her corpse to give offence.

'She needs some sheets,' Ella informed them. 'The last lot I washed were worn out and one of them had a long rent in it. I replaced it with one of mine, but all her linen is old and threadbare. Most of it belonged to her mother. Auntie Flora would never buy anything if she could help it.'

Marcia got up without a word and left the room. A few minutes later she came back with an armful of sheets and pillow-cases and gave them to Ella. 'Let her have these,' she said.

'Thank you. Are you sure you can spare them?'

'Of course,' Marcia said expressionlessly.

Only one thing was agreed upon: that Sibyl should arrange for Flora to have a telephone installed, and they would all share the rental.

'It will be up to her whether she uses it or not,' Sibyl said, 'but at least we shall be able to keep in touch with her.'

Everyone promised to visit Flora more often and do whatever was necessary for her comfort. Ella stated that she was going to sound her out about going into a nice residential home by the seaside. It would be ideal for her.

Tom and Stuart discussed this idea on the golf course the following weekend.

'Those places cost an awful lot of money,' was Stuart's opinion.

'She's got plenty, hasn't she?' Tom asked.

'It wouldn't last long if she went into a home.'

'It wouldn't have to. She's seventy-seven, after all.'

The next time Stuart visited Flora with his wife, he took her a present of a bottle of her favourite sherry. Sibyl disapproved, but, as he told her, it was the poor old girl's only comfort. He also told his wife something else. Tom was making a fool of himself with one of the women at the golf club, a flashy blonde who had been eyeing him for some time. Stuart was annoyed by this turn of events. He and Tom used to go for the golf; now Tom was more interested in getting back to the clubhouse. In consequence, his game was suffering badly and this was having an effect on Stuart's own performance by making him irritable with his friend and viciously wild with his swings.

'It's a pity about Marcia,' Stuart observed to his wife. 'Tom never used to look at another woman.'

How typical! Sibyl thought. It's Marcia's fault for being unwell.

'I wonder what excuse men give when there's nothing wrong with their wives,' she remarked tartly.

'You know what I mean,' Stuart said. 'It can't be much fun for him, with Marcia the way she is and those two girls to look after. Kate is becoming quite a handful according to Tom, going out with a different boy every night and coming in at all hours. He's worried about her, but Marcia doesn't seem to care; in fact, Tom reckons she encourages her.'

'I'm sure she doesn't,' Sibyl answered, springing to Marcia's defence. 'She doesn't seem to be able to feel deeply about anything or anyone now. It's very sad.'

'Yes, it is,' Stuart agreed, thinking about Tom and his deteriorating golf.

'Are you going to Lapcombe on Saturday?' Bart asked Una over lunch the next Thursday, in their usual restaurant.

She answered that she was.

'Then come with us,' he suggested. 'We are going to visit Louise's parents. I can drop you off at Mrs Macfarlane Brown's and pick you up afterwards.'

'Then you would have to take me all the way home,' she protested. 'It's silly to add all those miles to your journey.'

'It's not silly, at all, Una. I want you to come back to my place and spend the evening with us.'

'And the children?'

He smiled. 'Yes. The girls are going to cook the supper. They want to impress you.' He waited, looking into her serious brown eyes, while she considered the implications of this invitation.

'Thank you,' she said politely. 'That will be very nice.'

'Why don't you want to come?' he teased her.

'I do,' she protested, but she was not telling the truth. Meeting his daughters would mean setting off on another stage of their association, and it made her feel apprehensive. It was eighteen months since Luke had backed into the library van and in that time Bart had become an attentive, fondly sympathetic friend. She would miss him if she were to lose him, but she would not be devastated. Una could not face the thought of further devastation. The years following such traumas are painful in the extreme, a nightmare that gradually loses its intensity yet leaves one nervous of a recurrence. She was afraid to take a further step towards intimacy with Bart, because one tentative step could lead to a succession, propelling her into a headlong rush. She was desperate for affection and did not want to be offered something she knew she was too weak to refuse, but would probably live to regret. It was ironic, but she had become more of an accepted member of Neil's family since his death than she had ever been before, despite all her efforts. Their need of her had grown in proportion to her involuntary separation from them, as she turned inwards to dwell upon her unhappiness. Gradually, Bart was drawing her out of that long period of introspective sorrow, drawing her away from the only family she had. Instinctively, she was resisting him.

Bart could sense that resistance, but he did not understand its cause. He thought that it was her nature to be cool and aloof. When, occasionally, she put a hand on his arm, a brief touch, it was not so much an affirmation of their friendship, he felt, as a warding off. Having been used to Louise's spontaneous hugs and kisses, Una's mental and physical reservation was tantalising. He kept wanting to ask her what she was thinking, but knew she would resent the question as intrusive. Her husband had seemed an uncomplicated, straightforward type of fellow and, according to Louise, had

142

been kind, with a good sense of humour. How had Neil coped with the subtleties of this woman's character? Had he loved her and understood her, or just loved her? It had taken no great effort to understand his Louise. She had been eager to explain her emotions and make light of frequent disagreements.

'Drink your coffee,' Bart urged Una, 'or we shall be late back. I don't want Frank giving you a ticking off.'

They laughed at the absurdity of the idea. Frank Truebody was more likely to be gently reprimanded by his efficient secretary, than vice-versa.

'He retires next year,' Una said regretfully, putting down her cup and reaching for her handbag. 'I'll be fortunate if my next boss is even half as nice.'

Bart did not answer. He placed her jacket around her shoulders and hurried her out to the car.

When Una answered the door on Saturday, it was to find Luke standing on the step.

'Are you ready?' he asked her.

She looked past him towards the road, but the car was hidden by the garden hedge. 'Come in while I fetch my coat,' she told him.

Luke stood in the hall and had a good look round.

'It's a tall house, isn't it?' he observed, as they walked together down the path. He thought he ought to say something about her home, and that was the only adjective that came to mind, which did not sound too critical. He liked the house and felt sorry for it, or for Una, he was not sure which. It was too tidy and quiet, like its owner. Left in the hall, he took a quick look into each room while she was upstairs, and was overcome by an urge to shout and rush about a bit, just to liven it up. He always felt a similar urge with Una herself. She was so controlled and pensive.

Una waited, glancing towards the car, while Luke un-fastened the gate. Dolcis and Angela were sitting in the back. Bart smiled at her. She was encouraged and walked past Luke to join the solemn young ladies.

143

'You have to go in the front, Dad said,' Luke informed her.

Una walked round the car and got in beside Bart. 'Hello!' she said cheerfully, to the other passengers.

'Hello!' they echoed, without enthusiasm.

Luke got in and sat between his sisters. Una could feel their appraising eyes on the back of her head. Bart drove off, remarking on the beauty of the Summer's day. When the weather had ceased to be a topic of conversation they were left in a constrained silence, until Una summoned the courage to say how much she was looking forward to having supper with them that evening. She turned her head as she spoke, and smiled in turn at the two young women. They smiled back politely.

'What are we having?' Luke asked them.

'Mind your own business,' Angela told him rudely.

'If I'm expected to eat it, it is my business,' Luke replied.

'Nobody's asking you to eat it,' Dolcis remarked. 'You can go to bed if you prefer.'

'Thanks,' he said bitterly. 'I probably shall. Move over, fatty!'

'Little beast!'

It was almost seven years since their mother had died. Dolcis was nineteen and at the London School of Economics. She was a fine looking girl, with a good, full figure, brown hair and large, hazel eyes. Her sister, Angela, was seventeen and still at school. She had Bart's colouring— vivid blue eyes and black hair. She was thinner and taller than Dolcis, with quick movements and an even quicker temper. Luke was the only one who resembled his mother in looks.

'Whatever we are having will be delicious,' Bart said proudly. 'Both my daughters are excellent cooks.'

'Then we take after Mummy. You always said she was the best cook you had ever known,' Angela said.

'So she was,' Bart agreed equably.

'Do you like cooking, Mrs Favory?' she was asked sweetly, by Dolcis.

'Not a lot,' Una admitted. 'I do it, because I have to. My greatest pleasure comes from gardening.'

'We have a man to do that for us,' Angela informed her.

'I don't think Una was offering her services to us in that capacity,' Bart put in rather sharply.

'Or in any other capacity, for that matter,' Una said with good-humour. 'I'm sure you all manage very well.'

Dolcis and Angela exchanged significant looks across their brother. Luke glared at them. Mrs Favory was his friend and he did not see why they had to be so cool towards her.

When the car drew into the lane leading to Flora's house, Bart said they would be back to pick Una up in about two hours. 'Will that be convenient?'

'Perfectly,' she answered.

They watched her walk towards the house, while Bart was backing the car down the lane. He swung into the farmyard entrance to turn.

'I like her sandals,' Dolcis conceded. 'I wonder if her hair is naturally wavy?'

'Why don't you ask her?' Bart suggested, amused.

'I don't know her well enough,' Dolcis said stiffly.

'I do,' Luke said. 'I'll ask her.'

'You'll do no such thing,' Dolcis warned him. 'It would be impertinent, especially from you.'

Flora was at her most cantankerous that afternoon. She had been watching for Una from the landing window and had been surprised to see her arrive in the car belonging to Louise's husband. Imelda had told her a few months ago that Una was becoming very friendly with him, but Una had never mentioned it.

'Has your car broken down?' were her first words on opening the door.

Una realised immediately that she had some explaining to do. She hung her lightweight jacket on the hallstand and followed Flora into the living-room. 'Will you let me wash your hair this afternoon?' she asked, viewing the back of it with consternation. Evidently Flora had been hacking at it with the scissors.

'No,' Flora said, easing herself into her usual chair. 'I have a cold.'

The effects of years of dyeing had gradually worn off, leaving her sparse white hair drily unmanageable. She had dusted powder liberally over her face for Una's visit. The collar of her black dress was whitened and so was her lap, where she had dropped the lamb's-wool puff. She was looking gaunt and faded. Her eyes had lost their intensity and were a watery blue.

'I thought I might come across and go to church with you next Sunday. I can't manage tomorrow, I'm afraid,' Una said, pitying her.

'Don't bother. I've given up going.'

'Altogether? I didn't know that.' Una was concerned.

Flora sniffed disparagingly. 'We all have our little secrets.'

Una took this as a reference to her means of arrival. 'Bart Pascall will be calling for me later,' she explained. 'I'm going to have supper with him and the children. I've become quite friendly with them.' She did not like to say 'with him'.

'Evidently!' Flora remarked with hauteur.

'Why do you disapprove, Auntie Flora?'

'I don't disapprove,' Flora declared, but she was thinking how unfair it was that this woman, who was not a patch on Louise in looks and personality, should have been preferred by Neil and chosen as a substitute for her by Bart Pascall. A man did not see a woman regularly for months on end and then invite her to his home to have supper with his children, without the desire for a closer relationship. Flora wasn't daft! All her life she had looked with respect towards the people at the manor. They held a special position in the life of the locality, dating back to the time when they were the principal landowners and employers. Nothing would have delighted her more than to have become closely associated with them through Neil's marriage to Louise. Who would have thought that it would be Una's fate to be drawn closer to the Pope-

Wessingtons? Una, a quiet nonentity who had not even been able to give Neil a child and so had effectively rubbed out the name of Favory from generations yet to come.

'Ella says I would be better off in a home,' Flora remarked expressionlessly.

'Would you like that?'

She looked slowly round the familiar room and sighed heavily, without answering.

'I'll make some tea, shall I?' Una asked.

'You won't find much to do out there. Jessica and Sibyl were here yesterday, fussing around the place. I wish people wouldn't bother. Ronald keeps on at me to do something about repairing the roof, but it will last me out. Since he started doing my accounts I have had nothing but expense. I'm sure he adds noughts to the bills. Lavinia managed much better.'

'Everything costs more now,' Una explained. She had sympathy with Ronald who, since Lavinia's death, had managed Flora's finances out of the goodness of his heart and received little thanks and much aggravation for his trouble. Lavinia had been paying many of the bills out of her own savings, rather than trying to get Flora to part with her own money, which was a painful business for all concerned.

'Would you like to go for a walk?' Una asked. 'It's a lovely day.'

'No. I was going to suggest a drive,' Flora said, giving her a direct look.

Una was amazed. The only time she had persuaded Flora into the car since Neil's death was when they had gone to visit his grave together. She supposed, quite correctly, that Flora was being contrary.

'I'm sorry I haven't got the car. We'll go out in it next time I come.'

'Whenever that might be. No doubt you will be spending more time with your friends up at the manor.'

'The Pope-Wessingtons are not my friends,' Una explained tolerantly. 'I've never been to the manor.'

'It's not as old as this house,' Flora informed her with satisfaction, 'neither is their name as old as Favory—but it will be!' She stared at Una accusingly.

Una flushed with annoyance. Flora persisted in blaming her for being childless, once even going so far as to remark, pointedly, that Louise had managed to produce three children, despite recurring ill health. Now she was saying, darkly,

'Other people's children are small compensation, but no doubt you will find that out for yourself.'

'In what way?' Una asked crossly.

Flora chose not to answer. 'I think I will have a cup of tea,' she decided.

Chapter Seventeen

Lapcombe Manor was not a pretty house. It was square, with solid walls of grey Portland stone and a slate roof, which was smudged with golden lichen and surmounted by squat chimneys. It had tall, narrow windows, set geometrically around the central doorway. In fact, it looked rather like a house a young child would draw, only with twice as many windows. Its uncompromising outline was softened by the many fine trees, mostly elm, which grew around its elevated position. At the back, the house was not square. It had been added to by Claude Pope-Wessington's father, in brick, so it was fortunate that only those who wandered the acres of densely-hedged farmland could be offended by it. The heavy front door was never used. It would open only with great difficulty and it took ages to persuade it to shut again. It was going to be fixed one day, but in the meantime everybody used the back entrance, which was more convenient anyway, because then nobody had to answer the summons. Occasionally, strangers rang the strident bell at the front, but, unless they were insistent enough to investigate further by wandering round the outside of the house, they just gave up and went away, presuming that there was no one at home.

There was a small park on either side of the drive which curved up to the house from the main road into Lapcombe, and it was there that the annual village fête would be held in a week's time. As they were driving through it, Luke spied Mr Forbes, the gardener and odd-job man, lurking with a wheelbarrow near a mound of rhododendrons. He was slow of speech and movement and not very good at doing anything; that was why there were so many odd jobs about the place —including the front door which only needed a bit of planing on the bottom and a few screws tightening in the massive old hinges. Claude Pope-Wessington knew exactly what needed to be done, but it would never enter his head to have a go at it himself. When things were really desperate and expertise with a screwdriver or a shovel became a necessity, he showed his wife the problem, suggested the solution and left her to get on with it. Jane would tackle most things in an emergency—even the lethargic Mr Forbes, who could move with surprising agility after a ticking off by 'the missus', as he called her.

Bart drove round to the back of the house and parked the car beside a large barn which did duty as a garage and store-room. Claude Pope-Wessington emerged from it, dressed in an open-necked Vyella shirt and old flannels, a black standard poodle at his heels. He was carrying a rake and beamed with pleasure to see the visitors. The dog bounded forward to greet them.

It was a perfect Summer's day, the kind of day that stretches in one's imagination to encompass all the Summers of childhood. All was warmth and sunny brightness, beneath a light breeze which gently wafted the scent of grass and flowers to mingle with the mellow sounds of the countryside. The lush pasture in the water meadows and the fields of ripening wheat were alive with creeping, crawling, flying insects. Shrill grasshoppers leaped before the feet of grazing cows; all things were intent upon their low-level existence, a world within a world.

The young people jumped eagerly from the car, glad to get out of its stuffy confinement.

'We've broken up,' Luke told his grandfather, grinning with delight and patting the poodle. 'What are you going to do with that rake?'

'Not a lot,' Claude confessed. He did pick up gardening tools occasionally, but more as an excuse to be out in the sunshine than from any serious intent.

The young women kissed their grandfather on the cheek and hurried into the cool house to find their grandmother. Bart and Luke stayed to chat to Claude and inspect the garden at a leisurely pace.

Jane Pope-Wessington was in the drawing-room, reading. It was a faded, pretty room, in pinks and greens, facing the park through two long windows. Jane was curled up in a shabby, comfortably dilapidated armchair, which was covered in cretonne to match the curtains. She looked very much a part of the room, prettily faded and dressed in a pastel green cotton dress, patterned with large pink flowers. She shut her book when Dolcis and Angela entered and greeted them fondly, confessing that she had not heard the car.

'It must be a good book,' Angela remarked, kissing her.

'It is rather,' Jane agreed, putting up her face for Dolcis to kiss. She watched the two young women as they plonked themselves upon the sofa, thinking how lovely they were and wishing they would sit down less heavily.

'We gave Mrs Favory a lift,' Dolcis said. 'She is visiting Mrs Macfarlane Brown.'

Angela asked, 'Did you know she's a friend of Dad's. She's coming to supper this evening.'

Jane did know. Luke had told her all about Una Favory. However, all she said was, 'That will be nice, dear.'

Her grand-daughters were not so sure.

'Actually, Gran, Angela and I think Dad would like to marry her.' They waited, their wide, clear eyes fixed upon Jane's face, watching her reaction.

'Would that be such a bad thing?' she enquired mildly.

They looked at one another and then back at her, considering.

'You mustn't be selfish,' she cautioned them. 'You have your lives in front of you. In a few years you will probably both be wanting to leave home to get married yourselves. Your father will have years of loneliness left. I know how lost I should be without your grandfather, even though I love you all dearly and see you often. It's the hours in between that would be so long, waiting for you all to visit.'

'We don't want anybody to replace Mummy!' Angela stated.

'Of course not,' Jane agreed hurriedly. 'Nobody could do that. I'm sure Mrs Favory wouldn't be so presumptuous as to think she could.'

'Do you think she's nice?' Dolcis asked wistfully.

'I think she must be very nice, the way she bothers with Flora Macfarlane Brown.' Jane had endured years of community affairs hindered by the outspoken, insensitive criticism and astute meanness of Flora Macfarlane Brown, who could be relied upon to support any scheme for raising other people's money in a good cause. Nothing had been too much trouble for her, provided Lavinia Favory was capable of doing it. Flora had made the commitments on her various committees in the church hall and Lavinia had been mobilised to carry them out. The trouble had been that Lavinia sometimes became confused over her many tasks and someone else had ended up doing her allotted share, rather than let Flora discover her sister's well-intentioned incompetence. Over the last two or three years, Jane had seen increasingly little of Flora, who had turned her back, first on the village and then on the church. Mr Laston had looked sheepish when Jane enquired about her at church about a month ago, and she suspected he was not altogether sorry to lose Flora from his faithful flock. Fortunately for Jane's peace of mind, Flora had her nieces and Neil's widow to support her in her unsociable old age. She would be all right, unless she fell ill. She had never got on with Dr Cowper: everybody in the village was aware of that fact. On the rare occasions when she had been ill enough to consult him—in her house, for wild horses would not have dragged her to his surgery—she considered that he had scored some kind of victory over her and never gave him any credit for her recovery, which she always professed, preferably in Mrs Cowper's hearing, had happened despite his remedy. Lavinia, constantly ailing, had been made to feel a traitor to be so reliant upon the doctor's skill and had taken her medicine and pills discreetly, in order not to give offence. Jane had often wondered what would have happened if their brother's five children had been sickly. It was through Louise's friendship with Marcia and Sibyl that Jane had been given an insight into the domestic scene of their two bizarre aunts.

Angela jumped up from the sofa and walked across to one of the windows. She was a quick, restless creature, like her mother had been. She put her forehead against the glass for a few minutes, deep in thought, then swung round to state defiantly, 'I know it's selfish, but I don't want to share Dad's love with anybody else, neither does Dolcis.'

She expected her grandmother to reprove her, instead, Jane was amused. 'You talk about love as if it is a commodity, rather than an emotion. It would be very sad, wouldn't it, if, in order to love someone new, we had to deprive our first loves? Thank God it is one of the few things we never need to ration. Come on, let's make some tea and take it into the garden. I expect your grandfather is ready for a cup.'

There was a black metal table and four chairs set beneath the shade of a generously spreading oak tree, beyond the barn. Tea, bread and butter and a large cherry cake were carried out to it. Jane shouted at the top of her voice, 'Tea!' and the three males appeared miraculously from the path leading down to the stream and sauntered across the lawn towards them, the two men deep in conversation. The dog loped ahead of them to be the first to welcome the food. Luke and Angela sprawled on the fine, dry soil and twiggy bits between the worn roots of the tree, leaning their backs against the great trunk. The others took seats. Dolcis began pouring the tea.

'I love it here,' Luke said dreamily, throwing a stick, which the poodle ignored. 'If you don't fetch it, Potter, you won't get any cake,' he told him severely, but the dog did not believe him.

Jane and Claude exchanged smiles of happy satisfaction that their grandson should be so fond of the place, which would one day belong to him. 'Are your hands dirty, Luke?' Jane enquired.

'No, Gran.' He did not bother to inspect them.

'Why don't you bring Mrs Favory to the fête next week?' Jane suggested to Dolcis. 'I don't believe she has ever come.'

'So that you can get to know her better, Gran?' Angela asked slyly, her eyes upon her father.

'I'll ask her,' Luke offered.

So Bart was made aware that his daughters had been discussing Una with their grandmother and that Jane had not been disapproving.

'We'll have to go as soon as we've finished tea,' he said. 'Una will be expecting us.'

The talk turned upon the preparations for the fête. Luke was to be in charge of the coconut shy, Dolcis the cake stall and Angela the bric-à-brac.

Jane said, 'Mrs Cowper has promised to make two cakes for your stall this year, Dolcis. A chocolate sponge and her speciality seedy cake, which no doubt Forbes will buy, he usually does. When you've finished your tea, Angela, we'll go and have a look at the pile of stuff in the barn. I hope it will be enough for your stall.'

'I have some things in the boot of the car,' Angela told her. 'We had a turnout at home. I'll go and put them with the rest.'

Fifteen minutes later, they were ready to depart. Luke opened the car door and gasped as he was assailed by the heat, which had lain inside it like the fetid breath in the tin lungs of a mechanical dragon. He stepped back a pace. 'Phew,' he said, 'you should have left all the windows open, Dad. I'm not sitting in the middle this time. Angela can.'

'Why me? Why not Dolcis?'

Bart ignored them and started the engine. They quickly climbed in, with Dolcis in the middle, resigned as the eldest to being the peacemaker.

'See you next Saturday. Come early,' Jane called after them.

Una sensed a distinct change in the atmosphere in the back of the car as they drove away from Lapcombe. Dolcis and Angela were more relaxed and their conversation was friendlier and spontaneous. When Luke asked her if she would go to the fête with them next Saturday, both girls added their voices to the request. Dolcis even wondered if Una would mind making a contribution to her stall. Una said she would gladly bake a cake and also look out some oddments for Angela; she knew she had a vase she would love to give away.

'Grandma hates the fête,' Luke informed her. 'She can't stand all the litter. It takes me and Mr Forbes ages to clear it, and when we think we have finished, Grandma points out all the bits we have missed.'

'Would you mind if I ask Auntie Flora to come?' Una asked. 'She hasn't been since her sister died, but I think I might be able to persuade her.'

'By all means,' Bart told her.

None of them knew Flora, except by reputation and the occasional casual meeting, while they were waiting for the Pope-Wessingtons to have a few words with her, but even that had become a thing of the past. They were quite keen to meet her again and decide for themselves whether she was as intimidating as she looked.

'She's changed a lot recently,' Una said sadly. 'People will have difficulty in recognising her. For a start, her hair is now pure white.'

There was disappointment on the back seat. Flora Mac-farlane Brown sounded as if she now resembled every other elderly person and was probably quite ordinary. But Flora hadn't changed as much as that!

When he drove her home that night, after supper, Una invited Bart in for coffee. It was the first time that he had been inside her home and, for the first few minutes, while he sat waiting for her in the living-room, he felt like an intruder. Her husband was very much in his thoughts, surrounded as he was by Neil's possessions and reminders of his and Una's life together.

Una came in with the coffee and, as she handed him a cup, she said, 'I enjoyed my evening very much, Bart. Thank you.' She sat in the armchair on the other side of the fireplace.

Bart regarded her steadily, until she blushed beneath his look. 'Did you feel like an intruder in my home, Una?' he wanted to know.

'As a matter of fact, I did,' she confessed.

'I understand,' he said. There was a silence, while he looked around the small, tidy room, with its colour scheme in subtle shades of creams and greens, then he said, 'The girls like you. I'm glad.'

'So am I,' Una smiled. 'I hope we'll be good friends.'

Bart did not express the wish that Una and his daughters should become closer than friends. The time was not right. He was ready to tell Una that he loved her, but he was waiting for some encouragement. It had taken her long enough to invite him in for a coffee. While she kept her distance from him, he ought not to make a sudden movement in case it caused her to ward him off. He desired a mutual coming together.

Una was perturbed. She recognised the sentiment in Bart's vivid blue eyes and kept her own downcast, in case he read her response. More strong than the desire to be loved by him was the fear of loving and losing all over again. Her life was tolerably comfortable now. Why complicate it with precious possessions? There was another reason for her wariness. Una suspected what Flora had hinted at, that she would be a pale substitute for the spirited Louise in Bart's and the children's lives.

Bart did not stay long. When Una opened the front door to let him out, he gently pulled her into his arms and kissed her before hurrying out to his car without another word. She did not object. He had expected her to stiffen against him, but she was soft and pliant and the kiss, meant to be a brief salutation, lingered with promise.

Bart did not recall the long drive back. He was putting his

key in the door before he realised that he had arrived home.

Una went to bed thinking, he should not have done it, it was not fair. When she was loved, her logical mind had little power over her aroused sensuality. A kiss was a beginning. It invited progression. Where would it end? she wondered, with the pessimism of sad experience.

Chapter Eighteen

The fête was opened, at 1.30 p.m. precisely, by a local celebrity, a friend of Jane Pope-Wessington, who appeared on television once a week in a popular panel game involving much intelligent guessing and witty repartee. He was middle-aged and smoothly handsome, with a small moustache and an air of being well manicured. He had an appreciative eye for the ladies, whom he courted with half-smiles and outrageous, softly spoken flattery. He was a bachelor and celibate, but only he knew that. Jane found him amusing company. Claude did not. Denzil Lake was not popular with his own sex. When he had delivered his short, expert speech, saying just the right things to make the industrious feel proud of their efforts and the bystanders feel generous towards the causes of succouring the parish needy and replacing the cracked church bell, Jane accompanied him round the various stalls and side-shows. She induced him to part with some of his money on her grand-daughters' stalls and hurl a wooden ball, ineffectually, at one of Luke's coconuts, before taking him indoors for a drink and an intimate chat.

Bart saw them approaching the house from the drawing-room window and escaped into the adjacent library, where he continued his watch over the heads of the strolling crowd in the direction of the drive. Ten minutes later, he saw Una and Flora Macfarlane Brown walking towards the trestle table where Mr Laston was selling admission tickets. He hurried out to meet them. He had no sooner set foot on the lawn when he was accosted by an enthusiastic woman with a bee-hive hair-do, bearing a gigantic fruit cake wrapped in cellophane, who begged him to guess its weight and write it down on the pad being held out to him by her acolyte, a small boy with a cheeky grin, one front tooth missing and the dirtiest pair of knees Bart had ever seen. He obligingly tested the weight of the cake on the palms of his hands, whistled appreciatively at its heaviness and handed it back with due reverence. He took the pad and scribbled a weight, which was one ounce more than the preceding guess, then he strode off through the crowd to find Una.

Dolcis saw him walk past her stall as she was handing over a cardboard plate of macaroons to the wife of the landlord of the Black Bull. Una Favory must be someone special, if she could entice her father to join the gathering in the park. In previous years, he had either kept to the house or joined her grandfather in the barn, pottering about amongst the junk and discussing the dairy herd of guernseys. Mr Forbes had been one of Dolcis' first customers. He had come for the seedy cake made by Mrs Cowper, the doctor's wife. One thing Forbes had in common with 'the missus' was his detestation of this annual event. He had grudgingly counted out his money for the round, golden cake, muttering about 'danged kids ruining me 'erbacious'.

'Two, please,' Una requested.

Mr Laston tore two blue tickets from a gratifyingly depleted roll and handed them to her in exchange for three shillings.

'They've put it up,' Flora observed with disapproval.

'Mrs Macfarlane Brown! How nice!' Mr Laston exclaimed with affected heartiness, pretending to notice Una's companion for the first time. 'How are you, dear lady? I've been meaning to call.'

'I know where to find you if I want you,' Flora said discouragingly.

'It's a lovely day for it, isn't it?' Mr Laston observed genially, determined to be pleasant. 'We have a good crowd.'

'You certainly have,' Una agreed, surveying the happily milling throng, patterned with colourful Summer cottons.

Lapcombe fête was one of the most popular in that part of the county, one of its main attractions being the skittling, with the coveted prize of a healthy, squealing, pink piglet. There was a queue of men of all ages, waiting to try their hand at it. With a sudden surge of gladness, Una spotted Bart making his way towards them, past the ponies from the local riding stables, who were patiently giving their services to the eagerly waiting children for sixpence a ride.

'I'm glad you came,' Bart said to Una, smiling into her eyes. 'Hello, Mrs Macfarlane Brown.'

Flora acknowledged his greeting with a stiff nod. She walked sedately by Una's side as the three of them made their way across the grass towards a group of young farm labourers, who were engaged in vigorous competition and good-humoured verbal assault. The object of their endeavour was to see who could knock large nails furthest into a block of extremely hard wood. Invariably, the nails bent under the hefty swipes of the hammer and had to be abandoned, only half-buried. The exercise was repeated with undiminished vigour upon another nail, taken from a half-filled bag of dirty brown sacking. Luke called across to them from his coconut shy, 'Come and have a go, Dad.' Bart shrugged and complied, with good-humoured resignation, but without success. Then Una had a go, which Luke cheerfully informed her was 'pretty pathetic', before encouraging her to have another try. He was determined to make more money than last year, when he had only been helping and not in charge.

It was a singular experience for Flora to be standing pass-ively by, a mere critical spectator, as she had been once, long ago, when she was a little girl and Claude's grandfather had been the owner of the manor. His children, home from board-ing schools for the Summer, would have been mingling with their village neighbours like superior young beings from another planet, carefully polite and affable to the natives. They were often accompanied by school friends, who were inclined to be condescending towards the locals and ready to laugh at them without joining in their simple fun. Flora recalled the year when Claude, in his early twenties, had first brought home the girl he was going to marry and how interested Jane had been in everything and everybody. How quickly she had learnt the names of the people who were to be her neighbours and tenants, and how easily she had become an active part of the rural community, always ready to help with organisation and help, yet remaining apart from the mainstream of village life; her liaison officer, the vicar, her observation post, the family pew in church, which she occupied on most Sunday mornings. Now, here were Claude's grandchildren. They were very much a part of the scene, as their mother, Louise, had been, with friends of their own age in the locality. Flora mused upon the years when she had been important to the village and its affairs, especially this fête, where she had presided over the handiwork stall with Ella, while Jessica helped Lavinia on the cake stall. Marcia, Sibyl and Neil had wandered about, spending their pocket money and getting into mischief devised by Louise—aided and abetted by Claude Pope-Wessington from his retreat in the barn, where the children invariably sought a guilty sanctuary to escape from the agile predecessor of Mr Forbes.

Flora picked up a heavy, amber-coloured glass vase from Angela's stall and examined it critically. Too late, Una remembered who had given it to her.

'It has a slight crack,' she explained with feigned regret, trusting that Flora would take her word for it and suppose that its apparent perfection was a figment of her poor vision.

Flora replaced the vase without a word.

Angela snatched it up, holding it against the sunlight. 'I hadn't noticed,' she said, then, catching Una's eye, added, 'Oh, yes, I see it now,' and put the suspect object out of reach and sight on a low shelf behind her.

They strolled from Angela's bric-à-brac, still piled high, to Dolcis' depleted cakes, where the paper cloth, covered in assorted crumbs, told a tale of what had been plenty. Only two plates of honey and oatmeal cakes, made by the wife of one of the farmers, remained.

'They taste better then they look,' Dolcis assured them, pushing the plates forward invitingly.

'They couldn't taste worse,' Flora remarked.

Dolcis giggled.

'There you are,' Jane Pope-Wessington called, walking quickly towards them. 'How lovely to see you, Mrs Favory. How are you, Mrs Macfarlane Brown?' She did not pause for an answer, but it would have been all the same if she had. Flora knew that when people ask you how you are, the last thing they want is to be told. 'I wondered if you would like to come inside for some tea. Denzil has just left. He has to get back to Bristol this evening, poor man.'

'They haven't seen everything yet,' Bart said.

'Are you too bothered?' Jane asked Una. 'It's the same old thing every year. I usually reappear upon the scene when I think people should be making tracks homeward, about five. Some of them would stay on forever, until the legs fell off the ponies, if I didn't say goodbye and thank you for coming in a rather pointed manner and begin directing the packing up. I expect you would appreciate a cup of tea, Mrs Macfarlane Brown.'

Flora admitted that she would, thinking how ironic it was that on this, the first occasion she had been invited to take tea in the manor, she owed the honour to Una. There was no doubt that Una was the centre of attention in the Pope-Wessington circle. Dolcis, Angela and Luke appeared eager for her approval, Bart Pascall was showing an air of proud possessiveness towards her, Jane seemed to be doing her best to get to know her better by a friendly, direct approach and, as they made their way around the house in order to enter unobtrusively by the back entrance, Claude emerged from the barn and walked by Una's side, remarking on the clemency of the weather and the prevalence of greenfly, which was spoiling his roses that year.

'Are you a keen gardener?' Una asked him.

Jane laughed. 'My dear, it will be Forbes or I who spray the roses and Claude will let us know whether or not we have done it well enough.'

'I love the garden,' Claude said, his kindly blue eyes smiling at Una beneath grey, bushy eyebrows. 'I love the land, it's so satisfying.'

'He's essentially an admirer of other people's labour,' Bart explained with a smile.

When Una, Bart and Flora ventured outside again, Dolcis joined them, having given up on the honey and oatmeal cakes and surreptitiously thrown them into the shrubbery behind her stall, for the birds to choke on. Potter got there first.

'I sold that vase,' Angela whispered to Una when they stopped to see how she was getting on. 'Billy Grant bought it for his mother, who's in bed with a new baby. Then he dropped it in the drive. Forbes was hopping mad. He cut his hand on one of the pieces when he was clearing it up. Unfortunately, I had to give Billy his sixpence back. He decided to get his mother a toffee apple instead.'

'Sixpence!' Flora sniffed in disgust, walking off to talk to an acquaintance she had just spotted. Angela watched her, grinning. She really was a weird person. She looked like a bleached old crow, very tall and slightly stooped with age. Her sparse, untidy hair was white, her face powdery white, her long-sleeved dress black and white, with large, blood-red buttons on the bodice, her stockings and huge, ungainly shoes were black. On her left arm she carried a bulging, black leather handbag, with a rapacious gold clasp which defied her rheumaticky fingers to prise open without great effort and snapped shut again with a painful noise like a bone breaking in half. Twice, Angela had seen Mrs Macfarlane Brown tackle that clasp and each time she had produced, not her purse, but an unsavoury looking handkerchief, to wipe perfunctorily across her beak of a nose.

Una followed the direction of Angela's eyes with her own. 'She used to walk like a ship in full, proud sail,' she told the girl. 'People instinctively stepped aside to let her pass.'

'They still do,' Angela said, laughing.

Flora had turned abruptly to walk back to them. The people standing immediately behind her scattered like small craft before an oncoming liner.

'The trick,' Una explained, 'is to walk in a straight line and never look down, but you need to be tall to be successful.'

'She makes me feel titchy,' Angela confessed.

Una knew what she meant.

'Don't ask me to come next year,' Flora told Una, as they were walking slowly homewards through the village. 'No doubt you'll be going, but it's not what it was, I can tell you.'

Una was disappointed. She thought Flora had enjoyed the outing. She had talked her into going, supposing she was doing her a kindness. It was eight years since Flora had last been to the fête, accompanied by Lavinia and her four nieces with their children. Una remembered guiltily that she and Neil had gone on a paddle steamer trip to Swanage instead. 'Has it changed so much?' she asked. Jane Pope-Wessington had said it was the same every year.

'Everything has changed,' Flora asserted disparagingly, 'and costs five times as much,' although she had not spent a penny, in the true meaning of the phrase, the whole afternoon. 'I remember it best when I wore long petticoats, with lace around the hems and black-buttoned boots. My father always won the prize for the weight-lifting. He was huge, my father was, with a long, black, curly beard and very red lips.'

Instantly, Una could picture that giant of a man and his two young daughters in their starched cotton pinafores, already tall for their age, watching him with pride as he bent his great back to the competition. 'What was your mother like?' she asked, intrigued.

'I remember my father best,' Flora said dismissively.

Una was left with a mental picture of remarkable clarity, except for one blurred corner where, presumably, a woman was standing, not loved enough to be recalled. They walked on a few more paces, then Flora said accusingly, as if it had been a crime, 'She was even taller than my father.'

'Oh!' Una exclaimed, surprised. She attempted to revise the picture with this startling piece of information, but it disintegrated with the effort. 'Was Neil's father tall?'

'Middling,' Flora said.

Did that mean average, Una wondered, or average for a Favory.

'That Angela's like her mother,' Flora declared. 'I can see Louise in all of them, but mostly in her. Not in looks so much, as in her ways. The boy looks like Louise. People never die completely when they have children.' She sighed deeply and trudged round the corner into the lane leading to her home.

Una was desolated. All the happiness of the afternoon vanished before the simple fact that Neil was dead—completely! For Bart, Louise lived on in their children. For Flora, Neil was utterly gone and it was Una's fault. What had happened to Flora's faith? It should be sustaining her with hope. Una was the one who should be hopeless. She pitied Flora. No wonder she found life sour and joyless. The bleakness in her watery blue eyes was matched of late in the eyes of both Jessica and Marcia. It was as if life had become an endurance to them, with nothing to alleviate the misery except death, and, apparently, Flora doubted even that exception.

The gaunt and rigid old woman and the slim, pliant younger one walked side by side towards the settling house. The late afternoon sun was shining dispassionately upon the slipping pantiles of the roof, the small-paned, dusty windows, the lush, overgrown garden and the two women, whose emotions were as tangled as the pink briar rose entwined about the sagging porch. An aura of fragrance hung about the thorny bower, which was so sweet, yet sharply painful to the touch—like the memories of the two women, jealously guarded.

Chapter Nineteen

There was a feeling of snow about the day. The bleached bark of a young silver birch in the next garden stood out with luminous intensity against the soft, grey sky, which was faintly tinged with pale rose. The pavements looked brighter and cleaner and the edges of walls and buildings were more sharply defined in the still, cold air.

It was a Sunday morning at the beginning of February. Una and Imelda had just left Una's house and were walking briskly towards the sea, muffled up in anoraks and scarves, scarcely exchanging a word. In five minutes they had reached the empty expanse of the promenade and a decision had to be taken. Did they walk towards the town, or away from it? They looked at one another, raised their eyebrows, shrugged as if it were of no consequence and walked away from it, turning their backs on the quiet harbour and their shrammed faces towards the cliffs, which swept in a series of white-faced humps in a long curve out into the Channel. The sea lay before them, pewter and sullen in the land's embrace, spewing its foaming grey bile onto the pebbly shoreline with a spasmodic rasping and retching.

Una took her hands from her pockets to pull her red scarf more closely around her throat. 'What's wrong, Imelda?' she asked, unable to bear the waiting.

Imelda did not answer immediately. She was reluctant to put it into words, as if saying it could possibly make it more final. Eventually, she uttered, 'Felix has gone back to his wife.'

'He never really left her, did he?' which was unkind, but true.

'I mean he has left the hospital and moved to one near his home in Portsmouth.'

'Oh, I see.' Una had been prepared for something like this, ever since she had received the telephone call from Imelda that morning, asking, almost beseeching her, to go out for a walk.

'I knew it had to end,' Imelda said flatly. 'We both knew it, right from the start. But it doesn't make it any easier to bear when it happens.'

Una wondered if Felix was feeling similarly devastated and what had prompted him to do it, after all this time. It was seven years since Imelda had introduced him to her and Neil. Since then, Una had met him only about half-a-dozen times and could not say that she really knew him. As to the relationship which had existed between him and Imelda, it remained a complete mystery to her. Una never had understood why they had both been so fatalistic about their eventual break-up and it seemed as if she never would. Imelda had only ever mentioned Felix, never actually talked about him. She had led two lives, one with her mother and the other with her lover. Now she was left with her mother.

'Poor Imelda, I'm so sorry,' Una said, commiserating with her from the bottom of her heart.

'Yes, poor me,' Imelda agreed gloomily. 'What are your plans?'

Una blushed. It did not seem the right time to talk about herself.

'Go on, tell me, for heaven's sake! One of us has to have a future. I am the type of woman who can devote herself wholeheartedly to her job. Luckily, I have that kind of job. You aren't and you haven't. It's not natural to become engrossed in a typewriter.'

'Bart and I are going to visit his parents in Newcastle at Easter, with his children as well, of course. We are going away, just the two of us, for a couple of weeks in June.'

Imelda looked at her closely, waiting for the rest. Una looked uncomfortable.

'Good!' Imelda said, settling for that. 'Have you seen Marcia lately?'

Una had not seen her since the week following Tom's abscondence with the blonde woman from the golf club, four months ago.

'She appears to be strangely happy,' Imelda said. 'She says she is relieved that he has gone. The rest of the family think it is because she is not right in the head and have a sneaking sympathy for Tom, but she seems sane enough to me. There's nowt as queer as folk, as they say.' It had been a favourite expression of Felix, when he was baffled by the unexpected behaviour of some of his patients and most of his colleagues. Imelda supposed, bitterly, that he thought his own behaviour was always perfectly rational.

'Will you never see Felix again?' Una asked.

'Never!' Imelda stated with conviction.

'How can you be so sure?'

'Because he has explained it all to me very patiently and logically. His wife needs him, I do not. Apparently, what I need is someone younger than he is, who will be able to offer me marriage. It doesn't seem to matter what I want, only what Felix knows I need. He is so wrong!' She turned her head away, looking bleakly towards the horizon, where sea and sky merged in a two-toned wash of dismal grey.

They walked on in silence for a while. There was a few people about now, isolated figures in ones and twos, nearly all of them exercising dogs. The town end of the beach was fine white sand, but here, past the pier bandstand, it was pebbles down to the tide's farthest ebb. Adjacent to the beach wall were double rows of open wooden huts, their strong, faded green canvas stored away in lockers, ready for the next Summer season. A seagull coasted low over their sloping roofs, clacking raucously, as if in harsh protest, across the desolate beach. Imelda squinted up at it with dislike.

'This was a favourite walk of my father's,' she observed.

'I know, Jessica told me.'

'When I was young, very young, that is, my mother was always losing me.' Imelda recollected having been lost amongst a crowd of holiday-makers near that very spot, next to the entrance to the public gardens and tea-rooms. 'She used to hold on tightly to Marcus, but I never liked being fettered, so I suppose it was my own fault. I stood close against a woman's skirt beneath a counter in Woolworth once, for ages, while she was waiting to be served, before realising it was not my mother. I used to have nightmares about her boarding trains and leaving me behind on the platform. She always smacked me and shook me when she found me, with relief, I suppose. By the time I was seven, I had learnt to look out for myself, which was just as well. Now there are times I wish I could lose her. I'm going to visit Auntie Flora this afternoon, do you want to come?'

'Sorry, I'm meeting Bart. Tell her I'll see her next week, will you? I think we should turn back now, Imelda. We've walked a fair way. Look, it's starting to snow.' A few flakes were descending gently through the still air, speckling the wide promenade and the women's hair. They turned about and began the long walk back.

'Would you like to come back for lunch?' Una asked, when they turned into her road. 'There's some cold chicken and we could start with soup to warm us up.'

'No, thanks. Mother will be expecting something cooked when she gets back from church. I'll take her to Lapcombe this afternoon. Perhaps between us we can persuade Auntie Flora to come and stay for a few days, while the weather is so cold. That house is too big and draughty to heat. It's like an ice-box upstairs. Going to the bathroom is a masochistic indulgence, It's more comfortable to wet oneself, and I suspect that Auntie Flora does, occasionally, if Sibyl's complaints about the state of the laundry she does for her are justified. You will come and visit me in my lonely old age, won't you? Yes, I know you will. It's not in your nature to abandon someone you love.'

'I'm eight years older than you. What makes you think I

shall still be around? Anyway, who says I love you?' Una teased.

Imelda pouted and hung her head, rubbing her eyes with her fists and buckling a little with knock knees. 'Oh, go on, Auntie Una, don't be mean,' she said in a little girl's voice.

The woman laughed and told the large child not to be ridiculous. For two minutes they both forgot Felix and the void he had left in Imelda's life—but only for two minutes.

When they were outside her house, standing next to Imelda's car, Una asked gravely, 'Is there any way I can help?'

'Just keep your door open, so that I can bolt inside occasionally.' Imelda got into the car.

Una watched her drive off, then turned into her whitened garden, where there were small signs of the coming of Spring. There were snowdrops around the black-budded ash tree and crocus shoots by the path. When she looked closer, she saw evidence of Neil's daffodils thrusting through the cold ground beneath the light coating of snow. It was five years since Neil had died. It had been Imelda who had helped her through the darkest patches of that world of numb shadows and painful reality. She had taken time from Felix to be with her. During that period, when Una had been adjusting to the loss of the only person with whom she had come first by rights of total commitment, Imelda had put her first. Una assumed that Imelda and Felix had made a similar commitment to one another, even though he had been married to someone else. Now Una must be prepared to let Bart take second place for a while, until Imelda had grown used to being on her own again. She wished she had accepted the invitation to go to Lapcombe. She could have telephoned Bart and explained. The pleasure of anticipating being with him in another two hours was spoilt by the thought of Imelda's tedious afternoon with Jessica and Flora; neither knowing about Felix, both thoroughly disapproving if they had known. I should have said I would go, Una told herself as she heated up some soup. Already I have failed her. I won't let it happen again. How can Felix bear to make her so unhappy? If he had to leave his wife, why didn't he do it properly? He has treated both women badly. At least I never lost Neil to someone else. Then a fey thought occurred to her. Perhaps I did. Perhaps I lost him to Louise. In which case, it is only right that I should have Bart, on loan, so to speak.

Una and Bart spent the afternoon house-hunting. Although she had not said as much to Imelda, the summer holiday was to be their honeymoon. Una was thirty-nine and Bart almost fifty. They had drifted together from hungry need for companionship, but there had already existed a nascent mutual attraction. They had liked the look of one another when they were virtual strangers and had usually exchanged a second glance at each casual meeting: interested and appraising. We all have people in our lives like that and we never expect, or even desire, to speak to them; yet, when we are close enough, we listen with fascination to their speech with others. Bart recognised Una's soft, West Country voice long before he heard her talking to Louise at Lavinia Favory's funeral. Una had sometimes heard Bart addressing his children outside the church at Lapcombe. She had listened to his deep, attractive tones, with the slight northern accent, while she was waiting by Neil's side for Flora and he and the children were waiting for Louise and the Pope-Wessingtons to finish their conversation with Mr Laston.

A strong love had grown between Una and Bart in the two years since Luke's brush with the library van; a love quite different from their first. It was different, because they had changed. A kiss was no longer the inevitable prelude to a fervent embrace; passion grew slowly now, it had to be coaxed into flame, yet when it did flare, it burned as fiercely as ever and in many ways was more satisfying. The hasty misunderstandings of youth, tearful and tempestuous, with apologies tendered in touch and forgiveness given in the bliss of total surrender, were things of the past, only half-remembered and barely understood. Una and Bart, with one love snuffed out and another patiently rekindled, rarely quarrelled, and when they did, it was regretfully. They made up with carefully chosen words of appeasement and gentle embraces intended to soothe as well as ravish.

'Is anything wrong, Una?' Bart asked, as they were driving to look at the first house on the list.

'Felix has left Imelda. He's gone back to his wife.'

Bart did not answer. He hardly knew Imelda. Una had introduced them, but he had made no effort to be anything but polite and Imelda, nearly twenty years his junior, had respect-fully kept her distance. Claude's whispered advice to Bart, on the afternoon of the fête, after Flora had been disagreeable to Una over tea at the manor, had been, 'Get her away from that family, Bart. The women have a tendency to crankiness. She's too sensitive and will get put upon.' Imelda's mother was a Favory, so Bart naturally included her in the group from which he was to rescue Una.

Una had sensed the coldness between them at that first meeting and was sorry that the two people she loved most should have little liking for one another.

The snow shower was over, leaving a fine dusting like icing sugar across the landscape of rounded hills, known as Bincombe Bumps. In a deep fold on their right, as the car was winding upwards out of the seaside town, was the railway tunnel where Bart's children had always confidently expected to see the round face of Thomas the Tank Engine cheerily erupting, followed by a flattened billow of black smoke. Their mother had read them the stories and encouraged that youthful fantasy.

'Which one do you want to see first?' Bart asked.

Una shuffled the papers from the estate agents, which were on her lap, and said rather irritably, 'Whichever is the closest, I suppose.'

'That's the one on top,' methodical Bart told her, glancing down at them to make sure she had not mixed them up. 'You don't sound very enthusiastic.'

This is Bart, not Felix, Una reminded herself. He doesn't

have to be punished for Imelda's unhappiness. 'I will be, when we see the one we like,' she assured him with a smile. 'Where's Luke this afternoon?'

'In my bad books,' Bart said shortly.

'Why?' She was ready to defend Luke, whatever he had done. Not only him, but Dolcis and Angela as well, when the need arose, which was not often. Bart was harder on his son than on his daughters, because he wrongly supposed that the boy was feeling the lack of a mother's influence more than the girls. Una had been delighted when the three had first appealed to her for arbitration and sympathy, playing on their father's weakness for her. She never sided with them too openly, but she put their case strongly when she was alone with Bart. On the occasions when she agreed with him, she said so and gave her reasons to satisfy them. Dolcis was away in London most of the year, at university, a young woman with an independent life to lead. Angela was old enough to stay out of her father's way and kept a considerable part of her activities a secret from him. Only Luke, at fourteen, was still suffering the full force of parental pressure and he was doing his best to wriggle out from under it. Una adored him and he was well aware of it. He was the only one of Bart's children who showed no sign of jealousy towards her and, in consequence, felt free to share his memories of his mother. Dolcis and Angela, on the other hand, kept Louise secreted within them, even hiding the precious hoard of memories from Bart, now that he had turned traitor. On the occasions when the girls did speak to him of their mother, they did so in an accusing manner, meant to shame him for unfaithfulness. Bart reacted with hurt anger and, at the first opportunity, talked it over with their grandmother. Jane counselled him to be patient. 'They like Una very much,' she explained, 'but they resent her importance in your life. One day she will be important to them as well and then they will be able to love her.'

Luke had already reached that stage.

Chapter Twenty

Una had paid her final visit to Flora at Lapcombe.

The day after Imelda had taken Jessica to see her, Flora, quite literally, got her knickers in a twist and fell heavily between the lavatory and the cast iron bath, bashing her head and breaking a hip. She lay there, thoroughly wedged, the thick, pink cotton drawers about her knees, drifting in and out of consciousness, her body temperature sinking dangerously low in the unheated bathroom.

Forty minutes after Flora had fallen, Ella rang her to tell her some exciting news. She let the telephone ring for a long while, in case Flora was upstairs. She tried again ten minutes later and once more in about another ten minutes, then became exasperated. Flora was suspected by her nieces of ignoring the telephone when she was feeling especially lonely, hoping that whoever was on the other end would be concerned enough to pay her a visit. They reckoned that it had worked at least twice, but they were not going to let it happen again. It was too infuriating to drop tools and rush the twenty-odd miles to Lapcombe, only to find Flora placidly watching television in her favourite chair next to the telephone. 'I must have been upstairs,' had been her feeble excuse. So they now rang twice or thrice to be sure to catch her when she eventually came down again. That afternoon the ruse did not work. Ella read another chapter of her novel and rang once more, but when she still did not get a reply, she dialled Sibyl's number. Sibyl, who had always maintained that Mr Laston should have done more over the last few years to rope in this particular recalcitrant sheep, explained the situation to him over the telephone and asked him very sweetly if he would mind dropping in on her Auntie Flora to see if she was all right, because neither she, nor any of her sisters, would be able to get over there before that evening.

Flora was not aware of Mr Laston entering her bathroom, so was spared the crushing humiliation of having the vicar see her in such an undignified state. Mr Laston did his best to move her, but hindered as he was by his portly size and lack of fitness, he could not manage it, so he hastened downstairs, puffing and panting, to telephone for Dr Cowper.

Flora was rescued by the two people she had made up her mind she could well do without.

Two days later, on the Wednesday afternoon, Ella imparted her news at Flora's hospital bed.

'I have something to tell you that will cheer you up,' she said to the person who hardly seemed like Auntie Flora, she was so weak and thin, as if she had shed considerable weight in forty-eight hours. Her face was white, without the usual addition of powder, and her nightdress, a birthday gift from Una, was a delicate shade of pink. It was absurd, but Ella had expected to find her in a black nightie. 'Tina is engaged. She will be getting married next Spring.'

Flora was not cheered up. She was feeling too poorly and lost. Her hip had been mended with a metal pin. She was not used to being ill and had never been in hospital before. She was frightened.

'Does Una know I'm here?' she asked Jessica, who was on the other side of the bed.

'Yes, but she can only visit in the evenings,' Jessica reminded her.

'When Sibyl comes, ask her to bring some nightdresses.'

'Is there anything else you need, Auntie?' Ella asked.

Flora surveyed her surroundings with bemused distaste and shook her head. The noisy ward was bright and airy, with snowy white counterpanes on the long rows of beds and pretty floral curtains draped beside them, to match the ones at the windows. Most of the bedside lockers held get-well cards and vases of flowers; the tables across the foot of each bed bore bunches of flowers, brown paper bags of fruit and packets of chocolates and sweets—gifts from the visitors, who, at that hour on a Wednesday afternoon, outnumbered the patients by at least two to one, and were beginning to give up on them, after ten minutes of their querulous medical problems, and chat animatedly amongst themselves.

As Flora did not seem very interested in Tina's engagement, but persisted in gazing at the cream-painted wall to her left, as if she could see the writing upon its glossy blankness, Ella began to tell Jessica all about it. 'She'll be the first one of the children to be married,' she finished triumphantly.

'What about your Donald?' Jessica asked. 'He has a steady girl in Worcester, hasn't he?'

'Yes, but they're not engaged. I can't say I care for her very much. When he brought her to stay last year, she was always offering to tidy up. I wouldn't let her, of course, but the very fact she offered meant she thought the place was a mess, so I had to keep doing it myself. I was worn out by the time they went back. Apparently she is very clever, like Donald, so I suppose they suit one another. Imelda hasn't found herself anyone yet?'

'I don't think she is looking,' Jessica replied huffily. 'What does she need a husband for?'

Ella could think of all kinds of reasons, the first one being to get away from her mother. God, Jessica was a misery! Look at her, a dowdy frump at fifty-one, with absolutely nothing to laugh about. She did manage to smile sometimes, but she did it sadly and apologetically, as if she no longer had the right to see the funny side of life. It made one want to shake her. Now she was gazing at Auntie Flora as if she was on her last legs—just the way to buck up the poor old soul.

'That's a terrible bruise on the side of your head, Auntie,' Jessica said in a horrified tone of voice.

Immediately Flora winced, as if Jessica had touched it, and said, with spirit, 'I don't like it here.'

'You'll soon be home, don't worry,' Ella consoled her, but even as she was speaking, she was wondering where she would go to convalesce. Broken hips in the elderly were not quick to mend. She could hardly go straight to Lapcombe and look after herself.

When Una arrived to see Flora, on the evening of the following day, Marcia and Kate were already at her bedside. Una had not seen Marcia for some months. The wild look, which had been so noticeable before, had left her eyes and Una was surprised to see how plump and complacent she had become. She made Flora look positively emaciated.

'Hello, Auntie Una,' Kate said, drawing the first attention to herself.

'Hello, Kate,' Una smiled, bending and kissing Flora on the side of the forehead away from the ugly purple bruise. She straightened up. 'Hello, Marcia.'

'I think there should be only two visitors at a time,' Marcia informed her after saying hello, smoothing her skirt across her knees in a settled manner.

Kate jumped up. 'I'll wait outside,' she offered eagerly.

Marcia gazed at her daughter with shining eyes which held an expression of besotted fascination; most unmotherly.

'No, I was the last here,' Una said. 'If anybody objects, I'll go and we can swop places at half time.' She turned to Flora, 'How are you?' she enquired gently.

'Poorly,' Flora admitted, still subdued by her alien surroundings. No matter how many people came to see her, no matter how often they came, she felt deserted and lost, as if they were visiting from the real world and she was in one set apart, from which she might never emerge, whereas they could come and go at will. She desperately wanted to go home. She did not say that, of course, because in her state it was not possible, so there was no point, yet she wanted to go just the same and was angry with her visitors for not realising the depth of her misery.

Una was worried by Flora's apathy. She had not even flinched away from her kiss. 'You'll soon be better,' she told her confidently, placing a bottle of blackcurrant cordial on the locker, conscious that Flora would have preferred a bottle of sherry.

Flora did not believe her. Getting better seemed to require an act of will and she was feeling too bruised and weak to make the effort.

Una, who had once lain in a hospital bed in a similar frame of mind, knew that it was possible to recover without willing it, but she supposed that it was different for the elderly, who lacked physical vigour.

'Have you heard the news, Auntie Una?' Kate said. 'Tina is engaged.'

'What's his name?' Una asked, for she had heard Tina mention quite a few.

'Barry something-or-other. I forget his surname. Sylvia fancied him first; now she is saying she can't see what Tina sees in him. Sylvia and I are going to be bridesmaids—and Shirley, of course.'

'How is Shirley?' Una asked Marcia.

Marcia's eyes dulled and her air of smug complacency was replaced by a vague shiftiness as she answered, 'Shirley is in excellent health, thank you.'

'Imelda says she's doing very well at school,' Una said, puzzled by her lack of enthusiasm.

'Oh, she's bright enough,' Marcia said coldly, as if that was not in question.

'I know Dolcis Pascall,' Kate informed Una, out of the blue. 'I used to play badminton against her. She's at university now, isn't she? Her father used to pick her up sometimes after a match. He's very dishy.' She smiled archly at Una, who blushed and glanced at Marcia, expecting her to reprimand her precocious daughter. She knew Flora never would. Kate had always been a favourite with her great-aunt, who approved her rude audacity. Marcia merely smiled enigmatically, not taking her eyes off Kate, who seemed to enthral her.

'She has a sister, hasn't she?' Kate went on, 'and a brother? We used to see them at Lapcombe sometimes, when we were at Auntie Flora's. That would be when their mother was alive. It must be awful for them not to have a mother.' She fixed her wide eyes on Una with a sad, innocent expression and Una had the sudden urge to smack her. If half the stories she had heard about Kate were true, a fat lot she cared about her own mother, although to look at Marcia now, one would suppose the girl had never caused her a moment's disquiet. Perhaps Marcia approved of Kate's endless succession of boy-friends, her blatantly flirtatious manner, her thick make-up and flashy clothes. Who could tell what Marcia thought about anything now? She was like a well-fed spider with a delicious secret, watching complacently while this female offspring spun webs to trap the prey they would devour together.

'Bart Pascall is a gentleman,' Flora said, 'which is more than can be said of Dr Cowper. He was here this afternoon.'

'It was kind of him to come,' Una said.

Flora sniffed. 'I dare say he enjoyed the sight of me lying here helpless.'

'All men like to see women helpless,' Marcia observed, with a touch of excitement. 'We mustn't give them the satisfaction, Auntie.'

'I hardly have much choice,' Flora snapped. 'I'm at everybody's mercy here.'

'Then you must get well,' Una urged her. 'You'll be your old self again by the Summer, you'll see.'

Flora refrained from answering. She had not felt certain about anything since Lavinia and Neil had gone, only that one day she would be gone herself and would know as much, or as little, about the hereafter as Mr Laston.

Over the next month, Una saw most of the members of Neil's family around Flora's hospital bed, which she visited twice weekly. Flora was up and about during the day, walking with the aid of a metal frame. Una listened to them discussing their affairs with each other and had an illusion of involvement. It was eighteen years since she had become a Favory. It was not to be wondered at that she should feel a degree of affectionate intimacy for them. Tina brought her fiancé, Barry, to meet Flora and Una felt as if the future they were all planning would in some way include her. In fact, she was drawn closer to them over that period than at any time since her marriage. She began to have a real sense of belonging in their circle and the thought of cutting those ties by marrying Bart filled her with regret. Imelda was coming to her home more frequently since Felix had disappeared from her life. In order to account for the extra nights she slept at home, Imelda had explained to Jessica that she had given up the fictitious room at the nurses' home; but that still left the occasional weekend and evening to be filled and she preferred to be with Una than at home beneath the pall of Jessica's constant complaining gloom. In consequence, Una was seeing less of Bart, but as they were meeting nearly every lunch-time, she did not think he minded.

'Have you told the Favorys about us?' he asked her, when Flora had been in hospital for nearly three weeks.

'Imelda knows,' Una said.

'That we are to be married at the end of May?'

Una blushed and admitted that Imelda did not know that.

'Isn't it about time you told them all? You'll be putting your house up for sale soon.'

'I'll tell Auntie Flora on Thursday evening,' she decided, but Bart could tell she was not enthusiastic about it.

'I can't understand your reluctance. I told Jane and Claude more than a month ago, soon after I told the children.'

'It won't make any difference to your actual relationship with them,' Una explained. 'When I marry, I not only get grafted on to a different family, I become severed from Neil's.'

'Not quite so dramatic, surely, darling? You'll go on seeing them as often as you wish. Which reminds me, my parents are looking forward to seeing you in Newcastle at Easter. You are still coming, aren't you?'

'Yes, of course,' she said, smiling to hide her trepidation. Yet another group of people who would be tacitly asked to accept her as one of themselves, strangers she must get to know well enough to correspond with and from whom she might, hopefully, poach a little of Bart's past. At least they won't be expecting more from me than I am able to give, she thought. They already have three grandchildren and should not be yearning for another.

'I'll come to the hospital with you on Thursday,' Bart said decisively. It was about time he showed himself at Una's side, her champion as well as her slave. He smiled.

'What are you smiling at?' she wanted to know, on the defensive.

They were tucked away in the corner of the restaurant at a tiny table for two. He picked up her hand, which was resting on the tablecloth, and quickly kissed her fingers, smiling into her eyes with adoration. The swift, surprising action made her heart falter in delight.

'It's strange, falling a slave to love at my age,' he confessed. 'Strange, yet wonderful. Sometimes, when I'm at a meeting surrounded by my staid, middle-aged, boringly married colleagues, I have the urge to yell, "Una loves me!" at the top of my voice and watch their faces for disbelief and shock. I quite frighten Luke by singing in the bath and being amiable at breakfast.'

'It won't last,' she warned him, smiling. 'By this time next year you will be as boringly married as all your colleagues and you'll be grumpy at breakfast again. I must tell Luke to make the most of it.'

Sibyl was waiting with the group of coughing, sniffing people, shuffling their feet impatiently in the corridor outside the ward, when Una arrived with Bart on Thursday evening. The sight of them together on such a visit had the effect that

Bart had intended. Sibyl would not be surprised to hear of their intentions.

'I wonder how much longer Auntie Flora will be here?' Una said, after they had said hello.

'She's walking quite well now,' Sibyl informed them. 'I had a word with Sister just now and she thought perhaps another week. She won't be able to go home, of course. We'll have to make other arrangements for her.'

Immediately, Una said, 'Let me know if I can help in any way. She could come to me at weekends.'

Bart was dismayed.

'We shall see,' Sibyl said briskly. 'Frankly, I think any arrangements we make for her will have to be long-term.' She glanced from Una to Bart, as much as to say that they probably had their own long-term arrangements. 'Thank goodness they are letting us in at last. I won't be staying long this evening. I've just brought Auntie Flora a clean nightie.'

As they were entering the ward along with all the other visitors, a young man in a duffle coat blew his nose and coughed in a manner that suggested bronchitis. Sibyl shot him a disapproving look.

'I hope he doesn't give his germs to Auntie Flora,' she said to Una. 'Another week of traipsing backwards and forwards to this place is about all I can stand. It's a terrible nuisance.'

Mercifully, the young man was visiting somebody at the far end of the ward, and was free to cough without feeling inhibited. The patient, who was his wife, expressed concern at his poorly condition and watched him with loving anxiety every time he had an attack, suggesting various remedies in the medicine cabinet at home.

Flora was bucked up to see a different face beside her bed. Bart enquired about her progress and told her how well she was looking. It was true. She had grown accustomed to the hospital routine and was familiar with the staff and some of the patients, not to mention their visitors. The world outside had become a little remote and the fear of being in the hospital had gradually been replaced by a dread of leaving it. Arrangements were being made for her welfare and she did not like the sound of them.

'Una and I have something to tell you, Mrs Macfarlane Brown,' Bart said, as soon as Sibyl had gone rushing off. 'We are getting married at the end of May. It will be a very quiet affair. Una doesn't want a fuss. We've found a house we like only two miles from Lapcombe. My children will be nearer their grandparents and Una will be nearer to you. I hope you approve.'

Flora said she did. She expressed the opinion that they were doing the sensible thing. People should not have to live alone if they could possibly avoid it. She had been fortunate to have her sister's company in the years after her husband's death. She did not say so, but she was convinced that Una's and Bart's marriage would be a purely practical exercise, and she would have scoffed at the very mention of the word 'love' between two such sensible, mature people.

'I hope you'll come and visit us as soon as we've settled in our new home,' Bart said when they were taking their leave of her. 'We'll come and fetch you, of course.'

Flora said thank you, that would be nice. She watched them walk from the ward, side by side, and then turned her head towards the glossy cream wall. The writing was definitely upon it, in huge letters, plain enough for her weak eyes to see, dimmed as they were by the difficult tears of old age, shed in solitude.

Chapter Twenty-one

Una, Bart, Luke and Angela travelled to Newcastle upon Tyne two days before Flora was released from hospital, which was a week before Easter. Dolcis was already there. She had taken the train from London at the end of the university term. Una had never been so far north before: the car journey seemed endless. There was very little motorway, only about forty miles, and they had to take the ring road around Leicester. She was appalled to learn, as they were approaching signs for Doncaster, that they had about another one hundred and twenty miles still to go. She shared the driving with Bart, which helped, but Luke and Angela became bored and headachy in the back and were already dreading the long return journey in ten days' time. It was a fine, bright day, with a strong, gusting wind which slapped the side of the car on exposed stretches of road and kept the clouds in swift movement across the heavens. Una expected the countryside to disappear in a morass of pit heaps the further north they went, but no, it extended on either side of the A1 in ever widening green vistas, with only here and there the black, conical shapes that betrayed the presence of coal.

'Northumberland,' Bart informed her, as they were speeding towards it through County Durham, 'is the least populated county in England.'

When they eventually crossed the historic Tyne Bridge, joining Gateshead on the south bank to Newcastle on the north, they had been travelling almost nine hours. Bart's parents lived on the outskirts of the city, which was to impress Una with its fine buildings and air of proud, insular tradition, tempered with the warm friendliness of its inhabitants, many of whom seemed to her to converse unintelligibly with each other, but patiently and coherently with strangers to their native tongue.

As they pulled up before the bungalow, Una became apprehensive. What if Bart's parents did not approve of his marrying again? However, her spirits were lifted almost immediately by the joyous reaction of Luke and Angela, who jumped from the car with glad cries the moment it stopped and rushed along the short drive to be met on the doorstep by Dolcis. Una hung back by Bart's side, clutching her handbag in tense fingers. As Luke and Angela disappeared through the doorway, Dolcis hurried towards them, smiling happily and, after kissing her father, turned to put an arm through Una's. 'Come and meet Grandpa and Grandma,' she said. 'Don't be shy. They are very sweet.'

'Una's not shy,' Bart laughed, following them.

Una was grateful to Dolcis for supposing that she might be, in the circumstances.

Mr and Mrs Pascall were talking to their grandchildren in the living-room, hearing all about the horrible journey and the smashing lunch they had eaten at Towcester, but that had been a long time ago and Luke was admitting to his grandmother that he was famished again.

'So this is Una,' Mary Pascall said, stepping forward to shake her hand the moment she entered the room. 'How nice to see you, my dear.'

Bart shook his father's hand and embraced his mother, who was similar to Una in size and had once been similar in colouring, although now her hair was grey. 'I expect you could all do with a cup of tea,' she said. 'We'll eat as soon as you have had a chance to unpack. Dolcis, show them where they are sleeping, while I put the kettle on. I'm afraid that you are in with the two girls, Una. I hope you don't mind. I know they are awful chatterboxes. They used to giggle half the night, but I expect they are too old for that kind of behaviour now.'

After five minutes' conversation with his parents, Bart went out with Luke to unload the car, and Una followed Dolcis and Angela to the room that had been allotted to them.

'Angela and I will sleep in the double bed,' Dolcis said.

Una placed her handbag on the single one.

'I hope I've put enough blankets on your bed, Una. If not, there's plenty more in the linen cupboard across the hall.'

'I'm glad that I'm no longer Mrs Favory,' Una smiled.

Dolcis smiled back. 'A bit formal, I thought, if we have to share a bedroom.'

'May I be less formal as well?' Angela enquired brazenly. She had always carefully refrained from calling Una anything. 'If you are going to marry Dad, I'll have to call you something and Mrs Pascall would be ridiculous, wouldn't it? You won't expect us to call you Mother, will you?'

'Certainly not,' Una agreed, shocked.

'Actually,' Angela said, crossing to the window and looking out while she spoke, 'you are not a bit like our mother and I'm glad. I wouldn't like you at all if you were. I hope you understand.' She turned back to Una with a defiant look on her face.

'I understand perfectly,' Una said, quietly. 'Let's be loyal friends, shall we?'

Dolcis, who had been most uncomfortable during this exchange, said with relief, 'Yes, let's,' and darted a look at her sister, which informed her that enough had been said on the subject.

They began unpacking their clothes in a constrained silence.

While they were eating the meal of quiche and salad and the family were conversing nineteen to the dozen, Una had a good opportunity to observe Mr and Mrs Pascall more closely.

Lloyd Pascall was a retired civil servant. He was tall and thin, with a balding head of white hair, mild blue eyes and a quiet, courteous manner. He was a good listener and was deriving great pleasure from the chatter of his grandchildren, particularly young Luke, who kept him entertained through-out dinner. Lloyd 'belonged Newcastle' and his speech betrayed this to Una's southern ears, just as she picked up the familiar Devon accent latent in his wife's voice.

'How long have you been living here?' Una asked her, drawn towards a fellow Devonian.

'Since my marriage,' she smiled. 'I only miss Devon when they have Spring and we are still waiting for it. My sister in Exeter has daffodils in her garden almost a month before ours flower. It's very frustrating. I expect yours are almost finished, aren't they?'

Una nodded. Yes, Neil's daffodils were fading. Suddenly, she felt homesick.

'You are from Devon as well, Dolcis tells me.'

'Plymouth.'

'I used to know Plymouth well, but they say I wouldn't recognise it now, so much of it was destroyed in the war.'

Bart said quickly, 'Una's home was bombed. She lost her family.'

'Oh, my dear, how terrible. I'm so sorry,' Mary Pascall said. 'We won't talk about it. I don't want your first evening here to be overshadowed by sad memories. Tomorrow, we'll take you to Durham to see the cathedral and castle. You'll love it. On Saturday we'll go to Hadrian's Wall. We drag our visitors about all over the region, determined to impress them. You southerners have such a peculiar idea of the north,' and she laughed.

By the time Una and the girls went to bed, all Una's misgivings about meeting their grandparents had vanished, and by the time the ten-day visit was over, it was a fact that she felt even closer to Bart.

During the tedious journey back to the south coast, while Bart was driving and she was taking a turn in the back with Angela and Luke, to let Dolcis have a spell next to her father, Una had time to dwell upon the holiday and put her many impressions into perspective. Bart's younger brother, Richard, had brought his wife and two sons to meet them on

Easter Sunday. One boy was Luke's age and the other was two years older. They had enjoyed an extremely pleasant family reunion and at no time did Una feel she was being assessed and found wanting, even though both Richard and his wife had laughingly informed her on being introduced that they had come 'to give her the once-over and see if they approved'. When they left, they had urged Una and Bart to visit them at their home in Alnwick, and in their turn had promised to visit Dorset.

In the course of the ten days they had spent with Bart's parents, his wife had been mentioned quite naturally and fondly during many reminiscences of former holidays and excursions. Louise had greatly admired Bamburgh Castle, insisting on visiting it every time they were in the north; she had lingered on Holy Island until they had only just escaped the tide on the causeway on their return to the mainland; one Autumn she had brought up pounds of sloes, so that Lloyd could make sloe gin—this told regretfully, as they sampled the last bottle of the delicious, piquant pink liquor, sweet and fruity. 'Can't find sloes round here,' Lloyd had sighed, licking his lips. 'I'll pick some for you next time, Grandpa,' Luke had promised.

Una relaxed and closed her eyes, thankful that any awkwardness that had existed between her and the girls at the mention of their mother had disappeared. Perhaps Angela would no longer see her as a threat, someone whose presence damaged her mother's memory. Una contrasted being presented to the Pascalls as a prospective daughter-in-law, almost forty years old, to being presented to the Favorys as Neil's young wife. At twenty-one she had been reliant, emotional, eager to please and idealistic, wanting to give all and expecting everything in return, to make up for all that she had so tragically lost. Now she was independent, tempered by further tragedy into resilience; cautious and with few illusions, willing to give only what was required of her. Love had once been a tremulous delight, unbounded; it was now a deep contentment, with limitations.

'Has Una gone to sleep?' Bart asked Dolcis in an amused tone.

Una opened her eyes. 'I haven't,' she declared, 'but Luke has. Let me know when you want a rest from driving.'

Una telephoned Imelda as soon as she got back. She was not in. Her mother answered.

'How is Auntie Flora, Jessica?'

There was a moment's hesitation, then Jessica replied that she was doing very nicely.

'Where is she? With you?' This seemed unlikely; nevertheless, Sibyl might have prevailed upon Jessica's better nature.

'No, as a matter of fact, she's in a home to convalesce. It's called The Lilacs. I expect you know it, it's just off the promenade.'

'How long is she likely to be there?'

There was another pause, slightly longer; then Jessica said, bridling a little, 'We thought it best if she remained there. She can't look after herself, Una. As you know, she has always relied upon other people to clean the house and do the garden.'

'Is she happy about it?' Una asked, dismayed.

'She seems to like it well enough. She'll soon get used to it. It's very comfortable and, I must say, the staff are really dedicated to the old people's welfare. It has close links with the church and I'm hoping that she will be brought back to God.'

'When can I go to see her?' Una asked anxiously.

'Whenever you like. It's a home, dear, not a prison,' Jessica rebuked her.

'And the house at Lapcombe?'

'Going up for sale, as soon as we have cleared it.'

When Una put down the receiver, she was utterly depressed. She had returned from Newcastle ready to put her own house up for sale and begin the sad task of clearing away her years with Neil. When Sibyl had mentioned making arrangements for Flora, Una had assumed she meant placing her with one of her nieces, not in an old people's home. How stupid she had been to imagine that she had been closer to them all since Flora's accident. Their talk and plans had been only for her ears, not for her participation. She was merely an in-law —hardly that now—and when it came to serious family matters they had discussed them behind her back, as always. The realisation that she was still of small consequence would make it easier to move away from them, yet it also made parting with all the old associations more poignant. She had been standing in the hall, gazing down with unseeing eyes at the telephone. She lifted her head and slowly looked around the narrow space, seeing the paper Neil had put on the walls, the water-colour painting they had chosen together at a dingy shop in Salisbury, the stair carpet they had taken so long to save for, when they first moved in. Una drifted sadly round the house, from room to room, surveying the well-loved objects. So many of the things had belonged to Neil and were of sentimental value, things which she could not justifiably include in the transfer to another man's hearth. To get rid of everything that had been Neil's was unthinkable, it would be tantamount to blotting out the years they had spent together. She must choose discreetly. She picked up a heavy ashtray made from a chunk of polished stone. It dated from Neil's pipe-smoking days, when he had decided to switch from cigarettes, because Una was trying to give them up and he thought she would not be tempted by watching him puffing away at a pipe. There he was, in her mind's eye, knocking his pipe upside down on the ashtray and admitting, ruefully, that somehow he could not get the hang of it. They had both gone back to cigarettes within two months. Now she did not smoke, because Bart disapproved. When they had started going out together, he had remarked that he was not surprised that someone so fastidious did not smoke and she had not liked to disillusion him. She imagined that he would have reeled back with distaste from their first kiss, if he had smelt tobacco on her breath—as pugent to the non-smoker as garlic to the garlic hater. Gently, she replaced the ashtray on the bookcase with a deep sigh. Perhaps Ronald would like it.

Una and Imelda went together the next afternoon to visit Flora. The Lilacs had once been a large private house and had been converted and extended into a home for the elderly at the end of the war. It was on a hill beyond the sea front and had fine views out across the bay. There was a small garden at the front, containing massive clumps of ornamental grasses, and an extensive garden at the back, mostly lawns, bounded by well-kept flower beds.

They were met in the hall by a jolly looking woman with a double chin and no waist, who was dressed in the staff uniform of yellow cotton dress with white collar and cuffs.

'More visitors for Mrs Macfarlane Brown,' she declared. 'My goodness, she is fortunate! I'll take you along to her, if you'll just follow me along this corridor.' It was often the way, she thought: all the family visited to start with, but it wouldn't last long. Soon the number would dwindle to those with consciences and, in her experience, most people had precious few relatives with those, some none at all. 'She's over there,' she said, indicating a corner of the rectangular day room, which was actually two rooms knocked into one.

There were elderly people sitting in small groups round the walls, in the manner of chaperones at a ball, whose charges had escaped them to live it up elsewhere. Curious old eyes followed the progress of the newcomers across the room; the conversation and knitting ceased until their quarry had been located, and then resumed in a fitful manner when Una and Imelda sat down in chairs facing Flora across a plastic-topped table, on which were ashtrays and empty cups and saucers. On the floor next to her feet was Flora's huge handbag.

Flora was looking well-cared for and mutinous. Her powder-whitened face and deep red lipstick shrieked defiance, but her hair lay acquiescently smooth from a staff-administered brushing and she smelled, unfamiliarly, of rose-scented bath salts from a staff-administered bath.

After they had both said hello and made enquiries about her health, which Flora treated as a mere formality and did not bother to answer, Imelda began to speak to her in the determinedly hearty tone of her profession, not requiring an answer, until the patient should feel inclined to respond. Una, on the other hand, did not know what to say. She was grieved to see the proud old person sitting bolt upright as if she was undaunted by her situation, when, in fact, she must be overwhelmed by its strangeness. Flora was an eccentric individual. Here she would become increasingly engulfed by the multifarious eccentricity of old age and be in danger of losing her identity. The handbag was a reassurance. In it was stuffed the proof of a time when she had been Mrs Macfarlane Brown of Lapcombe, a person.

'At least you won't be lonely here,' Imelda observed, glancing round at the inquisitive faces and exchanging smiles with some.

'More's the pity!' Flora answered, darting a venomous look to her right, where an ancient man, curled up like a tortoise, was watching her with a grin of bleary intensity and nodding his bald head from time to time in agreement with his thoughts.

'He's taken a fancy to you, haven't you, Henry?' a tiny, wizened woman said in a squeaky voice. 'He's glad to see a new face. We all are. It makes such a nice change.' She addressed herself to Flora. 'Why don't you take them up to see your room, my dear? You'll like that, won't you?' she asked the visitors, as if they were little children. 'It's a lovely room. Mrs Harris had it before, poor soul!'

Una and Imelda agreed that they would very much like to see Flora's room.

Flora struggled painfully to her feet with the aid of a stick, which had been propped against the side of her chair. 'We won't be able to stay up there,' she informed them bitterly. 'I can't have people in it. There's nothing but rules and regulations in this place.'

Once more the cynosure of all eyes, the three of them walked slowly across the room, with Flora in the middle, leaning heavily upon her stick, the bulging handbag on her arm bumping against her undamaged hip at every step. They crossed the corridor to a lift.

'This is very convenient,' Una said, for the sake of conversation, as they were ascending in it.

Flora gazed down at her, leaning over her stick like a malevolent vulture across a twig, her eyes cold and unblinking.

Her room was not large, but it was light and lofty, with a wide window that looked out over the back garden. Whereas, downstairs, walls had been knocked out to give more space, upstairs partitions had been built to divide the rooms in half. Apart from a single bed, with a prettily patterned eiderdown upon it, there was a hand-basin set into a white plastic top with a mirror, which served as a dressing-table, a built-in clothes cupboard and a large chest of drawers. The surfaces and walls were bare, except for Flora's toilet articles next to the basin.

'You must tell us what pictures and ornaments you want from your house,' Una said. 'Make a list and I'll bring them next time.'

'Don't bother about pictures. I'm not allowed to knock nails into the walls. Just bring me the photographs off the piano. I forgot them when I went back with Sibyl on Friday.'

'Shall I take you back again to pick up a few things?' Una asked.

'No,' Flora said rudely. 'I couldn't bear it a second time.'

'You'll soon have this room looking more like home,' Imelda tried to console her.

The same woman who had shown them to the day room came bustling along the landing and called brightly through the open doorway, 'It's very nice, isn't it? I'm sure she will soon settle down here. They always do, eventually. Are you coming down for tea?' She stood pointedly to one side, waiting for them to leave the room. They complied, feeling like naughty school children who had been caught doing something forbidden in the dormitory.

Una and Imelda returned with Flora to the day room. They did not realise it, but there were two small rooms set aside on the ground floor for the residents to entertain their visitors in privacy. Flora had chosen, deliberately, to keep them in the communal room, in order that they would be made aware of the full horror of community living.

'I suppose I shall end up somewhere like that,' Imelda said cheerfully, when they were in the car on the way back to Una's home.

'What a depressing thought!' Una protested.

'I would be well looked after.' Imelda did not have the same distaste for institutions as Una; after all, she worked in one, no longer as a nurse, but as a nursing sister.

'You wouldn't be allowed to be special.'

'Certainly not, if that meant inconvenience to the staff,' Imelda agreed.

'Don't you think that's sad?'

'I've seen sadder things,' replied the eminently practical Imelda.

Chapter Twenty-two

'I'll have them,' Luke said.

'But they are far too big for you,' Dolcis laughed.

'I'll grow into them.'

'In a month of Sundays,' his sister scoffed.

Regretfully, Luke stepped out of the size eleven welling-ton boots and consigned them to the rubbish pile beside the back door. 'Dad might like them,' he suggested tentatively.

'I don't think so,' Dolcis laughed. 'Anyway, he takes a size nine.'

'He could wear thick socks.'

'Oh, forget them, Luke. What's so special about a pair of old wellies?'

Luke thought they might be special to Una; after all, they had belonged to her husband. He felt vaguely sorry for her, having to discard so much, just because she was going to marry his father. As far as he could tell, his father intended to move all his stuff, lock, stock and barrel, into the new house. Everything that had belonged to his wife, he had handed over to Dolcis and Angela. Luke was looking forward to moving into the other house. His father and Una had taken him and his sisters to see it, as soon as they had decided upon it. Although it had four bedrooms, the same as their present home, it was not so big, yet far more interesting; for a start, it was in the country, even though less than a mile from the town, and it was nearer his grandparents' home at Lapcombe. His father had promised that they could have a dog when they were settled in. Luke knew the offer had been made as an inducement to make the move seem more attractive. His father was worried that he was going to kick up a fuss, like Angela and Dolcis. They had pretended to hate the house at first sight. They liked their old modern one, they said, and did not want to leave it. Dolcis had been sad at the thought, but Angela had been truculent and angry. She had sulked for days and declared that having a dog would not make up for leaving all her friends, as if they were moving to another planet. Luke had been disgusted. It was not the house the girls were objecting to, so much as the position Una would have in it as his father's wife, a position they felt she was usurping from their mother. They were jealous, especially Angela. Luke was eager to have Una as his father's keeper. Bart was a different person under her gentle influence. Sometimes, when Una was at home, being nice to everybody, he forgot to look critically at Luke for the duration of a whole meal. Once, she had actually complimented Luke on his manners and his father had stared at him in astonishment, as if he was seeing him as a normal human being for the first time in his life.

Una came into the kitchen with something in her hands. 'Would you like these, Luke?'

'What is it?' he asked.

'A pair of binoculars.'

'Smashing!' he cried, taking the case from her and eagerly unfastening it. 'Now I can take up bird-watching.'

While Luke was examining the binoculars, the door bell rang. Angela, who was halfway down the stairs, went to answer it. The next minute she appeared in the kitchen, followed by Sylvia and her younger brother, Peter.

'Mum thought you might like some help,' Sylvia said to Una, rather put out to discover the Pascalls already there. 'Imelda said you were starting to pack up.'

'It's going to be a slow process,' Una told her. 'I have six weeks to do it, so there is no great hurry. I was just going to make some coffee. Would you like some?'

Luke caught Peter eyeing the binoculars and put them back

in the case. Una wondered what she could give Peter. She would find him something else that had belonged to Neil. With his light brown curly hair and wide blue eyes, Peter bore a strong resemblance to his uncle and, because of that and his good nature, Una had always been especially fond of him.

It had been at Imelda's suggestion that Una had asked Bart's children to help sort out her possessions. 'It won't be such a sad business for you, with them around,' she had said. Una acknowledged that it had been a shrewd move: already she could feel a lessening of the girls' natural resentment. They liked her, they were even showing signs of growing used to her, but they were not sure they wanted her to live with them. Now, they could have their father to themselves for days at a time. All too soon they would have to compete for his attention. Dolcis would be away most of the time, so would notice it least. She was returning to London at the weekend, that was why Una had thought they should make a start on the house that evening. She had gone to their home after work and had tea with them, prepared by Dolcis, while Luke and Angela did their homework, then she had brought them back for a couple of hours. Bart would be collecting them about 9 o'clock.

While they were having their coffee and biscuits, Una became aware of a remarkable thing. By constantly drawing her into their conversation and referring to her by name, the two sets of young people were vying to claim the closest connection with her.

'Auntie Una has had that for ages,' Sylvia said, when Dolcis admired a delicate china teapot on the dresser.

'You won't get rid of that, will you, Una?' Angela instantly appealed to her.

Una promised that she would keep it.

'This is delicious shortbread, Una,' Dolcis said. 'You'll have to show me how you make it.'

Una recalled that Louise has been a superb cook and that her daughters took after her. She was amused.

Peter took a second piece, remarking, 'Auntie Una is famous for her shortbread.'

Goodness, Una thought, even more amused, I hadn't realised I was famous for anything.

'I've been lucky,' Sylvia observed a little later, when the conversation turned upon clothes, 'Auntie Una and I are about the same size and, occasionally, I've come in for some of her cast-offs.'

Angela glanced critically at Sylvia and then at Una, comparing them. Sylvia was taller by about two inches. She decided there was no way that Sylvia was going to get the sweater Una was wearing. It would fit her better.

'I believe you know my cousin, Kate Hastings?' Sylvia said to Dolcis.

'Yes, we used to play in badminton tournaments together. She is very pretty.'

'Yes, isn't she,' Sylvia agreed unenthusiastically.

'Is she the one who is getting married?' Dolcis asked.

'No, that's my twin sister, Tina. Kate doesn't want to settle down yet, if ever. She is only just nineteen and, with her looks, she can afford to be choosy.' At twenty-two, Sylvia was beginning to feel that her own time for being choosy was fast running out. Her sister had snaffled the young man she had been mentally nurturing as a prospective mate; now she would have to start looking all over again. It was somewhat demoralising to be one half of an identical twin and have the other half preferred by the man you had marked out for yourself.

Angela, who had been covertly glancing at Peter from time to time, took another biscuit and remarked that there was more to life than chasing boys.

'Being chased by them is preferable, I suppose,' Dolcis said, smiling at her.

Angela blushed. Peter grinned at her discomfiture. Luke allowed himself a slight smile and almost had it turned to stone upon his face by his sister's flashing eyes.

Una began collecting the coffee cups. 'Perhaps you would

help Angela clear out the cupboard in the small bedroom,' she suggested to Sylvia. 'If you pile everything on the bed, I can sort it out later.'

'I'll wash those,' Dolcis offered, moving over to the sink. 'Would you mind helping Luke to move that pile of junk out there into the garden shed?' she asked Peter.

Peter did not mind at all. His mother had sent him to be useful.

Bart arrived just before nine. 'How's it going?' he asked, when Una let him in.

'Slow but sure,' she answered.

He was about to kiss her, when a young woman, whom he did not recognise, appeared at the top of the stairs.

'Hello,' he said.

Sylvia answered, 'Hello,' thinking, as she slowly descended into the hall, that for an old man of fifty, Bart Pascall was not bad looking, quite distinguished, really. Oh well, there was hope for her yet. If she waited long enough, a widower with umpteen kids might fancy her. He would need to have plenty of money, of course, to make the proposition attractive. This one was obviously immune to her charms. He had eyes only for Una, whom he appeared to find quite fascinating and amusing. It occurred to Sylvia that this Una was a different person from the one who had been married to her Uncle Neil. It was as if she had acquired confidence from the power she was so effortlessly exerting over this handsome, self-assured professional man.

The 'For Sale' sign was up in the front garden and someone was coming to inspect the house on Saturday. Una was both excited and unsettled. Watching the children leave with Bart later that evening, she envied them their secure position in his life and longed to be departing with them, as one of the family. She exchanged a long, lingering look with Bart as he prepared to drive away and walked slowly back along the path to the house, with a sense of having been deserted. 'Not much longer,' he had whispered when he kissed her goodbye.

Before going to bed, Una went into the small bedroom, to see whether the girls had finished emptying the cupboard. The single bed was covered with an assortment of cardboard boxes, tennis racquets, linen and clothes. On top of the pile was the fur jacket she had been wearing on the night of the accident: Neil's fabulous birthday present to her. While she was in hospital, Sibyl had sent it to the cleaners to have the blood stains removed and some damage to the lining repaired. Una had not been able to bring herself to wear it again. She picked up the soft and heavy fur, cuddling it close to her face, remembering Neil. Tears filled her eyes, but they were no longer for herself, only for him. Deep within her was the irrational idea that she was betraying him, just as Dolcis and Angela thought Bart was betraying Louise. It could be stifled, but it would never disappear. She had loved Neil so passionately, needed him so desperately, yet his memory alone was not enough to sustain her through the years ahead. Lonely humans are frail and fickle: it is love that strengthens their will to survive. Una carried the coat into her own room and hung it in the closet. She would wear it to Tina's wedding, not her own.

Chapter Twenty-three

Mr Truebody and Una retired from the office on the same day. They were both entering upon new phases in their lives—one into a tranquillity bordering on downright boring, with only Mrs Truebody's constant companionship and mindless chatter for diversion; the other to the challenge of a ready-made family, in which the words 'tranquillity' and 'boring' would come to have a wistful sound.

They both left with regret the jobs they had enjoyed doing for so many years. They would miss their colleagues and one another. Mr Truebody had been a kindly, understanding boss and Una an efficient, agreeable secretary, attractive enough to be a pleasure to behold, but not so glamorous that she was alarming either to Mr Truebody or his comfortable wife.

Una's close friends were no longer at work. One had left to have a baby and the other had accompanied her husband to the Middle East. Una was keeping in touch with both of them. She occasionally met the former and she was corresponding with the latter.

It was the end of an era for the clerks in the outer general office and they were looking forward, apprehensively, to the arrival of the new personnel in the large room belonging to the chief officer and the adjacent small one belonging to his secretary.

There was the usual farewell ceremony, which both Una and Mr Truebody had been dreading. Complimentary things were said about them in short speeches, stilted with embarrassment, and best wishes for their respective futures were chorused as they were handed their parting gifts. Una was encouraged by Mr Truebody to speak her thanks first, which she did, briefly and emotionally, conscious that she had reached a crucial turning point in her life. Even Mr Truebody, an accomplished public speaker, found it difficult to say what he really wanted to say, or even make up his mind what it was he really wanted to say. He soon gave up the attempt and began shaking everybody vigorously by the hand and wishing them all the best.

Una left her office to drive away from the car park for the last time.

Mr Truebody had another farewell 'do' that evening, when he and his wife were being entertained to dinner by the other chief officers and their wives. Bart Pascall would be there, of course, accompanied by the woman he was going to marry in a week's time. Una and Mr Truebody would meet again, briefly, before taking their divergent ways.

The noon-time marriage ceremony, with Imelda and Dolcis as witnesses and Luke, Angela, Jane and Claude Pope-Wessington as guests, was soon over. Before she knew where she was, Una was standing on the steps outside the registry office, with her arm through her husband's and the marriage certificate safely folded into his inside jacket pocket. She was smiling into Claude's camera in the bemused fashion of one who has reached a miraculous stage in her existence and knows not how.

Twenty minutes ago she had been Una Favory. Now, after a prosaic ceremony and a chaste kiss, she was Una Pascall. She turned to look at Bart. He smiled into her wondering eyes, delighted with his achievement and, for the first time since Neil died, she experienced the warm glow of those who are lovingly possessed.

'Look at me, Una!' Luke shouted impatiently, having a go with his grandfather's expensive camera.

Una looked at him and laughed, joyful at the thought that she had become a fixed part of this boy's charming family.

'That should be a super one,' he declared, regretfully parting with the camera. 'Are we going to have lunch now?' he asked his grandmother. 'I'm hungry. It's ages since breakfast.'

They were having a celebratory lunch in a nearby hotel. Una and Bart were to spend the night there, before setting off for Scotland for two weeks. Dolcis was returning to university on Sunday, which meant that Luke and Angela would have to stay at the manor house in Lapcombe.

The lunch was a happy affair. Luke was allowed a glass of champagne to toast the newly married couple. Afterwards, they sat over coffee in the lounge, until it became evident that the young people's euphoria was wearing off and all the inconvenience of being without their father for two weeks was beginning to surface. Jane decided that it was time to go.

Una drew Imelda to one side. 'Thank you for being here,' she said warmly.

'I wouldn't have missed it for the world,' Imelda answered. 'You are a very fortunate woman, Una.'

'I know. I wish you could be as happy.'

Imelda laughed. 'As a matter of fact, I might be. His name is Giles, he has no wife and he has met Mother and the cats. What more is there to say? If I had insisted on taking Felix home, he would probably have been driven back to his wife a lot sooner and I would have been spared a lot of heart-ache. We live and learn, don't we? I hope you have a wonderful honey-moon, Una.' She did not give Una a chance to express her delight at the news, but called goodbye to everyone and left.

For a moment Una stood alone, looking after her, suddenly swamped by a sense of unreality, then someone said, 'This is for you, Una, from the three of us.'

She turned. Dolcis was standing there, holding a small, prettily gift-wrapped box. On either side of her were Angela and Luke. They were all smiling broadly in anticipation of her pleasure. They were not disappointed. Una opened the package to discover a pair of ear-rings in the shape of two tiny gold leaves. She was enchanted and touched by their thoughtfulness; as Jane, when making the suggestion to Angela, had trusted she would be.

'Thank you,' she said, 'they are beautiful.'

'We chose them together,' Angela told her. 'Luke wanted to get some huge diamanté ones. You should have seen them!'

'I did not!' Luke cried indignantly. 'I have as much taste as you have—more, probably. Girls think they know everything.'

Jane intervened to tell them that they must be going. While Bart was having a last word with his children, advising the two younger ones to behave themselves at their grandparents' and his elder daughter to mind what she got up to in London and get stuck into her studies, Jane and Claude took their leave of Una.

'Bart is a fine man,' Jane said. 'I know you will be happy together. Louise was a very special person and it has taken Bart a long time to find someone else with that special quality.' She kissed Una on the cheek.

'I've been told that I am not at all like Louise,' Una said, troubled by the comparison and wishing it had not been made on this particular day and at such a moment.

Claude sensed her distress. He took her hands in his, saying gently, 'My dear, my wife means that you have the gift of understanding people and making them happy.' He paused for a moment, choosing his words, then he said, 'We want you to know that we have room in our hearts for another daughter.' He did not give her an opportunity to reply, but turned away to call the children. It was just as well, for Una did not know how to express her gratitude for such kindness and felt the tears coming to her eyes.

As Claude's car turned out of sight round the side of the hotel, Bart put his arm around Una's waist and drew her closer to him. 'We have two weeks to devote to one another. Will it be long enough, I wonder?' he said, as they walked back into the hotel.

'Yes,' she answered seriously. 'No one can stay on holiday forever. Anyway, Luke and Angela won't want to remain at Lapcombe any longer, they have too far to travel to school.'

She was right, Bart acknowledged. Honeymoons were time out and must not be confused with the routine of reality.

When they were alone in the lift, ascending to their room, Una beseeched him, 'Promise me something, Bart.'

He raised his eyebrows at her earnest tone. 'What's that?'

'No comparisons! I mean, don't let's think it used to be like this, or like that, or they never said such and such a thing. You know what I mean.'

'Yes, I know. No comparisons,' he agreed. It would not be fair to Louise and Neil, he could understand that.

One lesson both had learnt. It was that the exciting person with whom one spends one's honeymoon becomes gradually metamorphosed into the familiar person with whom one spends the rest of one's life. In contrast to fairy tales, handsome princes all too often turn into toads and beautiful princesses into scullery maids. Only time would tell.

Women who have had children often have the edge taken off their sexual appetites, unless they desire more children, of course. Una could still abandon herself to the pleasure, without a thought for the consequences. She and Bart rediscovered the ecstasy of a shared bed and the secure contentment of a shared subsistence. By the end of the two weeks, they were ready to face the world as one.

★　★　★

It was raining, a soft, steady downpour through a mild Autumn air; the crisp and yellow leaves were turning into slippery-wet masses of shining dark umber beneath Una's flat-heeled shoes. She was walking along a narrow, fern-bordered path in the woods, which stretched either side of the river on the west side of Lapcombe. Every now and again, her legs brushed against a low branch or broad fern leaf and were spattered with fat drops of rain water beneath the generous overhang of her showerproof coat. Way in front of her rushed

Potter, the large black poodle from the manor. He had recently sired a litter and Luke had been promised one of the puppies, when they were old enough to leave their mother, a handsome brown bitch belonging to the village butcher.

Una had driven from her own home, which was on the road between the county town and Lapcombe, to the manor to see Jane, who had the 'flu; at Potter's urgent request, she had offered to take him for a walk. Potter appreciated Una's walks, because she appeared to forget to turn homewards. They set off from the back of the manor, across the garden to the stream, and followed it until it met the narrow river and the woods. Una took a path through the trees, diagonal to the river, and in another half-mile they emerged onto the lane not far from Flora's house. She put Potter on the lead and they made their way along the lane, towards the main road through the village. When they reached Flora's gate, Una stopped. Of course, it was no longer Flora's gate. The house had been sold. Workmen were inside it, gutting and modernising it. The roof had already been mended. The old brown pantiles were blotched with darker patches of clean, new ones and the chimney looked as if it had never been inclined to fall. Where the garden met the corner near the road there was to be a drive, leading up to a garage in cream brick, already partially erected. The hedge was broken down in readiness and a large red van, with 'Coyning and Son' on its side in white lettering, was standing on the churned-up lawn. The ancient porch and all its intricate mass of supportive climbing roses had been torn down to make way for a more imposing one, in cream brick to match the garage, with pantiles to match the new blotches on the roof. According to local gossip, the Macfarlane Brown place, or the old Favory place, as some of the oldest inhabitants still referred to it, had been bought by someone with pots of money. Once it had slumped with comfortable ease under its considerable weight of years; now it was pulled erect by a modern stiffening of its sinews.

Una thought it was an appropriate time to view this transformation, when all the world looked dismal in the rain. She gazed dolefully at the end of the newly glazed conservatory, where once the children had been allowed to run riot amidst the clutter of plant pots containing scruffy geraniums, the shabby and odd assortment of chairs and the rickety trestle table, covered with leprous green baize. It was now waiting to be filled with smart cane furniture, covered with cushions of pastel patterned cotton, and handsome plants in expensive pots would be placed upon cool Italian tiles. Una recalled the last time she had visited Flora in her new home, The Lilacs, and her mouth drooped sadly as she fought back the tears.

Potter heaved himself into the hedge and lifted a leg. Una took her gloved hands from the decrepit gate and tugged on the lead, 'Let's go, Potter,' she said, dragging him off on three legs, still widdling. No doubt next time they walked in that direction, the gate would have been replaced as well.

She did not go back along the lane, but took the more direct route through the village, past the straggling outlying cottages to the compact centre, where the church looked down with haughty grandeur from its rise above the village green towards the Black Bull and the handful of small shops. Mr Laston's large green car was on the road in front of the vicarage, and the white mud-spattered mini of the doctor surged through the rain-covered street towards his own home, hitting a puddle as it passed Una and sending up a wide spray which showered the dog. Potter shook himself with disgust. Una leaped aside, too late. Not that it mattered, they were both thoroughly soaked.

'Lovely weather for ducks, Potter,' she observed to his trotting form.

They approached the manor along the front drive. On either side stretched the tree-dotted park, deserted of even Mr Forbes' wheelbarrow. Only two months ago, it had been a busy scene of rural pleasures and fund-raising activities, with Una presiding over the second-hand book stall, selling mostly tatty comics and *Readers' Digests*. While Jane did the honours in respect of the visiting celebrity, Dolcis, Angela and Luke had supervised their own stalls, and Bart and Claude had kept out of sight somewhere behind the house, probably in the barn.

Una had not intended becoming involved in the fête, but then she had become involved in a lot of things that she had not intended since her marriage in May, almost five months ago. She would not have believed it possible that in such a short time anyone's life could change so drastically. Settling into a new home and an entirely different pattern of existence at the same time had been both challenging and hectic. She had loved every minute of it, even those minutes—and there had been quite a few—when there was family friction, in which she inevitably became entangled now that she could not entirely divorce herself from it. After years of cooking for only herself and Neil, and then only for herself, she was now expected regularly to produce filling meals for four, sometimes five when Dolcis was at home, sometimes six or more when school friends were invited to stay. There was always washing and ironing to be done and the house did not stay tidy. In fact, Una was amazed most mornings just how untidy it could become overnight.

Ella and Ronald had dropped in to see her soon after her marriage, long before she had got herself organised, and Ella had almost rubbed her hands in satisfaction to find Una wearing an apron, with a wooden spoon in her hand, in the middle of a kitchen which looked as if a tornado had passed through it. There was a delicious smell of liver and bacon casserole, a favourite dish of Bart and Luke, at one time never to be attempted by the faddy Una who found the sight of raw liver absolutely revolting. There were many things Una did now from necessity that she had avoided doing before from fussy singularity; except eat some of the dishes she was obliged to cook.

Potter had been let off the lead as soon as they were back on his home ground. He was leading the way round the house to the rear entrance. As Una was crossing in front of the drawing-room to follow him, she raised her eyes to the first long window and there was Jane, smiling wanly down at her, one hand holding back a heavy curtain. Immediately, Una's spirits lifted. She was always sure of a warm welcome and a sympathetic hearing from the owners of this fine old house. She came to it with a sense of returning home and always left it eager to return.

Chapter Twenty-four

The night before her silver wedding anniversary, Una found it difficult to get to sleep. The various aches and pains, which were a legacy of the car accident, were troubling her more as she got older and she toyed with the idea of getting up and searching in her hand luggage for the pain killers which she had already packed for fear of forgetting them. She turned over to ease the dull ache in her shoulder and began gently rubbing her right knee. Bart was asleep beside her, coughing every now and again, without waking. He had suffered a distressing attack of bronchitis last winter and the cough had persisted. Una was hoping that the sun in Singapore would help to clear it.

Samantha was coming to take her to the hairdresser in the morning. Una no longer did any driving. She had stopped about three years ago when she began to be severely troubled with arthritis in her hands and feet. Giving up had not been much of an inconvenience. Since Bart had retired, they went out and about together most of the time and he was content to do the driving. They rarely went very far now. Their visits to Newcastle had ceased fifteen years ago, with the death of Bart's mother, who had survived his father by only a short while.

Una turned onto her other side and put an arm round Bart, trying to relax against his warmth. This was the sleeping position she had favoured over the past twenty-five years. Twenty-five years! She had a presentiment that she had reached a milestone in her life and that tomorrow heralded change. No doubt it was due to the exciting anticipation of the holiday and the pleasure of soon seeing Angela and her husband, Colin, again, but first there would be the party at the airport hotel. All the rest of the family would be there: Dolcis, Graeme and their three married sons with their wives and children; Angela's daughter, Samantha, and her younger brother; Luke and his wife, Claudia, with their two girls; and Imelda.

Thinking of Imelda brought back a host of other people who had gradually vanished from Una's life. Through Imelda, Una had heard of the events in the Favory family as they had happened. The last time she had been amongst them all had been when she and Bart attended Tina's wedding. When it was Sylvia's turn to get married, Una had been unable to accept the invitation because of ill health—possibly the 'flu, but she could not be sure, it might have been that year she had the gastric trouble. Una withdrew her arm from Bart's waist and turned onto her back, staring at the shadows on the ceiling, recalling the years, month by fateful month.

January, her birthday month. The car crash had been on her thirty-fourth birthday. Neil had been killed and she had been widowed. February. That was the month in which her home in Plymouth had been destroyed by a bomb. It was also the month when Felix had left Imelda and gone back to his wife in Portsmouth. In March, Marcia had become temporarily deranged, after being shut in a cupboard—a most peculiar business that had been—and then, years later, Jane, Louise's mother, had died. Marcus had been killed in a far-off Korean April. May? Nothing horrible had happened in May and it remained a blessed month. She had married Bart in May. One June, Marcia had taken an overdose of tablets and killed herself—definitely not a cry for help but, judging from the note she left, a shout of farewell. No one really knew why she had done it, although there was some talk that she had been out of her mind with worry about Shirley. She had certainly become morbidly engrossed in her unresponsive and ungrateful daughter, after Kate left home to follow her lover to

America. Then there was that terrible hot July when Ella and Ronald had gone to Italy to sample one of their own tours and check up on the itinerary, which they did from time to time. The coach had crashed on a mountain road and they had both been killed, along with many of the other passengers. What had happened in August? Oh, yes, Lavinia had died—ages ago that seemed, as if it had happened in another existence. Both Jessica and dear old Claude had been chosen to die of natural causes during September, but not in the same year. Una could not remember exactly which year Jessica had died. Then five years ago, in October, Flora had eventually succumbed to extreme old age, well over ninety she was, and had died penniless, her fortune consumed in supporting her in The Lilacs for over twenty years. Her funeral had been a particularly dismal occasion, with none of the reassuring sense of coming together usually experienced by the mourners on such days. She had outlived most of those who were nearest to her. The small group huddled around the grave in the pouring rain had been composed of Sibyl, recovering from the first of her operations and looking ghastly in black; her husband, Stuart; Ella's son, Peter, a married man of forty, doing nicely in the motor trade; Imelda, Bart and Una. The following October, almost a year to the day, Sibyl was once more wearing the black outfit, this time at Stuart's funeral. He had been carried off by a stroke, a disappointed man, robbed by Flora's stubborn longevity. November? Poor, sad Hugh had died in that month, staggering towards the sea, perhaps to drown his shame and unhappiness. In December last year, brave Sibyl had died of cancer.

There had been so many funerals. The name of Favory had vanished.

Jessica, Hugh, Ella, Ronald, Marcia, Tom—whatever had happened to Tom? He had been so arrogant and handsome. Had he died as well?—Sibyl, Stuart, Neil, and then there was Una. How strange, to think that, of the ten of them, she was the only one still about. Stranger still that she should be in the centre of a loving, growing family of children who called her grandma. It had been explained, to those who were old enough to understand, that she was not really their grand-mother, and there were plenty of photographs of Louise for them to gaze upon with wonder, when their curiosity about their ancestry prompted them to ask for details of their family history. Children love to work out intricate relationships and, in the painstaking process of putting everyone they loved into their proper place, Una was firmly established as Grandma Pascall, even by the great-grandchildren, of whom, so far, there were three. She had Dolcis and Angela to thank for creating that special place for her.

Una wriggled with discomfort and turned over yet again. Bart stirred in his sleep, muttered and coughed. I must get to sleep, she thought wearily, I shall look tired and haggard tomorrow if I don't, just when I want to look my best. What was it that Imelda had once said about chameleons and leopards? Oh yes, that was it: chameleons change at the whim of outside influence and leopards won't change a spot for a stripe for anyone, whatever the inducement. Was she right? Perhaps! Imelda had once changed her hairstyle to please Felix, but it had been only a superficial change, a token gesture of love; there had been no fundamental alteration in her character and outlook. If she had possessed the facility, or even the desire, to change a spot for a stripe, perhaps her marriage to Giles would not have ended in divorce.

Una, the chameleon, admitted that she had changed. She seemed to have the ability to be what people expected her to be. Married to Neil, she had been expected to be satisfied in her role as a Favory wife. She would have fulfilled that expecta-tion, had not a perverse fate deprived her of children and thwarted her best efforts. She had been too anxious to be grafted onto the Favory clan; the tender graft had not taken. She had visited Flora regularly until the last month of her life, but Flora had resisted her well-meant overtures to the last.

How different had been her ready acceptance, just as she was, by Jane and Claude Pope-Wessington and by Bart's elderly parents in Newcastle. For them she had been a godsend: a companion and a housekeeper for Bart and a stepmother for their adored grandchildren.

Drowsily, Una concluded that there was no such thing as the same woman married twice. A different man called forth a different wife and circumstances dictated that wife's response. Una Pascall was most unlike Una Favory. She was self-assured, independent and, being well-loved and much needed, less concerned to be liked. Gone were the days when she had tried by effacement to match her environment; now she moulded the environment to suit herself. In fact, come to think of it, she had turned from a chameleon into a leopard!

Una gave a deep sigh and, settling once more against her husband's back, fell asleep at last.

Chapter Twenty-five

There were fifteen adults and five children around the huge oval table in the private room that had been set aside for the celebration. Bart and Una were sitting opposite one another halfway down its length and around them were assembled Bart's elder daughter, Dolcis, with her husband, Graeme; his son, Luke, with his wife, Claudia; three married grandchildren, with their wives; four grandchildren who were not yet married; and three great-grandchildren, two of them in highchairs and one in a buggy; and then there was a niece of Una's from her first marriage.

All these people, Una thought, looking round at them while everyone's attention was upon Graeme, who had risen from his place at one end of the table with the intention of making a short speech—all these people and, with one exception, they all belong in my life by courtesy of Bart.

Graeme cleared his throat in preparation. The talk and laughter eased to a hush. One of the tiny children sneezed rather messily. Imelda, who was sitting next to him, opened her handbag and produced a neatly folded handkerchief, edged with lace. Instantly Una was reminded of another family occasion, another family. They had all been walking back from Shirley's christening in Lapcombe. Una and Neil, hand in hand, were bringing up the rear, when Sylvia had fallen into the ditch at the side of the road and Imelda had used her clean white hankie to rub most of the mud off her knees. Now she was dabbing gently at the snub nose and rosy mouth of this cherubic three-year-old, who had sneezed with his mouth full of raspberries and meringue. She did not replace the hankie in her handbag, but put it in her skirt pocket, no doubt trusting that she would remember not to use it.

Graeme waited until he once more had everyone's attention, then he said, in his loud, rather pompous manner, 'On behalf of us all, Una and Dad, I congratulate you on your twenty-fifth wedding anniversary and thank you for inviting us to share this happy occasion with you. It was a splendid meal and we have all thoroughly enjoyed ourselves. We hope you will have many more happy years together.' He picked up his half-empty wine glass and said, 'Let's drink a toast. Una and Dad! Here's to their golden wedding!'

This was endorsed with lifted glasses, smiles and thanks from around the table, which bore evidence of a feast consumed. Now, only coffee cups, assorted glasses and a scattering of gold and green chocolate mint wrappers remained amidst the stains and the crumbs.

While their guests were standing about them with their glasses raised, Una smiled across at Bart, thinking that if they lived to see their golden wedding, he would be one hundred and she would be eighty-nine—not a very likely event! When they sat down again, she looked around with delight at all the dear faces, some, she admitted to herself ruefully, dearer than others. Samantha caught her eye and got to her feet again, pushing back her chair.

'What do you think of the gear, Gran?' She swung the long string of pearls, which she had borrowed from Una that morning, nonchalantly between two slender fingers and gave a short, saucy rendition of the Charleston.

'You look beautiful, Samantha,' Una said.

The dress, which Samantha had purloined from her friend's great-grandmother, was a soft, slinky, silver *crêpe-de-Chine*, with thin shoulder straps and a low-cut vee neckline that plunged even lower at the back. Samantha was lean and leggy and she was wearing the dress bra-less, as it would have been worn by its original owner. She was provocative and naughty, full of life and adorable.

'You're a little minx,' her grandfather told her fondly. She gave him a big kiss.

'She's an awful show-off,' her eighteen-year-old brother declared. 'Good job Mum's not here!'

Samantha gave him a big kiss too and sat down again. 'Is there any more coffee in that pot?' she asked her Uncle Luke.

'I expect you are excited about going to Singapore,' Imelda said to Una. 'I wish I was coming with you.'

'I wish you were,' Una said. Imelda looked as if she needed a holiday. At fifty-five she was worn and faded. Her thick, fair hair had turned a lustreless grey and was plaited around her head in the style of her youth, before Felix. She was still nursing and contemplated without pleasure retiring in five years.

'We're going to have to go now, Grandma,' the wife of Dolcis' middle son said. 'The baby will need feeding soon.'

'I understand, dear. Thank you for coming. It's been lovely to see you again. The baby is gorgeous.'

'Don't forget to give Auntie Angela and Uncle Colin our love,' her husband said.

'We won't,' Una assured him, gazing down at Bart's youngest great-grandchild, plump and pink-cheeked, fast asleep in her buggy. 'She's been very good.'

Dolcis' other two sons, with their wives, one of them with two tiny children, soon took their leave as well. Samantha and her brother departed at the same time. They were going on to a night club with some friends.

Remaining around the table, besides Una and Bart, were Dolcis and Graeme, Luke and Claudia with their two teenage daughters, and Imelda.

The talk turned upon Angela and Colin and the long journey to Singapore.

'I'll miss you both,' Imelda smiled wistfully. 'A month is a long time.'

'Yes, it is,' Bart agreed. Privately, he still thought that it was too long, but Una had insisted it was not worth going for a shorter period. 'Don't forget to water the stuff in the green-house,' he reminded Graeme for the umpteenth time.

Luke and Una exchanged smiles. 'How are things at the manor?' she asked him quietly.

'Fine,' he answered, but that was not strictly true and they both knew it. Claudia was not the stuff of which ladies of the manor are made. She found the house too big and incon-venient; it was cold and draughty in the winter, despite all the improvements Luke had made for her comfort, and too far away from the town, something he could do nothing about. As for the villagers, she wanted nothing to do with them, with the exception of her trendy friends who were living in the elegantly modernised house that had once belonged to Flora Macfarlane Brown. The rest were just a lot of busybodies and Mr Laston's successor was the worst. The fête was a thing of the past. She had tolerated it when they moved in with Claude, after Jane's death, and when Claude had died she had put a stop to it. Jane had not liked it either, but she had carried on the tradition as a matter of course and with a sense of duty. Claudia had a mania for privacy, yet loathed the isolation of country life. How could Luke be happy, loving his home and the farming life so deeply and being married to a woman who detested both?

He should have chosen a wife more carefully, Una thought dispassionately, but love had blinded his judgement, and at the start Claudia had seemed everything he most desired, until the inevitable move to Lapcombe.

Una did not like her. She had tried, but it was no use. Anyone who could not make Luke happy she was bound to find disagreeable. Now, listening to Claudia chattering to Dolcis, her kind and placid sister-in-law, about a 'dear little shop' she had discovered in Bridport, where she had bought 'the most charming suit imaginable' and 'at such a reasonable price, darling, an absolute give-away', Una could barely hide her irritation.

'Grandma?'

Una looked across into Louise's smiling grey eyes, only

they did not belong to Louise. Luke's eldest daughter was so like her true grandmother that it was not surprising she was a great favourite with Bart.

'What is it, dear?'

'Next time you see Samantha, will you remind her about the jacket she said I could have?'

'That won't be for at least a month,' Una reminded her.

'I know, but I don't know how long it will be before I see her again. I did ask her tonight, but you know what she's like, she keeps forgetting.'

Yes, Samantha was full of good intentions and generous impulses, but she was too busy to carry them all out.

'Don't forget to keep an eye on Samantha while we are away,' Una said to Dolcis.

'That's easier said than done,' Dolcis laughed. 'No doubt she'll turn up when she wants something. She usually does.' Her brother was at university; nobody in the family could keep an eye on him. Perhaps it was just as well.

'It will be a relief when Angela and Colin come home for good,' Dolcis said.

All too soon, it was time for everyone to say goodbye. There was much kissing and well-wishing and waving of hands from cars. Una and Bart stood side by side on the hotel steps, watching them all drive off. Imelda was the last to leave.

'Sorry I won't be able to see you off tomorrow,' she said, 'but I'm working.' Una and Bart were not leaving until eleven-thirty.

'Remember me to Angela and Colin,' she called as she got into her car. 'Have a lovely time!'

'With so many commands to enjoy ourselves, I wouldn't have the nerve not to,' Bart observed. He and Una turned back into the brightly lit warmth of the hotel. 'I just wish we weren't flying. I do dislike it.'

'Think how long we would have to be away if we went by sea,' Una said.

'True,' he admitted, trying to reconcile himself to the flight.

Only Dolcis and Graeme were at the airport in the morning. They arrived looking subdued and, as Una's and Bart's excitement and anticipation mounted with all the hassle of checking in amidst the hectic surge of arrivals and departures, it was obvious that, despite their cheerful and encouraging words, the younger couple's spirits were not elevating in sympathy.

Una guessed that they were disappointed not to be going as well. She knew that Dolcis would dearly love to see her sister again.

'Don't worry about the garden, Dad,' were Graeme's last words to Bart, as he and Una walked towards the departure lounge.

'I'll keep an eye on Samantha,' Dolcis called after Una, blowing a kiss.

Twenty minutes later, Dolcis and Graeme were standing on the roof of the airport terminal building, waving to Una and Bart as they boarded the plane.

'Do you think we were right not to tell them?' Dolcis asked her husband with a worried frown.

'Yes,' he answered firmly. 'We've been over all this, Dolcis. Una wouldn't have gone and what would be the point of them staying? There's nothing they could do except attend the funeral. We shall have to go on their behalf.'

Imelda had died of a brain haemorrhage, ten minutes before midnight.

May had not remained unscathed for Una after all.